C.H.I.S

By Jorge Gill

This book is a work of fiction and except in the case of historical fact, any resemblance to actual persons, living or dead, is purely coincidental.

DEDICATION

For

Karen, Sami, Charlene, Jason, Paris, Jayden, Jace, Mya, Mason, Archie, Rome, Jakob and Evelyn

ACKNOWLEDGMENTS

I would like to thank all my family and friends for their patience and support over the past few months. Love to you all xxxx

C.H.I.S

Prologue

CHIS : DEFINITION

Covert Human Intelligence Source, "CHIS" is defined as a person who establishes or maintains a personal or other relationship with another person for the covert purpose of facilitating anything below;-

- *Covertly uses such a relationship to obtain information or to provide access to any information to another person ; or*
- *Covertly discloses information obtained by the use of such a relationship or as a consequence of the existence of such a relationship.*

CHIS is the official terminology used for the word informant. Covert Human Intelligence Source. More commonly referred to as agents, if you work within the realms of Justice and Law. Historically, placed deep within the heart of organised criminal networks. Secretly talking to the authorities, telling them what they needed to know, without the consent of their day to day criminal associates.

Today they are even more commonplace in everyday police work. Ever wonder how the Police caught you? You thought everything had been so watertight! Only the people you trusted knew! Well let me tell you something, your trust was abused. Chances are you trusted an informant. Someone who needed something, a leg up at court, money, their own charges dropped, or someone who just plain and simple didn't like you.

Whatever you want to call them, one thing is for certain; they are and have been one of the most important sources of intelligence for the many law enforcement agencies that operate in our world. Some of the biggest *results* obtained by the authorities have, and could only have been achieved from the direct resourcing of such agents.

Of course there is the other side of the coin as well. Set ups, provoked by revenge, jealousy, greed, desperation, or one or more of a number of other selfish motives. Conspiracies that have led to huge miscarriages of justice. The CIA have indeed been heavily criticised for their use of drug lords and murderers as paid informants. Not only paid, but also offered a leniency towards their own criminal activities. Consequences that give grounds for why agents or informants are not the more familiar names used for such people. In fact by large more derogatory names are used. Names such as, *rats, snitches, snouts, stool pigeons, weasels, tell-tales, narks and grasses*, but to name a few. Did you know that the origin of *grass* comes from the rhyming slang for grasshopper, meaning copper or shopper? There are a million names I guess, most not very nice.

The world, however, no matter where you come from are full of informants. I know people who *grass* on cheating partners, dodgy neighbours, the rich guy, naughty kids, bad teachers, council workers, fellow employees; in fact the list is endless. People talk and give information for a motive. What's yours?

So let's talk about me. I was actually born to have no chance in life, fighting for some prospect all too often. Perhaps I was some evil person in a previous life, here now to be punished and make amends.

I inherited the position of third child to heroin addicted parents, brother to heroin addicts, brother to a prostitute and a pass-the-parcel for a number of other people from the same degenerate background. Not the ideal introduction to life. Of course this meant a childhood of chaos, uncertainty, mood swings, police raids, hospitals, social workers, mal-nutrition, neglect, learning to steal, learning to fight, learning to lie and least of all learning to survive.

Growing up in a world that hated grasses. Untrustworthy rats, who had made our already difficult life, even worse. Ever present when my old man suffered the search warrants. Executed by officers who always seemed to know what he was holding and where it was. Information provided by grasses that no doubt graced our company under pretence.

Threats made by the *Old Bill,* to take us into the care of social services unless our parents made it easier for them. *The Gavvers* willing to overlook the lack of food, hygiene and clothing available for Wayne, Sarah and myself if they co-operated.

My old man hated grasses, as did we all. Unfortunately they have always been, and will always be ever present in the world of drugs. Especially in the world of heroin. *Give us some information or go to jail.* It's a no brainer. No heroin addict wants to go to prison. He or she need their gear. My old man however, never grassed. Well that's what he told us. He hated grasses.

As for me, I have never touched or taken heroin in my life, largely thanks to my brother Wayne. In fact I hate drugs, all drugs. Heroin nevertheless, is the daddy of them all, no question. It is a killer, responsible for murdering my family. It is also to blame for me never having that normal cosy, warm, protected childhood. The one that the majority of you took for granted. It is responsible for my untrusting nature, my lack of trust in others, my need to deal with my issues using my fists. To blame for me running away and joining the army and then for leaving the Army. In fact heroin is to blame for everything that has ever happened in my second-rate life.

One thing though. Call me a grass and I will kill you.

One

1900hrs 2nd March

Peter Snugs howled as the lit cigarette burned deep into his manhood. This form of torture requiring some seconds of contact. Contact between the item producing the dry heat, in this case the tip of the cigarette, and human skin, in this case Snugs penis. Enough seconds to leave round punched out lesions.

Snugs wriggled and writhed in contorted motion to escape the pain. The cord wrapped around his wrists, cut deeper into the skin and bone of his undernourished arms. The restrained limbs were held tightly behind the wooden chair that he was bound to. His naked body convulsed in somewhat impossible directions due to the affliction.

The dehumanization of Snugs was not just necessary to them; it was also some sort of game. Snugs was an object of experimentation. An experiment and torture method that they had used before.

Nobody heard the screams coming from the top floor of the notorious Wallace Square block of flats in Northfleet, an impoverish estate just on the outskirts of Gravesend. A small flat in the small town, north of its County of Kent. A perfect location for their needs. No neighbours, just boarded up flats. No prying eyes.

Kent bragged the title *Garden of England*, which perhaps once upon a time it was. A title owing to the abundance of fruit growing and hop gardens in the region. The Borough of Gravesham, better known as Gravesend, has its own history. A town of about ninety nine square kilometres, with a population of about ninety nine thousand people. A town that houses the burial site of Pocahontas, who allegedly died of TB on a ship just off its river front. It brags of having one of the oldest standing market places in the Country.

Wallace Square however could brag of nothing. The welfare and residents of this estate had increasingly been neglected by the local authorities. A high rising, grey concrete block of flats, decorated only by the graffiti signatures of its past and present tenants. Even ignored by the local constabulary. It was almost as if the population of Gravesend had jointly agreed that it did not exist.

Snugs, with tears streaming down his face pleaded for the torture to stop. The three Jamaicans standing in the same room just grinned. Three self proclaimed Yardies. Today these people used the term *Yardie* to invoke fear. Yardies generally had no ties anywhere. The real ones were illegal immigrants. Very few actually know the origin of the name. A word that actually originates from a slang name given to the occupants of poverty stricken government yards built in West Kingston, Jamaica. Yards that were basically improvised shacks placed around a central courtyard with communal cooking areas. The yards just encouraged gang crime and violence and as such, *Yardies* were born.

None of the Jamaican Yardies had identified themselves, but had just referred to themselves as letters from the alphabet. It was impossible for Snugs to remember who was which letter. All of them stood about six feet tall and had identical muscular athletic builds. Each one equally evil and ungodly.

The one stood in front of Snugs with the lit cigarette, who had in fact introduced himself as B, showed off two gold front teeth while grinning. Savouring the tormented plea's coming from his captive. He said, "Yah need to be sure yah know who de boss man."

"Please, You're the boss; you're the boss," whimpered Snugs, still crying, tears streaming down his bony face.

One of them, D, stood over the filthy double bed, covered only by an unwashed duvet with no bed linen. It was coated in dark stains, dried blood, urination and an assortment of other aged marks resulting from an unhygienic lifestyle. D spoke in an unusual high pitched voice, which somehow did not suit his heavy build, "Nah Man. Yah got to KNOW."

D grabbed the long, unwashed blonde hair of the female he had sat on the bed next to him. Vikki Snugs. (Snugs being an adopted surname as a result of her relationship with Peter Snugs.)

She screamed, "Fuck off you mug," as he tossed her onto the floor, in front of her incapacitated lover of the last five years.

"Please Vik, just do as they say," pleaded the male Snugs, legs now crossed over, trying to compress the burns. She briefly glared at him before D spoke again.

"Yah got to learn too bitch." He now grabbed the beautiful long hair of the thirteen year old girl who was also sitting on the verminous double bed, Rebecca 'adopted name' Snugs, daughter of Vikki 'adopted name' Snugs. Rebecca was now screaming on the floor next to her Mother. No one outside could hear them scream. The wailing and shrieking continued when both females, child and adult were stripped naked. The heart wrenching anguished cries for help strangely dulled when all three Snugs were ravaged and raped again and again and again. No one heard them scream.

Two

1700hrs 10th March

I looked out again, through the begrimed window, through its dirty net covering. The lace net was stained yellow from the days when you could smoke in a public house. Perhaps the landlord still did. It wouldn't matter a lot. From the look of things customers in the once very busy Manor Ale public house had hit an all time low.

I turned back to my pint glass and took a sip of the Fosters lager in front of me, as I scanned the room for the third time since arriving. The decor was aged, deep-green painted woodchip paper stretched across all three customer walls, broken only by two old sash cord windows at the front of the pub and the entrance door. A worn pale green carpet with random stains of spillage from over the years, covered the entire floor. Despite the desperate look of needing to be replaced, the carpet did look free of dust and dirt. Recently vacuumed by the old upright purple Hoover which was still stood next to the bar. The landlord probably did his own cleaning; a paid employee would have put the Hoover away.

He stood at the corner of the bar furthest away from where I was sat. He was a stocky old boy in his fifties with a broad cockney accent. He still had a good head of hair, slightly greying at the temples, which he had brushed back into a quiff. He wore a tight white Lonsdale T-shirt that showed off his large pectoral and arm muscles. It also highlighted his round mid region. General tough guy in his time I guessed. He had looked me up and down when I arrived an hour ago, but I was used to that.

Only one other person sat on my side of the bar. A local alcoholic, known to me, only as Bill. We weren't friends, but we weren't enemies either. I just knew him. Bill could often be found sitting on the benches at the clock tower in the middle of the town centre with a bottle of white lightening cider, surrounded by a number of other individuals of the same ilk. Bill was buying beer for both the landlord and himself. *Just got his dole money,* (social security benefit) I thought. Still, neither person present represented any danger to me.

Between five and six, he had said, or choked if I wanted to be more precise. Speaking had proved difficult with my size ten boots pressing down on his skinny neck. An altercation that had occurred earlier in the day, an altercation that had led to me sitting at this window at the Manor Ale public house.

It must have been just after ten in the morning. I still exercised everyday, early if I could, so I had the rest of the day to myself. Even after everything had gone shit for me. No longer able to afford the rising prices of the local gymnasiums I had taken to outdoor training, using bodyweight exercises. This morning it had been a long run to the promenade, followed by an intense mixture of pull ups and dips on the outdoor apparatus kindly invested from the local council at various local parks. An initiative that was supposed to tackle the increasing problem of obesity. That said, I had never seen a single obese person using them, ever.

I had just dropped from the chinning bar after the sixth super-set, exhausted and pumped when I saw him. Ian

Piper. Skag head, a term used for heroin addicts. Piper had grown up here in Gravesend town. A bright kid who from the age of fourteen very quickly became a waste of space. He couldn't blame his parents, who incidentally, everyone knew were in fact righteous people. They had as any decent parents would, in the early years of his drug addiction, tried to help. Unfortunately you cannot help somebody who does not want it. Eventually after being the victims of numerous thefts from their own flesh and blood, they cut all ties. Painful as it was, they decided to move away with their other children. A daughter and a son.

Without his family to sponsor his self prescribed medication, Piper was forced to support his habit in other ways. Shoplifting was the beginning, but that has a tenured life. It does not take long for stores to become familiar with the habitual thieves. Once you became known to one store, you are as good as known to all of them. Nowadays all of them link up, they give each other information, photographs, descriptions and names. Eventually it had become impossible, his *sticky fingers*, resulting with his incarceration, courtesy of Kent Police. Even shoplifters eventually go to jail. But heroin addicts NEED their gear. Not like you or I need a beer after a hard day, or like you need that pair of trainers, but their need can only equate to our need of oxygen to breathe. As such the severity of the crimes they commit increase. Most follow the same general line. Thefts from vehicles, shed breaks, garage breaks, prostitution, house burglaries and eventually robbery. Piper had done all of them.

By the time I had sneaked up behind him he was already lying on the open air bandstand. A barren round concrete structure built in the late 1800's. I didn't have to sneak up. He was out of it. Lying on the hard stand, head and shoulders leaning against the metal rail surround. The spent syringe with traces of blood at the tip was still hanging out of his arm. The tip of the needle barely sunk into the blood vessel on the inside of his elbow joint. His eyes were now rolling up and his eyelids half closed. I knew there would be no conversation for a good few minutes. So I spent the next few moments going through his pockets. He was a thief. He was a drug addict. He should have something on him.

I found nothing. In due course, thanks to the odd slap and my size ten boots I was eventually able to get what I wanted. His dealer, B. No name just a letter. A London Yardie. Apparently he had come to Gravesend with D and H, to take over the heroin and crack cocaine scene. They had used violence to force addicts to buy their gear and as such, slowly forced other local dealers out of the picture. They never met customers themselves but employed local addicts to deliver on their behalf. The benefit of working for them would be having access to the gear first hand yourself. No more stealing or selling yourself. They were currently using Reader. Another sad story of a Gravesend kid gone wrong. Today, Reader would be meeting numerous customers by St. James Church in Parrock Street between five and six in the afternoon. His busiest trip of the day.

Grasses like Piper came in very handy in my line of work.

Three

I didn't personally know Reader, but I did know of him.
Most long term Gravesend boys know all the heroin
addicts, especially if you come from a family like mine. No
one sets out to be an addict, but once it's got you, you're as
good as done. Heroin won't discriminate. It will treat
everyone the same. Suppress your pain, generate that false
sense of well being, the feeling induced by *chasing the dragon*,
has been compared to that of having the best orgasm, even
better. Then it wears off. My brother told me once, 'It's like
you're in the deepest hole ever, impossible to climb out of.
Until you do it again.' No one likes a heroin addict, unless
you are in that world yourself.

At precisely five twenty, I had no difficulty in
recognizing him as he walked by the window that I had
been monitoring. He was a matter of two feet away from

me, just a flimsy pane of glass and stained net covering separating us. His once bright ginger hair was the instant giveaway. Naturally produced grease and the lack of shampoo had taken some of the brightness away. At five feet ten inches, surprisingly plump build for an addict he was not hard to recognize. He was wearing a matching ash grey tracksuit, which brand new probably looked nice. His however looked as if he had rolled around in a skip all night.

I called out to the landlord, "Back in a bit, just popping out to make a phone call." He just nodded his acknowledgment and he poured himself another pint courtesy of Bill's giro.

I stepped out onto the pavement. I pulled up the hood of my dark grey Nike hoodie, covering my thick mess of jet black hair. Hiding my tattooed neck. Reader was now about ten feet away from me. Not aware of anyone around, including me. I followed slowly, up Manor Road. A very narrow side street, with a cobbled road, bordered by a narrow pavement on each side. A variety of shops stood flat against the footpaths. Most of them now closed to business due to the hour of the day.

I stopped a few feet short of its junction with Parrock Street and watched Reader cross the road. I instantly saw the small group of junkies, stood beneath the large Church sign, *Praising The Lord.* Even more ironically, the deals were taking place a matter of feet away from the local drug addiction clinic. Six customers in all. Not bad. I mentally thanked Piper, *the grass,* as I watched money and small packages being exchanged.

I made a short phone call, six seconds later I hung up. I watched Reader roll up the right leg of his tracksuit bottoms and slide the money into his sock. He made sure the cash was sitting deep in the sock before rolling the tracksuit leg back down. I traced my steps back towards the pub, stopping short, at an alleyway that led to an adjacent multi story car park and tucked myself into the entrance. I waited. Reader walked past and I instantly caught his shoulder. Hard and firm. I almost lifted the blubbery addict off his feet.

"Drug search," I growled at him, my head next to his ear.

"This is harassment," he started to say as he turned to face me. His eyes locked on my face and I saw the fear as clear as I could see the colour of his blue eyes. It took me fifty five seconds to get what I wanted. The only resistance offered, "Please Samuel, don't, they will kill me."

Two minutes later he was gone. One minute after that I was sat in the Manor Ale public house, drinking my pint, the Landlord and Bill now engaged in deep conversation, not even glancing in my direction.

Gary Reader was sweating. What was he going to say? He was going to get beaten, that was for sure and he was also going to owe the money he had just lost.

"Fucking Samuel Jakobs!" he cried quietly. Reader stopped and looked back. He watched Jakobs enter the Manor Ale and quickly turned away. His mind was racing. What to do? If he grassed Jakobs to them, Jakobs would kill him. If he didn't they might kill him. Numerous scenarios shot through his brain, split second thoughts flashing in and out, he could just run away, but where to? He would need gear later. He could say he got nicked, or robbed by someone else. Then his phone rang. He looked at it, beads of sweat ran down his already wet salty forehead. Finally he answered, "B, I got into some trouble."

Four

0600hrs 11th March

The alarm sounded on the mobile phone, which was lying on the floor, next to the single mattress. It vibrated as it trilled, nestled inside the size nine left footed training shoe, the black sock that covered it loosely, slightly muffling the sound. Charlie Jackson fumbled around with his right arm, across the floor in an effort to find the phone. He was laying on the mattress face down, head pointing towards the wall that hugged the length of his makeshift bed. He eventually found the phone, having tossed the sock aside and switched it to snooze.

His eyes remained closed and he squeezed them tighter in an attempt to get rid of the dull pain set deep behind his eyeballs. Every morning was the same. Six years of solid drinking would take its toll on anyone. In the grand scheme of things, the headaches were nothing. It was the emotional turmoil that every night's sleep brought with it that was unbearable. Every morning brought exhaustion. Almost as if he had run a marathon, or worse, like doing twelve rounds with Mike Tyson. Some mornings he could not remember his dreams, but knew they had been the same. The inner feelings of fear, or helplessness were evidence of this. Dreams that were nightmares. Nightmares of reality.

Six years ago Jackson had lost his fourteen year old son, Jason, to a freak accident. An accident that should never have happened. Jason had been killed on a motorbike, bought for him by his Father, for his birthday. A motorbike that his father had allowed him to ride in the woods. Worse still, the woods that his father had driven them to. An accident that Jackson would never, ever forgive himself for. Three years later, his soul mate, the mother of his children, Karen, had killed herself, desperate to rid her tormented mind of the pain of the loss of her son. The very same pain that Charlie was forced to cope with, every day of his miserable life. He himself, probably would have gone the same way had it not been for the tremendous strength and support shown by his three remaining daughters. Not forgetting his joyous grandchildren who adored their relatively young Grandfather.

He finally opened his eyes and grabbed the phone from his shoe. Flicked through the notifications. Two text messages and five emails, none of which held any importance. He looked around the mess of his room. A small twelve feet by twelve feet self contained bedsit.

Jackson had lost his house soon after his son's death. Three years later, he moved out of their rented maisonette, the one that Karen had committed suicide in, not being able to bear to step foot in it again. Since then the offer of roof and food had come from all directions, especially from his daughters and five younger brothers. Jackson had known he could not take up any of these kind offers. His daughters were special and deserved better than having to cope with the alcoholic tramp that their father had become. Instead, he was now living in this small bedsit, but he did make great efforts to visit all of his girls as often as he could, at times that would sandwich between his working and drinking habits.

Jackson sat up rubbing his eyes. Still wearing his jeans and t-shirt from the previous day. He waded past the pile of clothes strewn across the floor, and flicked on the kettle, which was sat on a worktop next to the small sink on the far side of the wall. He caught the strong smell of whisky.

He looked down at the almost empty bottle of Jack Daniels at the end of the worktop. The neck was open. He took the bottle and put it to his mouth. He tipped it up, three gulps and the remainder of the reddish brown liquid was gone. He picked up the bottle top and loosely replaced it, before dumping it in the black bin liner on the floor next to where he was standing. The bottle clinked against the other empty bottles in the bag.

He then left the room and headed to the communal bathroom at the end of the corridor to the right of his room. The first floor, of the three story house in Lennox Road accommodated three separate bedsits, as did the top floor. The ground floor had a single bedsit at the front of the house. The rear of the ground floor contained another communal bathroom and a large kitchen shared by all the occupants.

Jackson brushed his teeth but didn't wash before returning to his room. He took off his t-shirt and threw it onto the floor to join the rest of his laundry. Underneath was a very muscular toned body. Regular exercise helped Jackson retain this appearance, despite the dangerous amounts of alcohol he consumed each night. He looked at himself in the mirror, which sat flush to the wall above the sink. He turned the tap on, wet his hands and finger brushed his slightly thinning black hair into place.

Jackson picked up a pile of t-shirts from the floor. Smelling them one at a time. He chose the plain grey one, which offered the least unpleasant smell, and put it on. He kept on the jeans that he had slept in. The kettle popped and he poured himself a coffee. He normally had two sugars but had ran out. He made do without, believing the hot black liquid would take away some of the alcohol rich smell coming from his breath. Jackson drank his coffee while he replied to the text messages from his girls.

Finally Jackson was ready to go to work. As he got to the door he patted his rear pocket to make sure his police warrant card was still in place.

Five

0610hrs 11th March

Kulwant Singh protested his innocence as he was bundled to the floor by six heavy handed Police Officers. The licensed Hackney Carriage driver's hands being forced behind his back to be handcuffed.

"I am not doing anything," he shouted. Although he had lived in England for just over twenty years he still spoke in broken English. The cuts to his face and hands were not as a result of being physically forced to the floor, but from exploding glass. His long black hair was tied into a bun on top of his head, covered with a black net. A short while earlier the black net had been covered by a black turban, which was now rolling on the footpath next to where he was being held down.

"Just be quiet sir," said one of the restraining officers, "If you really haven't done anything, then you have nothing to worry about".

"But it was me who was calling you! Check my phone, I call you for help," he protested, confused, not understanding their actions.

The officers lifted him to his feet and led him to the back of the marked Police Skoda, parked ten feet behind his taxi, helping the distressed, crying, handcuffed, taxi driver into the back of their car. A group of civilian commuters were now gathering outside Gravesend train station, where it had happened, some in shock, some laughing, some on the phone and some taking photographs. The incident, now taking a priority, above the possibility of missing their train or being late for work. The growing horde were being held back by a barrier, formed by other Officers at the scene, behind the scenes of crime tape that stretched along the length of Rathmore Road.

Singh's green Skoda Octavia licensed taxi was awash with blood. In particular on the front passenger side and windscreen. The front and rear windows were smashed to pieces. The headless body of Jimmy Swift, local cocaine dealer, lay slumped on the road next to the front passenger side. Jimmy's hysterical partner Wendy had said the Taxi driver shot him because they were refusing to pay their fare. Wendy was intoxicated. Very drunk.

The Officers had searched Singh, who had no weapon on him. Scenes of Crime Officers were now also at the scene taking swabs and samples. No weapon was found in the vehicle.

Singh himself, could offer no explanation. Swift was refusing to pay his fare, got out of the car and then according to Singh, just blew up.

Six

0635hrs 11th March

Jackson slammed the flimsy, hardboard door behind him, but didn't lock it. He figured he had nothing worth stealing inside anyway. He also knew that the other bedsit occupants in the house were wary of him. Nice enough people but he had little interaction with them, wishing to keep his occupation amongst other things secret. It took him thirty seconds to get out the main front door and a further minute to walk across to his dark blue X plate diesel Toyota Previa people carrier.

The inside of his vehicle was an equal mess to his flat. Empty cigarette boxes were strewn across the front passenger footwell along with discarded beer cans, sweet wrappers and parking tickets. He had piles of clothes, his clothes, spread out in no orderly fashion across the seats behind him. All smelling as bad as the ones in his room.

Five minutes later he was typing in a four digit code on the gate entry system by the rear yard of Gravesend police station. The heavy, blue metal gates slowly started to roll horizontally. Jackson waited until it was completely open, which gave him a chance to finish his cigarette. He flicked it out his window as he drove up the steep ramp into the police yard. A benefit attached to holding the rank of Sergeant was having his own parking space in the small courtyard. Jackson steered around in a clockwise direction, around the dozen white marked Police Skodas. His assigned bay was at the far side of the yard, adjacent to the portable cabins that he worked from. Five minutes later, after another quick cigarette, under the smoking shelter in the yard, and accessing another security key pad, he was in the *office*.

Kent police had pioneered the National Intelligence led Policing Model, in more particular Sir David Phillips had, after he took over as Chief Constable of Kent in 1993. Policing methods previously had largely been reactive. The new model, instead concentrated on recidivist offenders. By using more covert methods, such as informants and surveillance. More conscious efforts were made to target those criminals who committed numerous crimes on a day to day basis. Crimes that were measured. Crimes such as Burglaries, motor vehicle thefts and other crimes which would otherwise affect the confidence of the general public in its Police service. By targeting the small proportion of habitual offenders, labelled targets, the Constabulary had managed to bring crime rates down as well as increasing their detection rate (solved crime rate). These local targets were categorised as Cat Bs. Every local officer had the responsibility of producing as much intelligence as possible on each Cat B. A joint effort, to produce enough information to secure an arrest and thereby lock him or her up.

Charlie Jackson ran the team that held the largest chunk of responsibility for providing, disseminating and resourcing the information. Jackson's role as Detective Sergeant on the Covert Human Intelligence Source handling unit meant exactly that. His small team cultivated, recruited and managed informants per se. Not like in the old days either. Once upon a time, most Police Officer could have their own little narks. Nothing got recorded officially, but some very good arrests resulted. Unfortunately, mixed results, right ones and wrong ones.

Wrong ones, such as set ups had became far too common. Also too often informants got burnt. Found out by those that were being spoken about, with very little protection.

Today everything was documented. Secret and separate computer systems housed details of every CHIS. Separate from the general access computers, keeping each informants true identity secret, even from Police Officers. The specifics of each informant, known only by the teams dealing with them, in the case of North Kent, Charlie Jackson's team. Every contact made, tasking issued and payments made, needed not only to be recorded but also authorized.

"It's going to get worse. If you don't like it jump ship," was Jackson's automatic response to his team, when the complaints came in of how many hoops they had to jump through just to get things authorized. Of course nobody in his team would ever leave. Not through choice anyway. They were all on the team because they loved it. They also loved working for Jackson who led by example, never asking for anything that he was not prepared to do himself.

Jackson walked across to the kettle at the far side of the mobile hut, as he liked to refer to it, when his eye caught a light on, in the solitary office at the end of the room. A single glass partition separated it from the rest of the office and the blind was down. The office belonged to Jackson's Detective Inspector. Ian Thom. The Controller.

"Boss you in there?" Jackson called.

"Yes mate," came the reply from his old mate. Jackson always called him boss in the presence of others. Respect, but the friendship was close and when they were on their own, more affectionate terms such as *prick* or *cock* may be used. Right now, although he knew Ian was in his office, he did not know if he was on his own.

"Coffee?" Jackson questioned, only slightly curious as to why the Detective Inspector was in so early.

"Yes please," came the reply.

A few moments later Jackson walked in, carrying two mugs of coffee, he noticed that Thom was on his own and said, "Fucking hell, you look knackered. What's going on?"

Thom took the shining black mug of steaming coffee from Jackson's outstretched hand. "On call mate. Been up since just gone midnight." His head was concentrating on a crime report, filling the computer screen on his desk in front of him.

"Should have called me in," Jackson said, despite not knowing the reason why his Inspector had been called in.

"Yeah OK, I really needed a ninety percent proof drunken asshole in to help me out." Thom knew of Jackson's drinking habits. "Look at the state of you," he added.

Jackson just smiled, ignoring his supervisor's half serious, half jovial comments. "So tell me what's happened?"

"Punch up in a pub that's gone seriously wrong. Two black guys tried to bully a landlord and his customers. They get nasty but one of his punters steps in and smashes them both."

"Sounds fair enough to me," said Jackson still smiling, he had noticed that his Inspectors shirt was buttoned out of sequence, leaving a gap midway up his torso, revealing a thermal vest.

"Yes suppose so but -" he paused to take a sip of his coffee, getting slightly irritated by Jacksons smirk, "but," he continued, "one of the black guys have gone missing, don't know who he is or where he is from, and the other one is in intensive care. Less than five percent chance of living. The landlord and his other customers are all saying it was self defence. They reckon that one guy did the damage on his own, which I doubt to be true. The black guys aren't the smallest blokes in the world. They are also saying they do not know the attackers name. No CCTV working in the pub apparently. CCTV outside does not cover the boozer but does show someone walking away from Manor Road about the right time."

"Manor Ale?" Jackson guessed from the name of the road given by Thom and then asked for a description.

"White male, 30yrs, Six feet tall, large build with massive shoulders, according to both the landlord and the CCTV at the end of the road -"

Jackson interrupted and finished the sentence. "Jet black hair, with a scar down one of his eyebrows? Believe left eyebrow."

"How do you know?" Thom looked baffled as he looked up at his Sergeants eyes. Suspicion etched all over his own face. Thom's ginger hair, normally brushed into a neat side parting, was currently strewn all over the place.

"I know who done it," Jackson spoke with satisfaction and turned his back on his boss.

"Well come on then," demanded Thom,

"Drunken asshole wasn't it?" Jackson replied, still facing away from his Inspector.

"Just tell me you prick," ordered the Inspector.

Jackson stopped walking, still smirking. "OK OK, calm down SIR." He emphasized the last word. "Only person I know who has the capability of doing what you just said and has the biggest shoulders in the world, shoulders any gorilla would be proud of." He paused again, holding the suspense, enjoying his boss's desperation.

"Get on with it Jackson," growled Thom, standing to his feet. His face reddened, highlighting his freckles even more than usual, when his phone rang. He held one finger up, as if to keep Jackson from moving and answered it. He listened, pulled a face and listened some more.

"I'll be right up," he said and hung up the phone. He looked up at Jackson and went on, "Got to go out. We've had a shooting. Some taxi driver has shot a customer for refusing to pay his fare. I fucking hate being on call. Why does the wheel always come off when it's me? Anyway before I go. Name Jackson!"

Jackson sighed before he finally spoke, "Samuel Jakobs."

Seven

0925hrs 12th March

It must have been about seven in the morning when I had walked up to Gravesend Police station. The hour previous, I had endured a forty five minute cardio work out, at the outdoor facilities in Woodlands Park. It was a short walk from the small room I was renting in Lawrence Square, where I sometimes stayed the night.

The small room, in the small flat, belonged to an old friend, Tommy, who had moved into his girlfriend's house. The flat also belonged to Gravesham Borough Council and he didn't want to declare to them that he had moved out. Just in case things went wrong with the girl. So he let me stay there whenever I wanted, so I could air the place and make sure that it did not get burgled, I had a certain reputation and it would take a brave person to break into a place with my name on it. It was rent free as long as I kept it clean. I just used it to sleep in, I always ate out, so keeping it clean took very little effort.

I had told the desk clerk at the Police Station that I was apparently wanted for an attempt murder. My appearance and the word murder, producing a look of both fear and nervousness from the aging grey haired woman in glasses, sat behind the desk. People surrendering themselves for murder being a rarity. I tried to smile at her, but it did not help much. She asked me to take a seat, quickly turned away and picked up the desk phone. She tried to keep her voice quiet. I wasn't interested in anything that she had to say anyway and I wasn't offended by her reaction. In reality, a person who looked like me, thick set, scarred face and tattooed neck would always evoke such a response, a thing I had got used to throughout my life.

I sat down, choosing the empty chair furthest away from the reception. About ten minutes later I was surrounded by four burly looking Tactical team officers, dressed in their black, door bashing overalls. I wondered if a requirement for joining the Tactical Team was height, weight and size. They always seemed to be larger than the average officer, apart from the females of course.

I was handcuffed immediately and then walked back out
the building, through the main entrance, into the street. I
was then escorted around the outside of the police station
to the rear yard. An odd decision I thought, as I knew they
could have taken me through to their custody area via one
of the doorways next to the front desk. I realized why, once
we had walked through the rear blue metal gate. A few
suits, (CID) were stood in the car park, behind a row of
marked Police vehicles, together with a few more rogue
looking plain clothed officers, oh and one rather gorgeous
looking petit blonde. *Monkey in a zoo* came to mind, so I
waved at the group with a big smile on my face. The suits
for some reason turned away. The blonde and a rough,
trampy looking guy held my stare.

Moments later I had been processed through the custody
procedure. I had declined my rights to have both
somebody being informed of my arrest and the right to
legal advice. It had been explained to me that it was free
and that I should at least consider speaking to a solicitor
due to the gravity of the offence for which I had been
arrested. I had remained polite but adamant that I did not
need one at this stage. Solicitors prolonged the periods of
detention. For certain reasons, interviews took place far
quicker when you were not represented and I had no

intention of spending my entire day at the station. Solicitors nowadays, often advised their clients to make 'no comment' interviews, that is maintaining your right of silence and refusal to answer questions. If the Police had enough evidence to charge you that was what they would do. On the other hand if they didn't, answering questions, sometimes gave them the additional evidence that they required. As such if you refused a solicitor, the Police often got into interview as quick as they could, just in case you changed your mind. I didn't need a solicitor.

Other than the other formalities of providing my name and address as being of no fixed abode, everything was dealt with quickly. No property had to be listed as I had turned up, on purpose, with nothing on me. Now some half hour later, I was lying on a thin blue plastic coated mattress, in a brightly lit cell. The smooth concrete walls were painted white. Graffiti ruined the plain white look over all the walls. There were no windows. The mottled grey glazed stone floor was cold. My shoes had been taken from me together with my belt, *for my safety*? One grey metal door with a small hatch in its upper half separated me from the rest of the world.

The hatch opened and a jailor brought me a small plastic cup containing my ordered coffee. No words were spoken by either of us. I spent the next two hours splitting fifteen minute periods, exercising and then resting on the plastic mattress. I knew that all the cells were monitored by video cameras. Doing pushups, squats and burpees in a cell wasn't normal behaviour. It left feelings, unpleasant feelings within those dealing with me. A jailor had once told me that. Be polite but strange. It keeps the power crazy types away from you. That was not the only reason. I also thought clearer while exercising. Now was the time to reflect on my actions. Actions that led to the taking of my liberty.

Yes, I had returned to the Manor Ale pub, after robbing Reader of one hundred and thirty five pounds cash and two half balls of smack. Half balls and balls, priced at ten pounds and twenty pounds respectively, were how local heroin addicts currently bought their gear in Gravesend. I dropped the wraps of heroin down a drain outside the pub.

The reason I had returned to the pub was to await Readers actions, what would he do when he returned to his bosses and explained that he had been robbed. More than likely, the Yardies that Piper *the grass* had told me about. Yes Reader would be in trouble and would inherit the debt of the money and drugs lost. But the test would be; who was he more frightened of? Them or me? If it was me then he would either, not go back straight away and claim he had been arrested by the Police. Though, that would bring the additional problems of having no Police paperwork, such as charge sheets or bail notices, or he would say that he had been robbed and did not recognize the robber. Alternatively, he would give me away and they would come looking for me straight away. In all likelihood they would come and search the area anyway. I do not like looking over my shoulder, so my best option would be to wait and have it out, there and then, if I was ratted.

The next hour had brought a handful of new customers into the pub. All of whom appeared to be familiar with the landlord and must have been regulars. Bill who was still there when I arrived, staggered out, advice from the landlord who didn't want the drunk upsetting his regulars, despite having taken advantage of Bill's giro for the past hour.

I had stayed at my window seat, with a fresh pint of Fosters lager on the table in front of me. One hour fifteen

minutes after my acquisition I felt relaxed. He hadn't
ratted me out. I smiled. But, I had smiled too early because
seconds later, after I had turned my back to the window,
the door opened and in came two potential Yardies, both
of whom were at least six feet tall. Both were wearing tight
black T-shirts, baggy jeans that were hanging below their
hips, flashing the seams of their boxer shorts, almost as if
in uniform. Facially they looked similar too, could have
been brothers. The only difference being that one had a
shiny bald head and the other had long dreadlocks. Behind
them stood Reader. His nose looked broken, blood
smeared his face as if it had been partially cleaned. The
break looked clean, his nose bent sharply to one side and
he was clearly in pain.

They looked down at him as he scanned the room,
moving his right hand up, partially covering his face, a
feeble attempt at concealing his identity, his eyes briefly
locking on mine, but he continued his scan. He shook his
head nervously. Too nervously, and they noticed. They
whispered to him and he quickly ran back out. He hadn't
grassed me up but had probably been forced to bring them
down to the scene. I stayed where I was. The room had
gone quiet and I turned to look around. Everyone in the
bar had seen the entrance made by these two strangers and

were watching, while pretending they were not watching. Small glances from the corners of their eyes.

The bald one walked towards the bar. "Two pints of Stella," he spoke loudly in what I could only describe as a Jamaican ghetto type accent, but with an unusually high pitched voice.

The Landlord looked up from the far end of the bar, face screwed and you could tell that he did not want them in the pub. He puffed his large chest out as he grabbed two fresh glasses from the counter behind him, under a row of neatly lined optics. He poured the lager and carried them over. He spoke to his new unwanted customer in a quiet voice, "Seven pounds forty pence."

"No man," came the reply from the bald one. "My friend with the broken nose just got robbed by one of your customers in here. You see how frightened he got? So frightened that it made him run off."

Mr Dreadlocks then spoke, "You owe us three hundred pounds man, you and your pussy hole friends here are going to pay us and we are going to give it back to that poor man." His pronunciation of *that* sounded like *dat* and *three* sounded more like *treeeee*.

"Look guys, I don't want no trouble. I don't know what you are talking about. Your, err, friend has never been in here." The Landlord still had his chest puffed out in an attempt to stand firm, but you could almost see his balls shrinking away.

Dreadlocks knocked his whole pint back, slammed the glass down and wiped his mouth clean. He walked over to the nearest customers. A couple aged in their forties. The red nose of the male, dressed in a loose green polo shirt and jeans, showing his inkling for a drink. His female companion was wearing a similar matching t-shirt, but black. She started pulling back, away from the imposing gangster. She had a tired looking face, but there was an attractiveness about it. She looked frightened and leant over towards her boyfriend.

Dreadlocks grabbed the female by the back of her head, fingers locking into her blonde but slightly greying pony tail, staring at the weakening boyfriend. "Money," he demanded and then thrust his lips onto the females. The force of the locking of lips drowned the little shrieking noise emitted from her throat.

That was about it for me. "Hey!" I spoke loud enough for everyone to hear.

Everyone looked up. The Landlord's eyes told me not to do, whatever it was that I was going to do. I smiled at him.

Baldy smiled as well. "Ah a hero. You can pay first." They both walked up towards me. Dreadlocks pushing his right hand deep into his front trouser pocket. I saw the silver knuckle duster come out and he grinned as he slipped it on.

"Yeah Ok," I said, "But let's take it outside." This was my fight after all, not that anyone else in the pub knew that. Also they would have to come out one at a time.

I stepped out, instinctively feeling that they were about five feet behind me. I walked out and stepped immediately to my left, my back almost against the wall, facing the door which I had closed on my way out, for reasons. The door was opened by Dreadlocks, with the hand wearing the duster. *Idiot.* His head came out and I drove a vicious straight right cross, striking the bottom of his jaw. I felt the crack and I knew I had broken it. He fell, unconscious and his head cracked hard on the pavement.

Baldy had been too close behind him and had no option but to stumble over the falling man. *Idiot*. He fell in perfect timing to my knee coming up hard into his jaw. His bald head bouncing back like a rubber ball. He rolled, comically over his static associate, landing on his back. I walked over calmly as he struggled to get to his feet. I waited until his legs were firmly planted and smashed out a kick with my right leg, strongest leg, thrusting all thirteen stones of my weight behind my rotating hip. It connected with the outside of his left knee. I heard and felt the sickening shattering of bone and this fight was over. Over in seconds. Real fights always lasted seconds, not like what you see on television. Dreadlocks was still out of it and would be for at least twenty minutes, probably longer. Blood was seeping from the side of his head onto the concrete edge of the footpath, exactly where it had struck. I looked back at the door which was now filled by the Landlord and his patrons.

"Self Defence," I said, a statement wanting acknowledgement. The Landlord nodded in agreement.

"CCTV?" I asked, wanting a certain answer.

"Not working," he said. I didn't know if he meant it, or if he was doing me a favour.

"Call an ambulance." I said as I walked away.

Five minutes later I was stood in Brandon Street. Seconds away from my ex-girlfriend, Louise's home. Ex-girlfriend probably not being the right word. She was an ex best friend. A really cool friend until we had a one night stand. Sexual activity, which we had always said we would never engage in, as it would ruin our friendship. We were right. She was now the Mother of our two year old daughter, Eve. I selfishly had wanted her to have an abortion. I was not ready to be a father, or a partner to be fair. I was a man with no regular work and at that time was living in a camper van. Not perfect husband material. She refused, she didn't believe in abortions. She stopped seeing me, right up to when Eve was born. She wanted to raise the girl on her own and wanted nothing to do with me. It had taken me a good few months of pestering her, just to start talking again. Somehow, gradually she also allowed me to pay my way, as an Uncle. According to her, I had lost my rights of fathership when I had demanded the abortion.

I phoned her for the second time that day. Moments later I saw her come out of her house. Stunning to look at. Every inch of her five feet six frame. Her dark brown, wavy hair, hanging loose over her shoulders. Face smooth and tanned. She was wearing a baggy T-shirt and equally baggy grey tracksuit bottoms, which hid what I knew to be the most perfect figure. She looked tired and stared at me through her large brown eyes, overlined by long eye lashes. I really missed her.

She eventually spoke, "Sam you said within an hour, I was just putting Eve to bed."

"I'm sorry," I said. "I got caught up in something. How is she?"

"She's good Sam. You really don't have to do this. How long is this going to last?"

"Until I don't have to," I replied. I then counted ninety pounds of my ill gotten gains and handed it over. Forty five pounds would see me through a couple of days.

It was late afternoon the following day I got a call from Louise. The Police had been around her house, wanting to speak to me. Warning her that it was serious. An attempt murder and that if she was hiding me she would be in serious trouble herself.

"What trouble are you in now?" she had pleaded.

My *mistaken identity* excuses had been overused and all of the *nothing to worry abouts* had also been exhausted.

Somebody at the pub must have named me I thought, but I was confident that they would all agree with the case of self defence. Worst case scenario of being charged and sent to prison did not worry me anyway. I would keep my head down and hand myself in to them in my own time.

So here I was, cell number eight waiting for the keys to jangle on the other side of the metal door and some Detective to appear for his introductions.

Sure enough exactly two hours fifteen minutes after being placed into my temporary windowless concrete billet, I heard the keys rattling on the other side of the door and it swung open.

Two Detectives stood on the other side of the door. Both smiling, both wearing grey flannel suits, white shirts and dark ties. There were no pleasantries though, no introduction.

The older male spoke one word, "Interview."

Eight

I was escorted by the two suits, back to the Custody Desk, one of them in front of me and one behind me. It was far busier than this morning when I was booked in. Uniformed officers, suits and their detainees formed untidy queues waiting to be seen by a Custody Officer.

"Sammy boy, who you beaten up this time?"

I looked in the direction of the voice shouting out above the hum of voices. A man in his twenties, wearing a blue paper prisoner suit, that is provided to you when all your clothes are seized, who I vaguely recognised was grinning at me. Being led away towards the cells by a jailer. I ignored him and was led to the front of the queue by my arm by one of my escorts.

"Mate of yours?" said the older Detective.

"Don't know him," I replied. It might be just me, but I frequently found myself in uncomfortable conversations with people who apparently knew me really well and I couldn't even remember their names.

The raised platform on the other side of the desk, gave the impression that the Custody Sergeant on the other side was taller than he actually was. It was not the same Custody officer that had booked me in that morning.

The other one, the one that had booked me in was dealing with an Asian man wearing a turban. Accompanied by an Asian solicitor wearing a suit. The man in the turban was being bailed.

His solicitor spoke, "Sergeant. I cannot see how bail is an option. You have found no weapons that could possibly link my client with the murder. It is clear that your victim was a drug dealer. The only possibility is that somebody else from outside my client's vehicle committed the atrocity. My client should be refused charge immediately."

The Sergeant spoke, with a look of disdain. "Thank you for your observations Mr Ali but Mr Singh is going to be bailed pending further enquiries." He then looked at the man in the turban. "Mr Singh, in all likelihood, unless the investigators uncover further evidence you will be refused charge before the set date."

The solicitor went to speak again and the Custody Officer's glare stopped him in his tracks. Instead he turned to his client and whispered.

I drew my attention to the man dealing with me on the other side of the desk and looked at his force issue number, displayed on the metal badge pinned to the left breast pocket of his white shirt. Four digits starting with a seven told me that he was nearing his time for retirement. Every officer had their own individual force number, issued on joining the service. Today, a first digit of seven showed they were somewhere between twenty five to thirty years service. Close to retirement. Most of the street officers now had five digit numbers. New blood. The higher the number, the least experienced.

The Sergeant was broad, his thick dark curly hair greying at the temples. He wore glasses. He looked to be in his fifties. He looked down at me and the older Detective spoke first, "Can we book him out for interview Sarge?"

The Custody Sergeant turned around to face a row of A4 sized clipboards displayed behind him. He picked up the one held under the title Cell eight and placed it down on the desk in front of him. He took a few seconds to read through it.

"You OK with that son? Attempt murder and no brief?" His voice was gruff and had a hint of a northern accent about it.

Mr Ali half turned towards me, expectant.

"Yes guv," I replied with a smile. It must have seemed strange that I did not want a solicitor for a case of attempted murder.

He raised his eyebrows and handed the paperwork that was clipped on the board to the Detectives. The older one wrote something on it, handed it back and told me to follow the jailer, who was stood next to the desk. Mr Ali turned away, no longer interested.

The jailer led us away, carrying a huge metal ring, bigger than a large bracelet, about a centimetre thick, which had a dozen large metal keys thread through it. We reached a heavy metal gate, lined with bars, that led to a corridor. He selected one of the keys, a short fat key and unlocked it. A number of large metal doors aligned one side of the wall. We walked along the corridor, stopping at one of the doors which was marked *interview room 6,* into a small rectangular room.

A DVD recorder sat on a cheap wooden table in the corner of the room next to a bolted down table with two bolted down benches on either side of it. A budget cord carpet, which was grey in colour covered the floor. The walls had white perforated metal panels on them, which I knew housed the audio recorders and there were two video cameras up on two opposite corners of the ceiling. I watched the younger Detective unwrap two new DVD's and place them into the recorder. As he did this the older one spoke.

"My name is Detective Sergeant Pete Davis. My colleague here is DC White. We are going to interview you. The interview is going to be recorded by way of DVD. Have you any questions before we start?"

I shook my head, amused at his robotic mannerisms. I had been here before and was accustomed to interviewing officers talking to me before starting the interview. Conversations that hinted towards, *it would be better for me to co-operate and tell the truth*. Or promises that, *I wouldn't be getting bail if I decided to lie*. DS Davis was making no such hints or promises.

"OK, let's start Dave," he directed his statement at DC White who pressed the record button. A short buzzer sounded for a couple of seconds and then switched off.

Once again the DS spoke first, "The time now is nine thirty six hours on the morning of the twelfth of March. Ok, this is an interview taking place in an interview room at Gravesend Police Station. The interview is being video recorded. My name is Detective Sergeant Davis from Tactical CID, based here at Gravesend Police station. Also present is." He indicated for his partner to speak.

DC White said, "Yes, hello my name is Dave White. I am a Detective Constable from Gravesend TAC CID". He spoke in a far more relaxed manner than his supervisor.

Davis looked at me and said, "Can you please provide your name, date of birth and address."

"Samuel Jakobs, nineteen, ten, eighty five and I am N.F.A, no fixed abode." I sat, completely relaxed as I spoke, knowing that I was soon, very soon about to irritate the hell out of them.

The next few minutes led me through a preamble of formalities from the robotic DS advising me of my rights and eventually he cautioned me, "You do not have to say anything, but it may harm your defence if you do not mention when questioned something you later rely on in court. Anything you do say may be given in evidence. Do you understand?"

"Yes I do. I fully understand the caution. I need a pen and paper from you as I intend to write down a prepared statement while being recorded after which I intend to retain my right to silence."

The two officers looked blankly at each other, puzzled at my request. Prepared statements were not a new thing but a prisoner asking to do so, especially during an interview without a solicitor was new to both.

"Paper and pen please," I repeated.

White acted first, perhaps a little embarrassed that his DS did not know what to do and spoke for the purposes of the recorder, "Ok Sam, here you are." He handed me a black biro pen and a blank sheet of A4 paper, which he had ripped out of a note book in front of him.

I then took my time writing down what I needed to, largely in silence, apart from asking for a coffee. It was White again who agreed to leave the room to fetch my refreshments. Davis, I could tell was stewing. I wrote with my free arm protecting the contents of what I was writing from the officer, as if I was taking a test and did not want anyone copying my answers. Half hour later I handed the document to Davis.

White leaned in and Davis said, "I will read it."

'I make this statement of my own free will. It relates to an incident two days ago at The Manor Ale public house. I cannot remember the exact time but it must have been late afternoon or early evening. I was having a drink inside the pub on my own. I am not a regular at the pub but needed some space to go over some personal problems I am having, which I do not want to discuss. While I was in the pub there were other customers present who I do not know. At some point two black males came into the pub with a scared looking white man with

a broken nose. The man with the broken nose left after one of the black men appeared to threaten him'

A small white lie.

The two black men were very intimidating to everyone in the pub. They ordered drinks and refused to pay for them and then threatened to rob everyone in the pub of money. They even assaulted one poor old woman in the pub. Fearing the worst I intervened. I can't remember exactly what I said but I was asking them to leave. They both then threatened me and started to walk towards me. One put on a knuckle duster. Clearly I was frightened and left the pub. But they followed me and the man with a knuckle duster threw a punch at me.

Another small white lie, but you know what they say, every good lie should contain ninety percent truth, which my statement did.

I am an ex boxer and managed to dodge the punch. I threw a punch back in self defence. One punch as I could see he was still attacking me. He fell to the floor. The other man came out and fell over his friend. He was very angry and also attacked me but I managed to kick him and he fell over as well. I could see the first person was still lying on the floor so I told the landlord to call an ambulance and I left. This is the truth as all the witnesses who are not my friends, associates or known to me in anyway should confirm. My statement is an accurate record of events. My actions were purely self defence. I do not trust the current Police service and as such will retain my right to silence for the remainder of this interview'

"The note then ends with a scrawl which I can only take to be your signature and a smiley face!" DS Davis continued, "Is this correct?" He looked at me waiting for an acknowledgement.

I smiled and put my finger and thumb across my mouth as if closing a zip.

I was asked numerous questions from that point on, and reminded of the part of the caution relating to harming any defence used in court if I did not answer the questions now. I stayed still. No words uttered, no nods, no shaking of my head. Right up to the point of the recorder being switched off. I watched White seal the discs and signed where I was asked to sign. Still not speaking.

"Take him back," Davis said to White. His already red face, had reddened even more and I knew I had successfully managed to piss him right off.

White on the other hand showed no reaction of being offended. He just nodded with a smile, signalling for me to follow him out. He took me back to the cell and said "Nice one Sam." He asked me if I wanted another coffee just before he slammed the door shut.

Nine

Back in cell number eight, I knew that now I would have the long wait. I had successfully pissed off the officers investigating me and they would be in no rush to release me. That was inevitable and something I had no control over. But release me, they would have to. I could not see any of the witnesses giving any account that would refute my statement. Even the little white lies. It would have been impossible for them to have seen whether Dreadlocks had thrown the first punch or not. I settled back onto the plastic mattress and closed my eyes. I felt myself relax and could have dozed off quite easily, but for the rattling of keys in the lock again. I opened my eyes and stared at the metal door.

The door opened. Outside stood the pretty blonde and her rough looking mate that I had seen in the rear yard.

The ones that had been stood with the suits in the Police car park when I had been walked through into the Custody area.

"Need a chat," said the blonde. She had neat straight hair cut into a bob style. Blue eyes smiled at me and she showed a neat set of pearly whites (teeth). A tight v-neck white t-shirt exposed, smooth flesh over a pair of proud thirty six D cups. Her equally tight black jeans highlighted toned curves that can only be achieved in a gymnasium.

"Any time princess. Is your Dad coming as well?" I nodded at the older man, stood just behind her. He stood about five feet ten, maybe twelve, thirteen stones. Could be forty years of age, maybe younger but looked fit, athletic and muscular. His black hair was just a mess on top of his head with no real style to it. His tatty grey T-shirt and black jeans didn't look like they had seen a washing machine in a while. He stood there smiling at my quip. I don't particularly have any sort of fondness for *The Old Bill* but for some reason I took an instant likeness for this guy.

I hopped off the bed and walked towards the smiling princess.

"Where we going?" I asked, my nose catching the hint of perfume or maybe it was her hair. Whatever it was, it complemented her princess status.

"I know this great place," she said looping her left arm through my hanging right arm, just as a dating couple would. She smiled again, her face a matter of inches from mine. I could have melted despite knowing that she was just joking.

I was taken past the Custody desk, which was still busy, out of the custody area, without booking me out, and into another room, a similar size to the interview room I had been sat in moments before. This room however had no recording equipment and no video cameras. There was a table and four chairs. None of which were bolted to the floor. Two wooden doors. The one that we had entered and one on the adjoining wall. Plastered walls painted white, no graffiti. There was a small corner table, with a small green plant pot on it containing a green rubber plant. The chairs were wooden, with soft brown upholstery on the seat and back rest. More comfortable than the interview room benches.

"Nice place," I said, still bemused as to what was going on.

"Sit down," she said as she slid into a chair opposite to the one she had indicated for me to take. The older guy stood by the closed door that we had just come through, leaning back against it.

"OK, so who are you and what do you want princess?" I said.

"My names Julie and my Dad is Charlie," she smiled warmly as she spoke.

First name terms I thought. "OK I got your names but you still haven't answered my question."

"Well, we are from the intelligence unit and WE can do YOU some favours," her scent drifted over to me again as she swished her hair to the side.

I could have kicked myself. I should have expected this visit. The Intelligence Unit, almost as a matter of routine spoke to anyone who was anyone, while they were in Custody. They made grasses. They got criminals to rat on other criminals. *'Rat on a rat'* was the slogan. I hated grasses. I felt sick.

"Sorry Princess, there is nothing that you can do for me. It was self defence and you all know that. You can keep me locked up for twenty four hours just to piss me off, but then that's it. Refused charge written all over it. I can't see what you guys would be pissed off about anyway. It was self defence and those two assholes deserved what they got." I paused briefly and then added, "Even if I did need a leg up, I'm sorry it wouldn't come from you guys, no offence but I am not and will never be a grass. To be honest I am quite offended that you would think anything different. I got nothing against you lot, the Police, but me? I just am not a grass."

There was a moment's silence. She was still looking straight at me. Still with that gorgeous smile on her face, neat shiny straight teeth held together by bright pink gums. Hidden behind them was her equally pink tongue.

It was Charlie that spoke next, as he pushed himself off the closed door. "Sam," his voice was friendly, slightly husky and spoke my name with a familiarity about it. "You have got it all wrong mate, the grass bit that is."

He walked over and sat himself down into one of the two free chairs in the room. I didn't respond. There was no need to. I knew he had a lot more to say and at that moment, it did not matter to me what was about to come out of his mouth. I was not a grass, period. Also the view of his colleague was much better than that of the four graffiti covered walls in my cell.

He carried on, "We don't deal with grasses. Most coppers do but we don't. Grasses are the most untrustworthy people I know. They don't care who or what they talk about. I've lost count of the number of times I get a phone call," he then mimicked getting a phone call, putting his right hand to his ear and put on a squeaky slurred voice, "Charlie, Charlie I need a score man," He then reverted to his own voice still on the fictitious phone call, "What you got for me then?" Squeaky voice, "My Brother's picking up a nine bar." I knew a nine bar referred to nine ounces of drugs.

Charlie hung up the fictitious phone and continued, "My Brother!" he spoke with a hint of disgust in his voice. "That's a grass. It's true Sam. Grasses will talk about anything and anyone just to get what they want. You know that and so do I. As much as I know that YOU would never, ever, ever be a grass."

"So why are we even talking Charlie?" I studied his face as he spoke. He was looking directly at me. Sincerity in his eyes and his face. I didn't trust anyone but his whole demeanour was truthful.

"We are talking to you Sam, because of exactly that. You are not a grass and you are not like them. Before I go on, let me tell you about you. You are a good guy. You had a tough childhood. Real tough childhood. Drug addict parents and I won't say much more about them. Older brother and sister, both who unfortunately went that way as well. But your brother was also a good guy. He looked after you. He kept you away from the drugs as best as he could."

I did not like people talking about my brother, Wayne. He had saved me. That was true. Kept me well away from the drugs. Made sure I went to school. He suffered the intolerances of my parents on my behalf. Parents that would have preferred me to go out shoplifting instead of school, so I could earn them the twenty, thirty quid they would need to juice up for the day. Wayne had worked twice as hard to support their pitiful habit, just to make sure I was alright. Too late to save our eldest sibling, our sister Claire. Hooked on heroin from the age of fourteen, prostituting, for her bit as well as for the pathetic couple who had put us on this earth.

"Please don't talk about my brother. He was a druggie. Cops don't like druggies so I know you don't mean it. So please don't make me lose it, you seem like a decent bloke, but leave my brother out of it."

"Ok Sam, but you are wrong, I did mean it. He was a good guy. Druggies as you call them, still have characters. Wayne was a good guy." He still had sincerity in his voice. I could feel a slight wetness in my eyes as he carried on. I loved Wayne and the thought of him being buried six feet under churned my gut.

Jackson carried on, "I'll skip to after school then. You joined the Army. Three years of character building and becoming who you are now, not mentioning the massive IQ you possess. IQ level of a leading scientist they reckon. Then you came back and grafted. Your turn had come to support Wayne, every now and then bailing him out of trouble. Until he was gone. Built up such a hatred for drugs that you now rob dealers, weekly if not monthly. In fact it's got so, that if you have not been *Sam raided* you aren't even on the map."

I had heard of the slogan. Some smart ass had made a derivative of 'Ram Raid.'

Charlie Jackson carried on, "You got a great kid from a one night stand. You still stand by the kid. I know you pay your way. Good guy. But this can't go on forever Sam. It will end up bad, really bad. It will be prison or death. In fact it won't surprise me if them Yardies don't already have a contract out on you after this."

"When your times up your times up," was all I could think to reply.

"It doesn't have to be Sam. Like I said, I'm not looking for a grass. I don't like grasses any more than you. I'm looking for an agent. An agent who works for what he gets. Someone I can trust. Someone who won't talk about his family or friends just because it might pay. Someone who won't talk about me. A good guy who don't like bad guys. Someone like you." I was a good judge of character. I knew police regularly said what they thought they had to say, to get what they want. Like salesmen. Charlie was not selling. He was being truthful.

I went to respond but couldn't. The deafening explosion and shaking of the room put a stop to that.

Ten

The door opposite me shook violently. Not the one that Charlie Jackson had been leaning on. Julie Stokes was cowering in her chair, her body folded, pushing her head down, deep into her lap, arms covering her head as if she was being attacked from behind.

"What the hell!" Charlie shouted as he rushed to open the door behind him, the one that shook.

I had stood up straight away. My response to danger had always been to attack. I instinctively stood in my boxing stance, hands held high close to my chin, as the Detective opened the door. He raised his hand as if to ward me back, away from the open door. The screaming on the other side of the door got louder. A wave of heat filled our room simultaneously.

On the other side of the door, in the reception, I saw a splintered, smouldering counter at the front desk. It was the room I had entered earlier that morning when I was handing myself in. There was some smoke drifting heavily in the air, like smoke exhaled from a dozen cigarettes. The old lady was not wearing her glasses any more, she was the one screaming, pushing herself back into the far corner of the room as hard as she could, trying to push herself through the actual wall.

The heat was coming from a fire. The main part of which was on the floor in front of the counter. I moved closer into the gap left in the doorway from Charlie's exit. I could now clearly see what was on fire. A close to headless corpse was lying flat on the floor, tatters of torn flesh were visible, ripped clothing on fire. The room was splattered in a mixture of bright red and crimson liquid and pink fleshy coloured substances. Looking closer, the lower half of the body was almost perfectly intact, the head and part of the shoulders however were not there. An older man sat huddled against the wall next to the public entrance, he quivered, arms around his bent legs seated on the floor, face transfixed on his knees with a glaze in his eyes. Shock taking him away from the real world.

Charlie was screaming at the receptionist, "What the fuck happened?"

Her screaming had turned to sobbing and she repeatedly said, "I was getting him a pen. I was just getting him a pen."

"Charlie," I shouted, "He needs help," I pointed at the elderly man on the floor in the far corner of the room, who now appeared to be convulsing in a fit, his head striking the wall behind him, dangerously hard. I didn't wait for his reply and went to the old man's assistance, pulling him away from the wall, joined a split second later by Julie Stokes. Charlie proceeded to put out the ebbing fire on the dead body.

I had no idea what had just gone on, headshot? explosion? the damage just did not make any sense at all. What I did know was that my new found friends were in for a very long night.

The mayhem that followed involved numerous officers, different officers, uniformed and plain clothed, entering and leaving the area. Some efforts being made to keep the scene sterile, while simultaneously treating the traumatized witnesses.

It took five minutes for somebody, Charlie, to realize that I should not be there. I was quickly taken back to cell number eight by a young officer. His high five digit force number telling me that he was clearly only weeks into his service. His face was white. He had never seen a dead body before. That's what he had told me as he escorted me back to my room. Other officers were running around in panic, I heard the words terrorists, shooting and bomb explosion, being uttered. Other cell mates were shouting and kicking at their individual cell room doors.

Once in my room, I laid back on the plastic mattress and tried to reflect on everything that had just taken place.

Eleven

0930hrs 12th March

Nicholas Tucker was sat on the fifth carriage of the South Eastern train, travelling from Gravesend to Chatham. He checked his Samsung Galaxy mobile phone screen again. Searching for the time again, five minutes after he had last checked. He was going to be late for his appearance at Medway Magistrates court and cursed the fact that he had overlaid, he also cursed the untold amount of alcohol he had consumed last night. A leaving drink with friends as he expected to be sent to prison for six months today. Being late would only serve to anger the Magistrates, who he had already upset during the course of the trial yesterday.

The charge was Burglary of a dwelling, which in reality, was Tucker breaking into his Aunt's, on his Mother's side, house and stealing two gold rings, a gold neck chain and a bag full of bracelets, also causing over five hundred pounds worth of damage, by forcing the patio doors open with a crowbar. He had known that her entire family had gone away on holiday, and he knew exactly where her jewellery was kept.

Stupidity and desperation for money had allowed him to pawn the jewellery at a national chain pawn broker. He had used the branch in Medway. Now Medway Police were dealing with his case. He had used a false name but did not know a video camera captured the image of everyone selling items at the premises. Despite the notices that said exactly that, on open display at the till. *CCTV OPERATES IN THIS STORE.* A routine check at the broker's by the local resident Police Officer, PC Redbridge, had matched the jewellery to the reported Burglary. A circulation of his image captured on the CCTV soon identified him.

The prosecution had made an application for the case to be heard at Crown Court, largely because of Tucker's previous convictions for burglary offences and the likelihood of him receiving a lengthy custodial sentence. Luckily for Tucker, the Magistrates had agreed to hear the trial themselves. Persuaded by his solicitor, Mr. Ali, who had gone through a torturous whole day of bullshit, outlining Tucker's mental issues, currently being treated by his Doctor, and that a Crown court hearing for such a trivial matter would seriously disrupt his treatment. A huge backward step in the rehabilitation of a man trying to change his ways. All of which was rubbish of course, but it would make the difference of receiving six months as opposed to three years at Her Majesty's Prison.

Tucker sat on his seat, flicking through his Facebook App, oblivious to the other passengers, a middle aged woman with a baby in arms sat in a seat, on the opposite side of the aisle that ran along the centre of the carriage. A man in a suit sat directly opposite Tucker, reading from a copy of the days Sun newspaper.

Rush hour had gone, so passengers were minimal, but there were still too many for him to spark up his joint of marijuana, which he really wanted to do. It might be his last joint. Instead he sat there chewing furiously on his gum checking his mobile phone for the time again, thinking that he could spark up his reef before walking into the court. He was going down anyway, so it wouldn't matter if he was late.

A minute later, 0940hrs, the train started pulling into Strood railway station. Two more stops. The train eased to a halt, clicking in rhythm, slowing down and then coming to a complete standstill. The doors gasped open as if desperate for a breath.

Tucker flushed, suddenly feeling an intense burning heat inside his head, inside his mouth. That being the last sensation he felt because a split second later he felt nothing at all. He could not hear the screaming that followed, he could not see the man in the suit sat opposite faint, splattered by bits of flesh, blood and bone matter.

Tuckers headless corpse lay across the aisle, still, dead, the mobile phone that had been in his hand seconds ago bleeped and lit up as it received a message from his Mother, *Good luck darling xxxx.*

Twelve

1230hrs 12th March

Robert Pond sat at his computer chair, what hair he had left on his balding head, moist with a mixture of grease and sweat. His bulbous, chubby face was equally wet from the salt water excreted at moments of excitement. Palmar Hyperhidrosis setting in the palm of his hands, due solely to the over stimulated eccrine sweat glands, trying to control his body temperature.

He sat there naked, apart from the blue checked boxer shorts, which were partially covered by his overhanging glutinous belly. The computer room was situated in the converted attic at the top of his three story town house, on the new housing estate built off Derring

Way at the South Eastern side of Gravesend. A family town house that was once occupied by his wife, three children, Staffordshire Terrier and tropical fish tank. Now inhabited solely by him.

Despite his carefulness for his new found fetish, his darling wife Maria knew somehow that something was wrong. No, not just wrong, but seriously wrong. Too wrong to share. Robert had just let them leave with a limpness. No fight, no argument, no attempts of persuasion. After all he actually knew it was very, very, very wrong.

The screen in front of him jumped to the requested page, the secret page, known only to him and others like him. Others who were wrong. He licked his lips in anticipation chewing on the gum in his mouth faster and faster, excitement causing a small movement in his nether region.

The child pornographic pictures appeared but Pond did not get to see them. His body had collapsed as his head exploded. Blood dripped down the screen covering the illegal images. The small flames at the severed end of his torso did not catch on the wooden floorboards, which was probably unfortunate. Unfortunate because that meant his predicament was not soon to be found. No family, no friends, in fact nobody ever came to visit Robert 'wrong, very wrong' Pond.

Thirteen

0320hrs 13th March

Natasza was probably the cutest six year old girl you could ever want to meet. Her long wavy bed hair, covered her otherwise pretty small featured face. Natasza was unfortunately one of the twenty percent of child sleepwalkers in the country. She generally sleep-walked when her Father was away. It had become a bit of a problem, so much so, that a child gate had been installed at the top of the stairs by her Mother, just to protect her. The steps were pretty steep in the purpose built flat above the corner shop in Perry Street. Today her Father was away.

The Mother, Lena Barela had moved to England from Poland eight years ago with her husband Marian. He had got some excellent work with a large contractor. A skilled carpenter, or chippie as they called it in England. Marian was an excellent carpenter, as had been his Father and in turn his Father. Right now, he had been sent to Wales for two weeks. The development of a new hotel and his employers had obtained the contract for installing the doors and windows.

Lena never liked it when she was left on her own. Although Gravesend had a large multi cultural society, animosity towards foreigners was slowly but surely growing. Blame being put on them for taking work from the local natives. In truth those Englishmen complaining, never actually wanted to work. They would rather stay at home living off the benefits provided to them by the very generous English Government.

Normally when Marian was away Natasza would jump in bed with Lena. But today their little *dzieciuch* (baby) had fallen asleep a little early watching her Frozen DVD in bed.

But right now Natasza was walking, in a trance, turning away at the stair gate. She carried on into the bathroom. A small bathroom painted white with a hint of green over thick woodchip wallpaper. It had a green linoleum floor over the entire eight feet by seven feet room. A small corner bath sat in the far side which gave room for a toilet and small hand basin, all of which were white porcelain.

Natasza walked over to the basin and picked up her frozen toothbrush from its holder. She turned the tap on and ran her toothbrush under the running water before dropping it into the basin. She then picked up a blue box with the word *Fresh* written across the front of it with a picture of gleaming white teeth.

She tipped the box into her small palm and a couple of capsulated shaped pieces of gum fell out. She caught them perfectly and put them into her open small mouth and started to chew. As she did this, smaller ampoules in one of the capsules broke. A mixture of treated alkali metals including sodium and potassium started to mix with a small amount of water released from within and her saliva. The reaction was heat first, then a small explosion which in turn, detonated the controlled amount of PETN, (Pentaerythritol tetranitrate), which structurally is very similar to nitro-glycerine and indeed one of the most powerful high explosive known to man. A combination that had been tested for years and years. A mixture measured out perfectly by its creator, to destroy by explosion anything within a foot of the centre of the reaction. Natasza's small upper torso exploded at the same time as her head.

Lena Barela, who had been woken by the running water in the basin screamed hysterically, and then she screamed and then she screamed, each scream containing the most wretched, heart breaking feeling of, *'it was the end of the world.'*

Fourteen

1900hrs 16th March

Peter Snugs laughed as he lost another game of cards to his
new tenants. He sat at an old thin white rectangular plastic
garden table. A makeshift, which the Snugs family had used
as a dining table, since moving into their unwanted flat in
Wallace Square. They had hoped for a house, with a
fireplace, two bedrooms, a living room, a dining room, a
conservatory and a large garden, but had already turned
down two offers. Gravesham Council didn't take kindly to
properties being turned down by allegedly homeless people
and had told them that they had to take the flat or risk
being taken off the housing list. Intentions of decorating it
and making the best of their new family home had
remained just that, intentions.

He was sat with B and another Yardie, K for King, he had been told. K was a smaller version of the other three. Five feet seven, very stocky and draped with gold chains. He also had a shaved head, shiny black skin and a very neat short goatee beard. Unlike the others he was always immaculately dressed.

After the beatings and the rapes, after they knew that they had full control of the Snugs family, they had eventually set them free. They, the Yardies, were now the ones in charge of the flat. They were now the ones in charge of the drug deals. Snugs, previously known as the main heroin supplier in Gravesend, and as such all his customers, now belonged to the Yardies. Heroin was just the beginning, in a few days crack cocaine would also be on the market, but the main money to be made was from something else. Something that had made them money wherever they went, something that went hand in hand with the cold dark world of class A drugs.

For the drugs though, Snugs would have to take all the risks. He would make all the arrangements. Pick the street dealers, make and take the phone calls, the drop offs to his street dealers and the cash pickups. All the cash would then be given to B, who in turn would give the money to K. K would be distanced enough to avoid capture, narrowing the window of risk only to the point when he collected the drugs from his supplier. This was something that he could not trust Snugs with. In return, as a favour, and only as a favour, the Snugs family would be given the occasional ball of heroin.

K had turned up the day after D and H had suffered their beating from Sam Jakobs. He, as a man, although smaller in stature, clearly out ranked the previous three. K had arrived with a fourth male. A man who never spoke. A man who apparently had no name. A man who by appearance, was a monster. The quiet giant stood at just over seven feet tall. He must have weighed about twenty stone. His appearance was both round and hard. The paler skinned Jamaican had short dreadlocks. His hands were huge, the size of two maybe three normal sized hands. The thick flesh covering his phalanges could not hide the mountainous knuckles protruding from them. His biceps, the size of basketballs were almost bigger than his head.

D had been sent off in a taxi somewhere, leg in plaster from the break suffered outside the Manor Ale public house. H had just walked out of Darenth Valley hospital two days after being admitted into intensive care. He had not been released. He had merely walked out in the middle of the night.

Having come out of his comatosed state, he had been transferred to a private room on a ward. H had not been in his bed for very long, before he decided to leave.

The fairly new hospital had only been operational since the year two thousand. As with all new build hospitals, the earlier years had seen problems. It had soon been labelled *Death Valley* by the locals, due to the number of mistakes and deaths suffered at its hands during its probationary period.

H had merely got up and walked out of his room. He was not challenged by anyone, at anytime. He left the building and walked across to the main public car park, despite the pain he suffered from his broken jaw and split head.

He stole an old beat up blue Ford Escort. The car was ancient, worthless ancient and had been left insecure by its owners. Probably due to the low value of it. Not worth stealing, which it wasn't for a normal car thief. For H though, it was perfect, he needed to get away before Police or Immigration turned up.

On returning to the Snugs abode, H spoke to B for a few seconds. He had then left and was not seen again.

Snugs today, had not long returned from collecting cash from the six street dealers they now had working around Gravesend and Northfleet. Two thousand eight hundred pounds. Money that he had to hand over to B, so B could give it to K, even though they were in the same room.

K called out, "Drink!" The instruction appearing to be given to the mute monster, who was just sat on a stool near the kitchen door on his own, in what could only be described a trance. He walked over to the table and poured a large whisky into Rebecca's empty pink plastic tumbler, which was sat in front of K. He placed the half empty bottle of Bells blended scotch whisky back on the table, a matter of twelve inches away from K. B leaned over and topped his own drinking vessel, not afforded the pleasure of the same hospitality as K. B topped his chipped black coffee mug with the whisky. Snugs clearly was not allowed to drink from the same bottle and instead swallowed a couple of gulps from the can of Holsten Pils lager in front of him. *Whisky made him ill anyway,* he had excused, before he could be refused.

"Deal again?" Snugs said and then added, "I'll be skint at this rate."

K motioned for him to deal, with a scornful nod of his head.

Vikki Snugs just stared at them from the window sill where she was sat. Her hands rested on the stained dusty white plastic sill, underneath her bony bottom. Feelings of hatred for everyone sat in the room, including her man. He was no real man. He had sat there and watched those disgusting fucking monsters rape her and her thirteen year old daughter. He had done nothing. Even though she knew he couldn't stop them, he didn't even try. He didn't love her, he was a coward. Now he was sat at the table playing cards, laughing and joking with them, like they were best friends, despite the knowledge that Rebecca was gone, run away she hoped, run away to tell someone she prayed, but she feared the worst. Those paedophile scum had savaged her little princess. She had wanted to call the Police to report her missing, but the resulting knife wound across the top of her thigh had put a stop to that. She was a coward too and hated herself for it. But she hated them more.

"I want another bottle of Bells," shouted K and the nameless monster went to struggle off his stool again.

"I'll go," Vikki said as she jumped off the sill. Needing to get out. She couldn't stand being in the same room as any of them any longer.

K looked at her and just stared, but with a smile across his greasy shining dark face. "Sure Victorious," which was a name he had chosen for her, on their first day of meeting, "Just remember this. Rebecca may come back," his smile was replaced by an evil grimace as he added, "or she may not."

His smile returned and he opened the palm of his hand showing her a ball of heroin, "Be a good girl. This is yours when you get back."

She took a twenty pound note from B, who was also grinning on the other side of the table, showing off his two gold teeth.

Vikki walked down the masses of stairs leading from the top floor of her block of flats, nodding the odd acknowledgement to other residents coming up the other way. Most of whom wanted nothing to do with the *druggie family.* Once outside, she headed towards the parade of shops situated within the neighbouring block of flats called the Hive. A few minutes' walk. Every now and then looking over her shoulder to make sure she had not been followed. She then pulled out her cheap Alcatel touch phone and dialled a number which had been saved on the contact list as *debt collector.* The number as usual went straight to answer phone. She spoke almost in a whisper, "Its Sally Tall, please call me back as soon as possible."

She hung up and entered the store. The shop was a grocery store run by a family of Asians. All the spirits were in neat lines, behind the cashiers desk, largely to stop them being shoplifted.

"How are you doing Vikki?" the thin aging Indian store keeper spoke with a welcoming smile.

About a year ago the two had fallen out, after he had caught her shoplifting some bacon and a bottle of Chardonnay. He had barred her from the shop instead of calling for the Police, for which she had been grateful. However a couple of months on, he had found her walking around in a drunken state with a bloody nose. She had fallen over, is what she had told him, but he knew her partner had beaten her again. He had taken her inside the shop and cared for her like a man would care for his own daughter. From that day they had spoken fondly to each other.

"I'm ok Jeet," she replied.

He knew she was lying, "If you need help you know where to come," replied the store keeper.

"Thanks Jeet but I am ok. Can I have a bottle of Bells please? The eighteen pound bottle."

"Oh dear Vikki, he will get drunk and violent. You must think of your little girl," Jeet spoke as he reached around for the large bottle. As he did this her phone rang. She looked at the screen. Withheld number.

"I'll be right back," she said as she answered the phone.

"I need help but I can't call the Old Bill," she spoke into the phone and after listening to the reply she carried on, "Yes I know you're the Police as well, but I got to go careful. I could die. Little Becs could die." She then went through exactly what had gone on with the Yardies, the rapes, the drug dealing and the threats. She told her handler that some punters were being forced to have sex as well as giving cash for heroin. Her flat was soon to become a crack house and they could do nothing about it. She reminded the caller that if it ever got out that she was talking to him she was as good as dead. The man on the other side of the call took notes, asked some questions and took some more notes.

Finally before she ended the call she said, "Oh yeah, one more thing. They have put five hundred quid on Sam Jakobs head."

She deleted the last calls from her phone list, the one she made to debt collector and the one she received from withheld number. She then rushed back into the store and purchased the bottle of Bells whisky. Vikki Snugs aka Sally Tall quickly hurried home, wondering what her handler could actually do to help.

On the other side of the phone, Detective Constable Eddie Phillips of the Source handling unit closed his book and called out to his supervisor Charlie Jackson, "Sarge, I think we've got another problem."

Fifteen

0100hrs 17th March

He stood to attention, five feet seven inches tall, wiry, hard muscular but bony body, wearing a skin tight black long sleeved compression t-shirt, which showed off his cut physique. A shirt similar to those worn by footballers under their football kits in the cold weather. Heavy black combat trousers tucked into black army style desert boots. The Balaclava had two small slits where his eyes were. The slits, not big enough for an outsider to make out his eyes, but big enough for him to look through.

The room he stood in was naturally dark, but a bright floodlight stood on a tripod over his shoulder. Halogen light pouring downwards and outwards, casting equally sharp lined shadows where the brightness ended. A purposeful set up designed for a more frightening effect.

There was one other person in the room. Invisible, behind the video camera where he stood. The man behind the camera moved his arm up high and he signalled with three fingers, then two and then one as he activated the record button on the video. The man in the balaclava spoke. His voice muffled through the balaclava, but didn't hide his Asian accent.

"I am Fatwa. I am your death sentence and I will take revenge. I will cause terror and destruction to all infidels. I have been patient. My family came to England in nineteen sixty two. We have worked hard and we have provided great services. Yet you still treat us like fools. You let our young ones slip through your hands on purpose so they can go and fight wars and kill on your behalf. My son died because of your foolishness. Because of your infidel ways. Your papers call him a traitor. But a traitor to who? You? You make me sick. You say that he was being watched by your so called secret services, yet he slips through to Syria. Now he is dead. Your war is now with me. Fatwa, your death sentence. I have as you know killed five in the fittingly named town of Gravesend. Five deaths leaving behind fivefold the sorrow that I was left with. Soon it will be tenfold and it will not stop. It will never stop while I breathe. There will be no negotiating, no ransom demands, no anything, but death." The man then appeared to stoop and produced a rifle. An AK-47 with an attached bayonet. He pointed the assault rifle at the camera and spoke again, "For over a thousand years we have suffered at the hands of all non Muslims, be it Christians, Sikhs, Hindus, Jews or whoever. Day by day I have read about Muslim terrorist plots foiled by your secret services. Let us see now. My threat is real, as I have already proved. No massacres of hundreds on railway stations or public events. Single kills. Single kills which will unleash more fear than ever. You will all be running scared. Who will be next? KHAYBAR KHAYBAR YA YAHUD!" (The armies of Mohammed are coming), " Fatwa had spoken."

Sixteen

0900hrs 17th March

Charlie Jackson walked out of the briefing room at Gravesend Police Station. Each morning representatives from the various departments at the station met at eight in the morning to discuss the area's requirements. The meeting was normally chaired by the Area Commander. The Commander ordinarily held the rank of Chief Superintendant. Today it was chaired by Detective Inspector Ian Thom. Temporarily made up to the rank of Acting Chief Inspector. Everyone of that rank and above had been called up to headquarters for an emergency meeting with the Chief Constable, in light of recent events. Namely Fatwa the terrorist's video.

The mood was unusually forlorn. They had tried to run the meeting in the normal format. Statistical counts of how many Burglary dwellings (houses and flats), burglary non-dwellings (commercial premises, including dwelling sheds and garages), Vehicle thefts, assaults and any other crimes of note, crimes that might affect public confidence. Then there were other issues to be discussed, with regards to victim satisfaction, another performance measurement commissioned by the government.

There had been two Burglary dwellings, which was very low, in comparison to the previous four weeks, when they had suffered seven to fifteen burglaries every day.

The Tactical Team Inspector had spoken up, after Thom had asked his audience if they had any ideas as to why the crime figures for the day were so low. Inspector Andrew Bale led the rufty tufty Tactical team. All large athletic types, who were also wholly gym freaks. Generally they were used to execute search warrants, make difficult arrests or flood an area that was suffering from a high rate of crime.

"Paul Baker," he said in his normal booming voice. Bale was a straight talking man, who had no liking for the namby pamby ways creeping into the force, through fears

of the Human Rights Act, and of the suing culture, slowly
but surely sliming its way into the courts of England.

Paul Baker was the man who had been decapitated by
explosion in the front office at Gravesend Police Station.

Everybody knew what he meant, but nobody said
anything. Charlie Jackson certainly knew what he meant, he
had inputted most of the recent intelligence received on
Paul Baker. Baker was a burglar, more recently he had
committed car creeper burglaries, every night, with a group
of younger kids. Baker at twenty two years of age,
already had an impressive criminal record, fifty three
convictions for a variety of offences.

He currently had a following of late teens, all of whom
he had taught the art of car creeper burglaries. An act
that entailed identifying rich areas, areas that enjoyed
desirable motor cars. An act intended only to target those
houses that had flash motors parked outside. No time was
spent in the houses after breaking in, just a quick search to
locate the car keys. Normally and obligingly, hanging on a
key rack by the front door. Some of his younger
apprentices went one step further, taking televisions, cash,
mobile phones and jewellery. The cars would then

be stolen and raced around just for the fun of it, bombed around the streets and fields without the tender love and care shown to them by their natural owners, before either being sold or burnt out.

Four weeks ago Baker had been arrested with limited evidence, having been found running, close to the scene of a burnt out Mazda MX-5. The car having been stolen from such a burglary in the early hours of the night. An offence that he had denied any knowledge of, stating that he was running home because he was late. He had been kept in custody for a lengthy period, despite the knowledge that no charge would ensue. It did however, give the Police some advantages. They could bail him with conditions of signing on at the Police station. A tool often used by investigators, which meant they could put a team of surveillance officers behind him after he had signed on at Gravesend. Which was exactly what Baker was doing when he died.

The rest of the meeting strayed from its regularity, discussions steering towards the explosive murders, and the new threat of terrorist activity in the small town of Gravesend. The video on the internet had gone viral and already been viewed by millions. A man wearing a balaclava claiming responsibility for five deaths. To date they were only aware of Baker, Tucker, Swift and a young Polish girl. Four deaths. Had he killed five? Had one of them just not been discovered yet? Had one survived? These were just a few of the questions being bombarded around the room. Questions with no answers.

Thom informed everyone that it was now a governmental investigation. Bigwigs from the secret services together with Kent Police's Major Crime Unit and SOCA (Serious Organized Crime Agency) were now jointly providing the investigation team. There would also be an input from SO15.

Everybody else, those not involved were told to get on with their normal day to day business, only with extra vigilance. The video was certain to invite reprisal attacks, on the local Muslims. The tabloids had not helped since day one. The aggressor was right. Fear was at the highest level it had ever been. The mood throughout the town, sullen and quiet, but almost volatile, like a volcano getting ready to erupt.

Jackson had stayed behind at the end of the meeting, at the request of his inspector, Ian Thom.

"They have asked for a local intelligence officer to join the team upstairs. They will be using the entire top floor for the operation mate. Can you get someone to come and see me and I will give whoever details of where to get briefed?" Thom was clearly stressed, the additional pressure of his temporary rank was telling.

"Yes boss, no worries. Any preference as to who?" Jackson asked.

"Send Julie if you can Charlie. Just not you. I will need you to run the ship while I'm up here. What's happening about the missing Snugs girl?"

"We have got a team set up from the Drugs Intervention Unit. Operation Alphabet, they will be looking after the Yardies. Looks worse than we thought though Ian. Word is from three other sources that these Yardies have raped young girls as well as their punters. Might be more than just the little Snugs kid missing. We've got hold of the girl's school. Rebecca apparently misses a lot of school anyway and it's currently being dealt with by the Education authority. She bunks school quite often as well. More than that, the school has said that Vik Snugs phoned to report Rebecca sick this time."

"Is she missing Charlie? Or does Vikki just want us to get rid of the Yardies, so Snugs and her can carry on with their dealing?" Thom was clearly too stressed to take on anything else.

"I'd go with its real boss. Too many sources have semi confirmed what the Yardies are doing. Anything we do though has got to be done carefully, to protect Sally Tall. She's petrified. If it comes out she has spoken, she is obviously a dead girl. She's hoping that the kid has run away, but is convinced that the Yardies have got her, just don't know where." Charlie winced as he spoke; knowing that kids being raped and kidnapped was heavy. But so was the protection of all covert human intelligence sources. Vik Snugs aka Sally Tall had worked for them for a couple of years now, albeit only when she was skint, or fallen out with someone, or had another selfish motive to do so. Sally Tall was a grass, not an agent.

"What are we doing then?" asked the acting Chief Inspector.

"A visit is going in today with the Education officer and a couple of our Tac team boys. If she is off sick genuinely they will get to see her."

"Ok Charlie let me know what happens."

Charlie nodded his acknowledgement. He had a bad feeling about the future right now. He was desperate for a drink.

Seventeen

Charlie Jackson came out of the Stations building and headed back across the car park, towards the mobile hut that housed his team, stopping for a quick cigarette on his own at the smoking shelter. His mind and body now demanding its ration of alcohol. Nobody else was about so he slipped out his small silver hip flask from his jacket pocket. He shook it and heard the liquid inside flop around. It felt about a quarter full. The lid popped as he released its catch. He took two big swallows of the whisky inside. He shut the lid and put it back into his inside jacket pocket.

The yard was sparse of Uniform patrol vehicles, all out on call. Reported incidents had risen dramatically since the terrorist killings. *Suspicious neighbours of Asian origin, racist assaults, information that may lead to the killer,* (none of which were proving right), all on top of the normal day to day incidents that had to be dealt with.

The door to his office opened for him before he had reached it. He covered his mouth as he coughed, not just because it was polite, but also consciously, to prevent the whisky aroma from his breath spreading too far. Julie Stokes stepped aside and let him in. All five of his Source handlers were in the room. Normal routine for them, after every morning area meeting they had their own office meeting. This was so they could go through the overnight crime and any issues raised by the other teams, as well as discussing his own teams agenda. Most of which as far too sensitive for the rest of the Police station.

His team sat around the room at their own desks. Eddie Phillips, the officer dealing with Sally Tall. He was currently running four good independent sources, all providing good actionable intelligence as well as the grass, Sally Tall. Eddie was always well dressed in smart casuals. Today he was wearing a blue polo shirt with blue jeans and a pair of black loafer shoes. His short fair hair brushed neatly into a side parting. Next to him sat his partner Jaspal Singh, affectionately called Jazz. The thirty five year old Punjabi had been with the Force for sixteen years and three months. He had joined Charlie's team about a year ago and had proved to be a valuable asset. He had the knack of speaking with criminals at their own level. He genuinely believed in the job he was doing, which made him come across with sincerity. A necessary skill required when dealing with informants. Jazz, as his partner was always immaculately dressed.

The other permanent partnership sat at their dual desk opposite each other. The pair, tagged with their own nickname, The Krays. As the name suggested both Crayston Bould and Ronnie Best looked like a pair of gangsters. Crayston's broad cockney accent, stocky build and cropped hair together with his dress sense made him look like anything but a Police Officer. Today he was wearing a short sleeved, black Iron Maiden T-shirt, black jeans and dealer boots. His arms were covered in tattoos. His partner Ronnie was very similarly dressed, in T-shirt, jeans and boots, but he instead looked like a rocker with long black shoulder length hair, which as normal was tied back into a pony tail. Both men were in their mid-thirties and had been on the intelligence unit for the past five years. They had worked together most of the time, separated only to break in new rookies on the team.

Finally Julie Stokes, Charlie's stand in partner. Her previous partner had passed his promotion exam and been transferred to Mid-Kent to perform the role of Acting Sergeant. He had not yet been replaced on the team. Staff cut backs meant that in all likelihood he would not be replaced.

Stokes was currently standing behind Charlie's desk. She let him take his seat and wrapped her arms around her supervisor's shoulders, just as a wife may do to a husband in a loving relationship, which of course they were not.

"You're sending me to the top floor Charlie, aren't you?" She spoke in a silky smooth, almost seductive voice and brushed her lips against Charlie's ear.

"You want to do that?" he asked, ignoring her normal flirtatious demeanour.

"Our Inspector asked me to ask, but no, I don't." She smiled as she slowly slipped into the chair next to him.

"Ok done," he said, reaching across and ruffling her hair in the same way a Parent would do with his child, which of course she wasn't.

"Right what have we got?" he asked and turned to the Krays first.

Crayston spoke on behalf of the pair, in his East End accent, "Yeah skip, looks like we got more trouble coming. I spoke to Tommy Foreman last night," Tommy Foreman was a pseudonym used for a long term CHIS employed by the Krays, "He reckons a group of them, what you call them, extremists, racist wankers are gonna kick right off coz of them bombs. I reckon we are gonna get some backlash from them," he then turned around to Jazz, "You better watch out mate." Crayston grinned.

Jazz just grinned back. He was a Black Belt Second Dan Karate expert, and was also an accomplished Wing Chun warrior. "No worries," he said.

"Get that bit of Intel in as soon as possible boys," said Charlie.

"It's already done Skip," replied Ronnie. Skip was slang for skipper, a term often used by officers with Ronnie's length of service for Sergeants.

Jackson then turned around to Eddie and said, "Any update on Alphabet mate?" Alphabet was the Operational name given to the Yardie drug dealing team.

"Not much Charlie. But we have got to get on it today, just in case it's right. That's three sources now saying that those Yardies are raping kids as well as the punters for gear. The only thing is a drugs warrant is not going to work if we want arrests. The gear is not held at Snugs address. Think short term, just to check on the Snugs girl we've got to go with the Education lot. I was thinking maybe me and Jazz can go in with them and the TAC team boys."

"Not a good idea Ed," said Jackson, "You don't know what Sally Tall's reaction will be when she sees you two at the door. She might give herself away."

"Fair point Charlie, I would just love to give them a dig." Jazz spoke up on behalf of his partner.

"Ok, we will get an update soon from the TAC team and we will work from that," Charlie said. "Right just to let you know, it's obviously gone crazy with the murders. Ian will be tied up working upstairs. So any authorities come through me for the time being. I'm conscious of the fact that we do not currently have any Muslims on our books.

I've got the analysts doing some research and they may come across with some names of people we can approach. Someone out there must know who this Fatwa character is. So I might be giving you a bell later to make a cold approach." He turned around to Julie, "You got anything to add before you go upstairs Jules."

Julie Stokes shook her head. She couldn't speak through the anger that was ripping through her. Thoughts of children being raped by the disgusting drug dealers still anchored in her brain. She got up to walk out but then turned around and said, "Don't forget Charlie, we got that meeting with Jakobs this afternoon. I'm going to go upstairs and feed myself in, but I will make sure I'm free to join you today. Got a good feeling about him."

Eighteen

1100hrs 17th March

It had been five days since my introduction to
them, Charlie Jackson and Julie Stokes. I had not been left
in the cell for very long that day. In fact nobody had. The
fear and panic of possible other explosions was bigger
than the severity of anything anybody was in custody for.
Deaths in Police Custody are treated very seriously,
especially by the IPCC, (Independent Police Complaints
Commission).

A decision had been made to bail all the detainees as
quick as possible. I myself had been bailed out for two
Months. To return to the Police station at 1000hrs on the
tenth of May. A date that they had just set without any
consultation with me. Not that I cared. I knew that I would
be 'refused charge' a long time before the date.

Hysteria on that day had taken over the station as a whole, uniformed officers and plain clothed officers running around carrying out their orders. Making the station as sterile as possible, as quickly as possible.

Charlie himself had seen me out the Police station's rear yard. He walked me past the cordon of Police Officers who were surrounding the entire building. Barrier tapes spread across the road, in all directions, preventing both pedestrian and road traffic entering the area. Charlie had slipped me a contact number, which he had written in code. Each number after the second digit seven had been increased by one number. Example an eight was really a seven and a nine would be shown as zero representing ten. Real cloak and dagger stuff I had laughed. My initial reaction was to take the number and dispose of it as soon as I had left the station, out of view. However intrigue had got the better of me and I kept it.

Immediately after being released, I walked myself to the Civic Centre, Woodville Halls, next door to the Police Station. A large building characteristic of its origin, 1968 when it was built. The exterior was clad with large aggregate faced grey slabs. A huge almost square block building. Inside, it was the main base for the local council but also shared with various other facilities such as the local theatre. It had a public area for computer usage, which was empty. Crowds had gathered around the neighbouring building, the Police station, in the hope of finding out more news of what was going on. I walked through into the reception and booked a computer from the receptionist. The usage of which were free. For the time being anyway, a benefit to encourage the unemployed to make online job applications.

I walked down three steps to the right of the reception desk where the computers lined up in neat rows. All were empty and I sat myself at the furthest desk. I fired up Google and typed in 'Covert Human Intelligence Sources.' The screen flipped to a list of web sites. The top one bringing me to a page outlining the Home Office Code of Practice for the use of informants. I soaked up the information. As always with such research, I ended up flying off at tangents, investigating all the different aspects of exactly what had been offered up to me. One thing Charlie was right about was that there was definitely a difference between an agent and a grass.

I ended up reading a biography on a French criminal, Eugene Francois Vidocq. July 24th 1775 – May 11th 1857.

A criminal, who got employed by the French Police as a spy, at a time when gangsters were ruling the streets of Paris. An agent. A bad guy turned good. Four hours of research had made up my mind. That I would give it a go. An agent. Not a grass. I would not talk about family or friends, as I was sure, neither would Charlie Jackson.

I had called Jackson on the number provided yesterday evening from a call box in the town centre. A number that I had memorised. He had answered it immediately. One ring. He had informed me that normal practise would be for the number to go through to a standard answering message. On a dual line that was pre-set on all his handlers phones. A message should be left for a return call. That was standard operating procedure. However Jackson's phone didn't. He knew people didn't like leaving messages on a machine waiting for a call back. A call back that might be urgent. So his phone was always switched on. He had asked if I wanted him to call me back to save my credit. I declined but informed him that I was *up for it*, for a trial period.

We had then arranged a meeting. Twelve in the afternoon at The Command Inn, a public house situated in Chatham town. About twenty minutes drive from

Gravesend. I of course had no plans on driving. The main reason being I no longer owned a car. I could have borrowed one, but that would mean paying for fuel. I chose to bunk a train and worry about ticket inspectors should I come across one. It was in any event a short journey and neither Gravesend or Rochester train stations were generally manned by ticket inspectors. Chatham was a short five minute walk from Rochester, the group of towns collectively known as Medway, famous for their association with Charles Dickens. The Command Inn was a pub close to the town centre but also out of the way. I had been there once before and knew what he meant. I was told to have a walk around the bar area and garden to check if I knew anyone. If I did, I was to leave and call him half an hour later. If not, I was to wait on the wall separating the car park from the front garden of the pub. The garden that overlooked the River Medway was a great pull for the business, especially when the weather was good. Charlie had also given me a false name to operate under. All contact with them from now was to be made using the pseudonym of Robbie Strange. A name that had no connection to Samuel Jakobs. A name that would be easy to remember but with no real meaning. Important because connections, such as Mother's maiden names, uncles, brothers etc. could always be linked back to you, by people wanting to know.

I knew that they would probably arrive half an hour early. One reason, to watch me come in and check my ability to follow instructions, and second reason, to ensure it was safe enough to carry on with the meeting. As such I arrived an hour earlier. Half hour before they would turn up. I did my walk around. The bar was only just opening and so there were no customers to worry about. The sun was out so I had no doubt, that around lunch time the local office workers would venture out in this direction. The view from the garden across the river was pretty awesome. I got myself a coffee and sat in the garden, facing the entrance to the car park, which was some five hundred feet away from me. I watched customers slowly roll in. As expected I did not know anyone. The Dickensian Medway towns were not a location I frequented.

Eleven twenty five I smiled as I watched a blue Ford Escort estate drive into the car park, purposefully slow. Julie Stokes sat at the driver's wheel and Charlie Jackson sat next to her speaking into his mobile phone. They parked up about thirty feet away from the entrance to the garden. I watched Stokes climb out the car. Tight fitting jeans and vest top and stunning to look at. She caught the attraction of the male part of a young couple walking across the car park. I smiled again as I watched the female side of the pair scold her partner for his wayward eye.

She parked the car in the middle of three vacant spots along the back row. About fifty feet from the garden. Jackson was still on his mobile. As he got out of the car he hung up the phone and Stokes electronically locked the car. They looked around the car park while Jackson spoke to his partner. I couldn't hear what was being said but whatever it was, clearly angered Stokes. I watched Jackson clamp his hand over her shoulder in a reassuring way. They walked into the garden. Jackson's eyes everywhere and he saw me sat at the garden table closest to the gate. He shook his head but grinned, pointing at the wall where I should have been. I just shrugged my shoulders as they approached me.

"I got here too early Charlie. Sorry mate but it would have looked strange if I sat on the wall for an hour."

"No stranger than seeing a bloke that looks like you sitting in a pub garden drinking coffee," he replied.

Julie Stokes lost her angered look and gave me that melting smile. *Just part of her job*, I told myself, feeling more and more attracted to this extremely gorgeous looking woman.

"I'll get them in," she said looking away from me towards Charlie, then back to me, "What are you having Robbie?"

"I'll have whatever the grumpy old boy's having," I replied without hesitation, reacting naturally to being called Robbie, which I knew pleased them both.

"Ok handsome," she said, blue eyes gleaming, still smiling and then she turned and walked off towards the building. My eyes followed her tight rear end for a few seconds before Charlie's approach to the table snapped me back to reality. He sat down opposite me. The wooden table-bench rocked slightly as he sat down, due to the unevenness of the grass underneath us.

"Just a few things very quickly Robbie while we wait for Jules," he said. "Firstly, if you see anybody come in that you recognize and it makes you feel uncomfortable, I want you to just get up and go. Give us a call back in an hour or so.

Secondly you have to have a story in your head just in case someone does recognize you, or worse recognize us."

"A cover story," I interrupted.

Charlie looked surprised, but carried on, "Yes a cover story. A story that covers both instances, of either you or us being recognized. One story that covers either eventuality."

"What do you suggest?" I asked more out of curiosity than being able to come up with a story myself.

"Could be something like you are trying to sell us something. A nicked car or something. Works either way then. If they recognize us, as far as you are concerned, we are trying to set you up for a sting. You can thank them for saving you a nicking. Other way if they don't know us it still doesn't matter. Just have some detail of any car in your head. Does that make sense?"

"Yeah that's ok unless they know you for what you do. You know deal with informants and that. Then I'm knackered really aren't I?"

"Not really mate. I make sure my team do nickings and stop checks and stuff normal coppers do as well. We do all that and anyone that knows me or Julie would know that too."

"So you cover the cover stories," I laughed but quickly realized that I was in danger of making the meeting non productive. "That's fine mate. Sorry about that."

"Don't be sorry son. Shows me that you're thinking. Other rules. You don't set people up. You don't set up jobs, just to tell us about them later. All you do at this stage is tell us about what you know, who you know etc etc etc."

A wolf whistle attracted our attention. A group of twenty something year olds had settled at two tables dragged together, about thirty feet from us. The whistle had been aimed at Stokes walking past with a tray, carrying three pints of lager. Stokes paid no attention and didn't even break her stride. She walked straight back to our table. Stokes then passed the pint glasses to each of us with her small but perfectly shaped hands. I could see her nails were immaculate. Not too long but not too short. They were bare of any nail varnish, yet shined of their own accord.

Her own pint glass looking comparatively larger than ours, in her dainty fingers.

Charlie took his glass eagerly and guzzled half the pint down straight away. He wiped his mouth and put the glass down, with a strange look of satisfaction.

"Pint drinker?" I questioned, looking at Stokes.

"You disapprove?" she replied, staring directly at me with a *how dare you* look, spread across her face.

"No Princess. Looks cool to me."

The next half hour was spent with them giving me names of various people from the criminal fraternity and questions with regards to my knowledge of those individuals. My information in return was very limited. Partly because I felt uncomfortable with this line of conversation and largely because I had little to do with these people. I was very much a loner. I was also informed that it was their duty to warn me that the Yardies had taken out a five hundred pound contract on me. They wanted me housed so they could sort me out.

"As I said before. When my times up. My times up. But looks like that could be my first job for you," I grinned.

"What do you mean? How are you going to do that? You don't buy drugs. You rob dealers. We can't have you roughing addicts up to get information. That defeats the object of why you are doing this. You are no good to us in the cells getting nicked for bashing people up." Charlie looked frustrated.

"Charlie calm down. We've done the ground rules. No set ups, no crimes. High IQ level, remember. I'll get what you need to get rid of them."

"It's more than that Sam, I mean Robbie," Stokes now spoke and I saw that angry look in her eyes returning. The same as before, when they were in the car park. "Something is going on with the kids. The heroin users kids. We think Vikki Snugs little girl has gone missing and there might be others."

"We still don't know that," Charlie interrupted. His eyes however told me different.

"Ok. I will see what I can do," I looked at them both "No bashings, no set ups. Just information. Got it."

"OI, FUCKOFF PAKI. GET AWAY FROM US. GO BACK TO YOUR OWN COUNTRY." The voice was loud and came from behind us. It was the same table that had celebrated Julie Stokes figure.

The pushed together tables had six men sat around them. One of them, a blonde haired pale and pasty looking male, with red spots splattered all over his face, was stood up. He was the one aiming the abuse at two young Asian students who were about to seat themselves at a table opposite them.

"I know him from somewhere," Julie spoke.

"Yeah so do I. Just can't picture where from," Charlie responded.

The two Asian's decided not to sit where they had planned and started to head away.

"Fucking black bastards. Go on fuck off out of here. Go and blow up your own country." The same blonde haired skinny offender screamed the abuse. This time however his mates joining in with vile jeers.

The two young Asian students quickened their pace but the blonde aggressor started to move around the table towards them.

"Sorry," I said and moved quickly, despite the protests from my handlers. I reached the skinny aggressor before he reached his Asian victims. My hand gripped his throat tight and I whispered into his ear. I smelt his fear and let him go. He backed away, not saying anything as he moved back to his table. I moved myself in the same direction. I stood square on, facing their table, facing all six men. My eyes saying it all. Eyes can tell a great story. I had learned this in the Army. None of them moved.

One eventually spoke. Another scrawny looking skinny boy, "You just assaulted a copper mate."

"Shut up," croaked the first blonde. Still holding his throat where I had grabbed him.

I glared down at the one who had just spoken to me. His eyes met mine, but for a split second, before he put his head down.

"Fucking bullies," I growled and walked away. I didn't walk back to my table but moved towards the exit. I walked back to Stokes car and was joined by my two handlers moments later.

"What the fuck was that?" Charlie groaned at me, "You may well have compromised yourself. Jesus, what were you thinking of?"

"One thing I hate more than drug dealers. Fucking bullies. What are you having a go at me for. You're the coppers. You should be nicking the mug for racism. Then if I let you do that I'm compromised anyway. This was the best way out of it." I remained calm as I argued my case.

"We would have nicked him. I was just about to tell you to leave so we could deal with it, but you turned into Superman before we could say anything." Jackson put his head in his hands as he spoke.

"You should have waited in there, just in case they started on the Indians again. I had to leave, before I did something that you really would not have liked. Anyway it's lucky you didn't do the nicking. The guy apparently is a copper."

"That's where we recognized him from Charlie," Stokes said. She was not showing any of the disappointment displayed by her Sergeant. "What did you whisper to him Sam?"

"Just told him to stop mate. That's all".

"Yeah right," said Charlie, "Oh my God, a bloody copper. We got to find out where he works Jules. If he knows what we do for a living, your career as an agent is over before it begun. For Christ's sake, a copper."

"He works Gravesend Charlie. He's a newbie. I've seen him walking around the Nick. He won't have a clue who we are. If he did, he would not have given me the whistle or behaved like that in front of us." Stokes just stared at me as she spoke, a satisfied grin all over her face.

"Well we got to do something about it; we cannot have a bloke like that working for Kent Police. We just got to be careful how we do it. Can't risk getting ROBBIE here in trouble," Charlie emphasised my pseudonym, as if to remind his younger detective what she should be calling me.

They offered me a lift back to Gravesend, once they had been back into the pub to check that the trouble had not re-ignited. But just as they walked in, the Indian students walked out. One gave me an acknowledgement of thanks and I gave them the thumbs up.

I left for the train station by walking along the river front towards town. I guessed the two of my handlers would now be talking about the pros and cons of having me on board.

Back in the blue Ford Escort estate Charlie spoke to his driver, "Don't know about him Jules. I know he's a smart guy but he is well set in his ways. Might be more trouble than he's worth."

"I like him Charlie. Like you said, he's a good guy."

"There's something else. He knows loads about our stuff. He said *cover story*, and *ground rules*. Our jargon and he used them with comfort."

"Do you think he's done this before? Snouting for someone else, maybe a different Police Force."

"No, we would have known that by now. As soon as we put his paperwork in, it would have flagged up."

"What then Charlie? Maybe it is that he's just clever. I reckon he would done some digging and research about it all before he signed up. He seems the sort of guy who needs to know what he is doing."

"You like him Jules, I can tell. Just remember the rules."

"What rules?" she said taking her eyes off the road.

"Three things get coppers in trouble. Special property, informants and," he paused briefly, "shagging informants." Jackson laughed for the first time as he spoke.

Stokes laughed as well, punching him on his arm with her left hand, "You are disgusting Sergeant Jackson."

Nineteen

Mark Shepherd, Police Constable five digit Mark
Shepherd was still sat at the joined up tables in the back
garden of *The Command Inn* pub, still holding his throat, not
because it was hurting physically, but because it was hurting
mentally. Grimacing with anger, anxiety sweat pouring
down his face, sweat caused by stress related adrenaline,
adrenaline that was now flooding his body. His group, his
associates, remained silent. Not because they feared him,
nor because he was a Police Officer. They merely liked his
money and upsetting him would take them off his list of
camaraderie. He didn't have natural friends, only the type
that money can buy.

Shepherd in reality should never have been a copper.
First of all, he should never have been accepted, should
never had got through training school. There had been

dozens of chances to boot him out, but he wasn't, he had a card up his sleeve.

His late Father Terry Shepherd had been a great Policeman. Old school. He had made the rank of, and retired as an Assistant Chief Constable. He never went for the big Chief's job, having been warned that it would be a futile attempt. The decision had already been made, particularly after his extreme right wing views had finally been aired. Views that had been carefully guarded, both by his close mates and himself, guarded until he had been told the job was going to a black candidate, an applicant from another force.

Kent Police wanted to be the first Force in the Nation to show off an ethnic Chief Constable. He was also by the way, an excellent candidate at that. He had all the credentials that were required. He was one of the few Chief Officers who had learned his trade. He had been both an excellent officer and detective during his career. A street cop who also had the ability to pass exams and interviews. That however would not matter. No one would see that side of it. For many, he would always be the one who got the job because of the colour of his skin.

After his retirement, Terry Shepherd set up his own high-tec Security business. Leaning on countless influential people that he had protected while in the Police Service. It was not long before 'Secretus Security' became one of the leading security companies in the world. Working for exclusive clients, obtaining government contracts, not just in the United Kingdom but around the World.

After his death, the whole company was left to his older son Jasper, a ringer for his Dad, but with a more ruthless streak about him. It was Jasper that had persuaded his younger sibling to join the Police Force. He had a need for somebody in the organization. It also kept the cretin away from him. Mark Shepherd suffered small man syndrome, officially known as *Napoleon complex*, a theoretical condition that occurs in people short of stature. He was a bully. A bully that had got used to having everything he wanted. A bully used to having everything his own way, right up to the point of their old man dying. Indeed he had been, as the youngest, the favourite child, receiving the favour from both his Parents, right up to the point that his Father had become critically ill. A time when Terry Shepherd knew that his favourite, his youngest had no inkling whatsoever on how to run a business. In fact the spoilt child had no idea on how to do anything for himself. So the whole shaboom had been handed over to Jasper. Mark was left with no lump sum, no status in the company, but just a healthy monthly allowance. An allowance, fortunately healthy enough for him to acquire friends.

He finally pulled his hand away from his throat looking up at his crowd. "Thinks he's hard does he? We'll see how hard he is. He's as good as dead."

None of his associates spoke but just nodded acknowledgment. Pathetic as Mark Shepherd was, he had the cash to do this. It would not be the first time he had paid for someone to get beaten up.

"Cheek of it, he even told me his name." Shepherd continued, "Well fuck you Sam Jakobs from fucking Gravesend. That's my Manor. Let's see who's going to bite who's fucking nose off." He spoke aloud before turning to his crowd grimacing. He raised his pint glass, "Come on, my round, let's get smashed." He grinned again, giving his throat one last rub, as his associates cheered with him, heading back to the bar.

Twenty

My train journey back to Gravesend had gone
smoothly. There had been no ticket collectors and so no
fines. I didn't get off at Gravesend though. I stayed on the
train to the next stop in Northfleet. Closer to my next visit.
I was never one to walk away from a fight. They had put a
five hundred pounds bounty on my head, so I had decided
to collect it myself. By now I was down to a five pound
note in my pocket and roughly two additional pounds in
loose shrapnel. Seven quid would not see me through the
rest of the day. I still needed to eat and visit the laundrette.
So I had a plan. One that would benefit both Charlie
Jackson and myself.

I stopped briefly at the bottom of the staircase. Dull grey
concrete stairs, surrounded by dull grey concrete walls,
smell of stale urine and putrescent old bins. These were the
stairs that led up to the Snugs flat. My eyes caught sight of

a small length of metal on the floor, just next to the first step. I picked it up. It was an old drill chuck. I placed the bar across my right hand, flat in my palm, letting the protruding chuck slip out of my closed fist between my first and second finger. I held it tight squeezing my fist, and headed up.

A few seconds later I was knocking on the plain UPVC front door that belonged to the Snugs clan. Both neighbouring flats were boarded up. Vacated by the previous tenants, who in all likelihood, couldn't bear living next door to heroin dealers, and probably got fed up of being burgled by their scum druggie visitors.

I saw a shadow grow in size through the frosted glass panel, it came towards the door, the shadow shaping into a figure. I stepped back into my stance. The door opened and Vikki Snugs stood on the other side. Her mouth opened when she realized who I was. Her gaunt pale face and dark sullen eyes adding to her feebleness.

She half shut the door again, so only her head was showing, "What are you doing here? Are you mad?"

"Where are they?" I whispered. She nodded over her shoulder towards a door at the end of the corridor.

The hallway was very narrow, barely wider than the door. The small width would give me some mobility problems, but also had its advantages, namely, it would also only allow them out at me one at a time. A door just inside the entrance to my left was partially open. I could see a stained unclean toilet. I pushed the door shut, not wanting any obstacles.

"How many?" I said.

She held three fingers up and whispered, "But one of them's Peter the wimp."

"Ok," I said. "Now scream."

She obliged with half a scream, like a poor amateur actress and I just shook my head at her, pushing her out of the flat. It did do the job though, I saw the door at the end of the corridor open. Peter Snugs stood at the door and I heard him shout back over his shoulders, "It's Jakobs."

"Jakobs get that coward as well," hissed Vikki as she leaned her head over my shoulder from behind.

I watched Snugs step back into whatever room lay beyond the door. A black male showed himself instead.

Five feet seven, stocky build, shaved head, goatee beard, dripping with gold. He stopped just in the corridor and said, "You got some balls man."

"I've come to claim my reward," I said keeping my eyes hard, glazed and fixed at the doorway behind him. "Five hundred quid, for giving me to you." I could see that he had no weapon in his hands.

"Ah, yes. That's very good of you. But you will not need money where you are going." He turned back towards the room and shouted, "Bring him to me." He turned back towards me grinning, "See you in a minute my friend. Come and get your money."

"Be in to collect it now," I said, walking towards the door, ready for a fight. I heard him shout for his phone as he vanished and he was immediately replaced by a giant. The replacement was so huge that he had to stoop as he entered the hallway, taller than the doorway. Head almost touching the ceiling. He was so wide that his shoulders pressed against both walls of the corridor. I grinned at him and I could tell that he knew why. His facial expression said it all. He knew that unless he managed to grab hold of me in the hallway there was little else he could

141

do, unless he could take the fight outside. Perhaps part of him hoped that I would back off. He must have been used to people doing that. He did look scary. But I was not going anywhere. I knew I had the advantage.

I slid forward remaining in my boxing stance. Three steps. Left hand forward, held up by my face and my right fist tightening around the metal chuck, alongside my other cheek. My bent elbows facing the floor. The way I had been taught.

He lunged forward at me unexpectedly and I stuck out my front hand with a stiff jab, punching upwards. It hit him square on the nose but he barely showed a reaction. It only just stopped his forward motion. I had a very strong, take you off your feet jab and I could see it had no physical effect on him. To the contrary, what he had managed to do was to make me take a step back towards the door. Another three steps and we would be outside, which would most definitely suit him. I had to be quick so I drove a hard kick with my front leg, aimed perfectly at his groin. No matter how big you are, your privates are your privates. No muscle or bone for protection and the pain is equal to all. He gasped and dropped to his knees. That brought his head level with my shoulders and I smashed my right fist at his face. Additional power being added from my rotating hip and shoulder. The chuck sank into his eye socket and the giant groaned. Leaning forward onto his giant arms. One more kick was going to do it. I kicked out hard, my heel connecting with his elbow, against the natural flow of joint movement. The crack was sickening and he groaned again. "Sorry big man but it was you or me," I said as he collapsed face down.

The slight scream behind me, which now was not acted, made me pivot to face the front door. Just in time to see a knife slashing down, aimed at where my back had been moments ago. The pivot had now put me into a southpaw stance and the knife nicked my wrist. It cut me, I could feel that unpleasant sense of tissue damage, however, *pain is temporary, victory is forever*, one of my favourite quotes. I ignored the blood dripping from my right hand and threw a left uppercut straight into the gold toothed Jamaican's jaw, who was now leaning forwards trying to maintain his balance from his lunging knife attack. The knife hit the floor before he slumped into a heap. I stamped down hard on his head to make sure he stayed down. He didn't move.

I picked up the knife and turned back towards the far door. Where my money was. Stepping over the monstrous groaning heap, still lying face down with his left arm positioned at an impossible angle due to the break. Real fights only last seconds.

I kicked open the door. I found myself in a kitchen-diner. The first black male was stood next to Snugs. A look of shock, not expecting me on my own.

"Where's my cash then son," I said as I shut the door behind me. I dragged a wooden chair over, from under a plastic table and angled it under the door handle to secure it as best as I could, just in case any of the two I had left outside fancied another shot at the title, which I very much doubted. Also they might have other helpers on the way.

"I give you five hundred pounds and you would have cost me a grand. How is that fair?"

"It's the way the mop flop's pal. You put the bounty up. I'm here to collect it. You could get it back though?" I said, using my mad dog eyes and my newly acquired knife to good effect.

"And how would I get it back?" asked the Jamaican.

"Well actually it's an either or. You either hire some other buffoons and put out a thousand pounds on my head and watch me come back down and claim it myself again OR you could hire me."

"Hire you?" he sounded as if what I said was ridiculous.

"You must need a debt collector or something. That way I don't have to keep robbing you or your goons, do I? Seems like I've wasted your heavy help anyway." I nodded towards the front of the flat, where his injured partners in crime remained. "Either way I'm taking that five hundred quid now."

I could almost see his mind working. That vacant look when deep in thought. "Interesting proposition," he grinned and he pulled out a wad of notes from his pocket.

"You can't be serious K? He's a nutter. He could turn on us any time," squealed Snugs.

"So who's going to collect my debts? You?" laughed the Jamaican. "Besides this five hundred pounds is being added to your tab you blood clot. It is all your fault."

He handed the money over to me, five hundred pounds wrapped in rubber bands. I didn't count it somehow knowing that he would not short change me. I put it in my pocket. He then picked up a carrier bag, which had been sat on the floor under the plastic table. He dipped into it and handed me a mobile phone and charger. "I will call you tomorrow to discuss this further. Right now I need to sort out, as you called them, the Goons outside."

I threw the knife onto the table, gave Peter Snugs a grin and left the flat. I met Vikki Snugs down at the bottom of the concrete stairwell.

"Have they gone? Are they going to go?" she asked hopeful.

"I'm sorry. No not yet. But they will soon," I promised, then carried on, "where's your girl Vik? You've got a daughter haven't you?"

Vikki Snugs burst out crying and threw herself on me, "I don't know. I don't know if they took her or if she has just run away. They raped her Sam, why didn't you fucking kill them? I can't run away in case they got her. I can't tell the Old Bill in case they got her. I am trapped Sam, if I do anything they could hurt her. I know I'm a shit skag head mum BUT I DO LOVE MY BABY."

She felt like a bag of bones, her arms didn't seem to have any flesh on them. It took all my sense and control not to walk right back into the flat for immediate retribution.

"Vik, I'm just here to earn some money, but I swear if they have got her, I will get her out for you."

I left her with thirty pounds and told her to eat something, even though I knew that it was more likely the money would be spent on some gear and booze; at least I had made the offer.

I decided I had one more visit to make before getting some shut eye. I caught a taxi to Brandon Street. Six pounds thirty. I paid the taxi driver a ten pound note and told him to keep the change. I then dropped off three hundred pounds to Louise.

"Thanks Sam," she said. Her gratefulness extended to the tightest cuddle I could have hoped for from my ex best friend. A complete contrast to her reaction when I last dropped money off to her. It's amazing what effect the threat of being cut off your power supply and having no food in the house can have. The affection shown towards me and the feel of her skin on my skin, when she kissed me goodbye had just made my day.

Twenty One

I felt like I needed to rest, which meant for me some time
without thinking or fighting. A time for recovery of
strength, both mental and physical. So I headed back to my
secret home. A place that few people knew about. A place I
would sometimes stay at for weeks, but also a place where I
could spend the odd random night, whenever I felt like
this. Plus it was only a short five minutes' walk
from Louise's house.

I headed back to Darnley Road. A long line of sizeable
houses bordered each side of the main road that headed
into town. I stopped at my destination. A large detached
house, almost in the middle of Darnley Road, favouring the
town side. The house, from the outside wept flakes
of green paint, peeling from the rotting timber roof fascia
and windows. Overgrown weeds had taken residency, both
in the garden and across the cracked concrete footpath that

led from the gate to the front door. Dark curtains were closed at all the windows. The majority of the front facing side of the house was covered in a pebble dash. It's forty feet square front garden consisted of an abundance of overgrown grass, unwanted plants and bushes. Broken garden gnomes randomly placed around the border.

I headed up the cracked concrete footpath to the doorway and rattled the door knocker. A large brass rapper shaped like a horseshoe. I gave it four loud bangs hoping that her hearing had not got any worse. It took one full minute before I heard the catch on the other side of the door. It squeaked open and she spoke before she even saw me, "Sam, Sam, are you well love?"

"Yes Nan been really good. I've just been to see Louise so I thought I would pop in and see how you are as well"

"I'm so pleased. Come in, come in. Are you hungry? I've got some chocolate cake," she gave me a huge cuddle as she spoke. Her frail arms barely managed to wrap around my shoulders, but it was as big a hug as the widowed Ann Margaret Bell could give.

"Thanks Nan. I am a little hungry and I could really do with a coffee as well." I gave my Nan and friend a soft hug in return.

Ann Margaret Bell was not my real Nan, but she had taken me in at a time of need. It was not long after I had returned from the Army. Three months after I had lost my brother Wayne. A matter of days after my Mother had overdosed on heroin.

I had met Ms Bell, Nan, by fluke really. As normal, it involved myself getting involved in other people's problems. The old girl had been putting up a fight against a Romanian pick pocket, after she had caught him dipping into her handbag. Dipping was a crime that had become common place in London and the South East. The offenders were generally Eastern Europeans. They had become skilled in the art of dipping into vulnerable people's handbags to retrieve purses and wallets. A lucrative activity that paid better than shoplifting, burglaries or theft. The elderly always took forever to discover that they had actually fallen victim to theft and not lost their purse or wallet. They also took even longer to report the matter to the bank or Police. My intervention of the potential theft of her purse on that day had been graciously received by the recently widowed and childless victim.

She was on her own, so I helped her carry her shopping bags home, and fixed her rear door lock while she made coffee. She had no remaining family and after finding out that I had no address at the time she virtually begged me to stay until I could sort myself out. *'We should look after our ex-soldiers,' she* had said.

Nan in return, had refused any type of rent money from me. All she wanted was for me to call her Nan, which was not hard for me to do. In fact having no normal family of my own, I had relished it. Instead of paying rent I would fix, repair or replace things that had run the course of their sell by date.

She had also given me a room, for my own use, at the back of the house, an old utility room which was now furnished with a single bed for me, a wardrobe for me, and a few of my belongings.

We had chocolate cake, coffee and then some more coffee while we spoke. Well she did most of the talking and I listened, in between fixing the blockage in her kitchen sink and emptying her Hoover bag.

A few hours later I was in my room plugging in my own pay as you go iPhone. I had left my phone charger there since my last visit a few weeks ago. I knew that I would soon be running out of call credit on the phone. I had received the standard text message from the provider after I had last used it. It would soon be time to change the phone anyway. I didn't like keeping the same number for more than a few months. I then plugged in the other mobile phone, a cheap small black Alcatel phone, the one that K had given to me. It made a small buzzing noise as it fired up. The screen lit up and I could see the battery icon run as it was being charged. It was not a new phone, the scratches on the black shiny plastic casing evidenced that. I thought of checking its call history but decided on waiting until it had been fully charged.

I had one call to make so I took my iPhone and dialled the number from memory. It rang twice before it was answered, "*Robbie?*"

"Yes," I replied, "Just thought I would let you know, I'm in with them Yardies."

Charlie paused before he spoke, *"That's great Sam. Well done. We'll have to speak tomorrow about what shit you pulled to do that. It's all kicked off here."*

"Why what's happened?"

"Found another body blown up."

"Shit who was it?"

"No loss really, some paedo," Jackson paused, realizing that he should not have given any information out. *"You don't know that though mate. Speak to you tomorrow."*

The phone went dead and I ran through what he had just said. '*No loss.*' The comment played on me, right up to when I fell asleep.

Twenty Two

0330hrs 18th March

I stood at the foot of the bed, looking down at Louise. She was fast asleep on top of the duvet cover, on her double bed. Her naked soft smooth skin glowing in the moonlight that shone through the open curtain-less window. I longed to touch her, to press myself up close to her, skin on skin, entwined so our two bodies made one. I could, I told myself. She will want this. It wasn't her that wanted to split. Not her, deep down she knew we should be as one. We were right for each other.

Then came the other voice. *'Stop being a fool Jakobs. You are too wild for her. You're just a tramp. You got nothing to offer. She wants what's best for the kid. She needs a proper man, not some fool without a job, a proper job, no house. Just get out of here you tramp before she wakes up.'*

I stared down at her face, wondering what she was dreaming about. A small frown appeared on her face. The frown made me angry. My Louise should never frown. She should be happy all the time. Who would dare give her reason to frown?

The voice spoke again. *'See what you've done to her Jakobs? You've ruined her life.'*

"Fuck off," I growled, keeping my voice down, not wanting to wake her.

Quiet as I was, she stirred. Not because of me, but because of the sound of the car alarm drifting in through the open window. I moved over to close it. But I couldn't. I felt as weak as a kitten. It took all my strength just to lift my arms. I pushed down hard but it wouldn't budge.

The alarm grew louder. Smashing against my face, like an intruder, wanting to get past me, just so it could wake her up. Wake her up so that she could see me. See the truth of how I felt about her. Just so that she could laugh at me. Laugh at even the suggestion that I could think that I was ever good enough for her. I pushed back against the sound, which was now taking a physical shape. The shape of a man in a suit. A distinguished man, handsome and clean. But he was strong. Too strong for me. I pushed back, he laughed, no normal laugh. The sound of the car alarm emitting sharply from his mouth. The sound filled my ears and it swam past me towards her.

I turned and tried to push her bed away with my feet, while holding fast at the window, stopping him from getting a clean entry. Too late, her eyes opened. She looked at me and screamed. The scream stabbed right through my body taking the physical form of a knife. It plunged deep. Deep into my heart. I could hear my heart beat now. Loud and clear. *Boom, boom.* Slowing down. I was dying. The alarm got louder and louder, my heart sounding duller and duller until that brief second when it stopped.

I jumped up. Sat in my bed. I was back at Nan's house, sweat dripping from my forehead. It was a dream. But I could still hear the alarm. I focused taking a deep breath and turned my head towards the shrilling noise. The phone was ringing. Not my phone. K's phone. I answered it but didn't speak.

"Good morning Sam. Time to earn your money son. Get yourself together. I will be picking you up in an hour. I've got a little job for you."

I pulled the phone away from my ear to check the time displayed on the top corner of the screen. Early but I was not going to make any noise about it. I never did when it came to work and this was work, albeit not really for K.

"I'll meet you by the Tollgate garage. Four thirty," I said.

"Don't be late Sam. There's money to be earned."

The phone went dead. I had picked the location on purpose. It would take me twenty minutes to walk and that would give me time to wake up properly. Also it was a twenty four hour garage, so I would be able to get a coffee and something to eat.

I didn't wonder about what job he had lined up for me. I was a debt collector. I did however start planning for a double cross. I had robbed his dealer, taken care of his heavies and walked away with five hundred pounds, a double cross was just as likely as a genuine collecting job.

Twenty Three

0400hrs 18th March

I had left Nan an apology note, telling her that I had been dragged away to a new employment opportunity. I knew that she would be disappointed. I was not there for breakfast. She would have already started planning what she was going to cook for me this morning. Plans that she would have made when she went to bed last night. As it was, I would have to make do with the garage self service latte, from the machine at a costly price of one pound twenty five pence and four hot sausage rolls for a pound.

I sat in the garage at a high counter on a tall stool to consume my early breakfast. The Asian male who had served me looked suspiciously in my direction, quickly looking away when I caught his eye. The coffee was hot and sweet thanks to the three sugar packets that I had added. The sausage rolls were equally as hot and flakes fell all over my denim jacket and black hooded jumper.

I kept an eye on the forecourt, which was brightly lit by the lights above the filling stations. I purchased a newspaper. The Sun, the biggest and most ruthless informant of them all, at a cost of fifty pence and sat there reading, while drinking the remainder of my coffee. The stories of the terrorist bombings were all over the front page again. It seemed weird that my small town of Gravesend was at the centre of National news. The whole country was in an uproar. It seemed that right now all Muslims were the enemy. Hatred was being fuelled by the extreme right wing groups and the UKIP political party. Muslim Mosques and shops were being attacked all over the Country. Muslim marches leading to small riots were also taking place. The headlines, 'CIVIL WAR' stretched across the top of the newspaper. It seemed crazy that all this was going on all around England apart from in Gravesend, the scene of the terrible attacks. Although for certain it would happen, sooner than later. Maybe that was why the cashier seemed nervous of me.

I managed to stay alert while reading the paper and noticed the black Mercedes saloon screech to a stop outside. It stopped bang outside the entrance doors. The front passenger door opened and the Monster I had taken out at Masters address climbed out. His left eye bandaged up and his left arm in a cast. His face grimaced in pain. Was it a double cross? Even if it was, this guy with one arm and one eye would be no threat. I watched him walk in and he stopped a matter of feet away from me. He stood square and now showed no emotion. If he was pissed at me he wasn't showing it. He didn't speak but nodded his head towards the door. I jumped off my stool and he instinctively stepped back with one foot.

"Let's go then big man," I said. "Oh and sorry about the injuries, but it was you or me."

He didn't reply. He just turned away to lead me out the door.

"See you man," I shouted out to the cashier. He was already looking nervous and I wanted to make sure he watched us for as long as he could, just in case things went wrong.

I followed him to the Mercedes where the monster opened the rear nearside passenger door with his working arm. I stooped to look inside. K was sat in the back with a big grin on his face. The driver had his head turned as well so that he could see me. It was the second guy with the knife who I had done at Snugs house. He didn't look good either. His nose was definitely broken and he had two black eyes, that were coloured dark purple. He looked angry and hurt. He immediately turned away. The monster climbed back into the front seat. He struggled shutting the door, having to twist around to use his good arm. Difficult because of the size of the man.

"Get in man. It's time to earn your money," K's grin vanished and was replaced by a more serious expression.

I got in, which also proved difficult, the seat in front of me was pushed back as far as it could go, allowing the sizeable front seat passenger room to get in. I managed to squeeze in but I didn't like it. My legs felt trapped. I could see both of K's hands, the driver had both his on the steering wheel and the Monster still looked in pain. I couldn't see anything that resembled a weapon or anything that could be used as an improvised weapon.

"So what do you need?" I said.

"You are now my debt collector. Is that not so? It must be clear then that I need a debt to be collected."

"Yeah that's who I am. I can see why they won't be able to do it," I sneered with a hint of sarcasm. The driver turned again and went to protest but was immediately silenced by K.

"I have a debtor, in the respect that he has damaged some goods. He owes me twenty thousand. He has said he needs a couple of weeks to pay it, but I want it now. It is also for his own good. In two weeks the debt would have doubled to forty thousand."

I processed his statement as he spoke. K was dealing drugs to local addicts. It would be impossible to raise a debt of twenty thousand or damage twenty thousand pounds worth of drugs. Unless he was also dealing to other bigger dealers that I was not aware of. Or something else. My brain told me it was something else.

Twenty Four

They drove straight out of the garage, onto the main road and then away from the town centre, we passed the junction that would lead us onto the motorway, heading straight towards the greener part of Gravesham. The Mercedes was smooth and quiet and smelt of patchouli oil, it was either from one of the passengers or from the dangling air freshener. Music was playing quietly in the background, perhaps a CD or a specialised radio station, some sort of rapping tune. I hated rap.

The drive took about thirty minutes I guessed, through the narrow country lanes, past Istead Rise, through Meopham and Vigo and then eventually into a thick wooded area. The thought of a double cross went through my mind again. We were out, rural, in a place I had never been to before.

"What's the matter Sam? You look worried," K grinned again as he spoke.

"Who me?" I said, staring directly into his eyes, "I never worry about anything."

"That's what I like about you man. Bollocks of a lion."

The car stopped close to the end of a driveway. Two large black iron gates stood sentry at the entrance. Security cameras looking down. The house appeared to be secluded. There were no signs of any other dwellings nearby.

"Who lives here then?" I said.

"A customer who has taken the piss," replied K.

"Afraid I need to know more than that son," I growled. Was this a set up?

"The man is a Muslim. That should make you happy, what with everything going on. Though he is not the suicide bomber type, but he is a barrister. He runs his own company. A real bad ass barrister at that. Can get anyone off anything. Mr. Mo Ali owes me twenty thousand today. Next week it will be double. So I want my money now. Twenty K is affordable for a man of his means, but forty might not be. When debts get out of hand people go missing and that is bad for my business."

"A law-man that does drugs?" I said, making it sound like a statement, but in reality it was a question.

"You don't need to know why he owes me the money. I told you, because of him I have damaged goods. That is all you need to know and he will understand." K shifted in his seat and ordered, "Door." It was directed at the big-man in the front.

The monster struggled again, to get out the car but once again managed to. I though, hadn't finished asking questions, "Family? Kids?"

"I don't know and I don't care. Just get my money. I'm sure you'll understand the reasons of why we won't wait here for you. Use the cash from him to get a taxi. Or get him to give you a lift back. Either way, I don't care. I will call you later to arrange picking up my parcel. Don't come back to Wallace Square, I can't afford it to be seized over a silly drugs raid." K turned away making it clear that was all he was going to say. My door opened and the big guy stood aside to let me out. I got out and left him to shut my door. He got back in the front and I watched the car drive off.

K wasn't a fool. He knew that by now the local Police would be aware that he had taken over the Snugs address. Sometimes the Police would execute warrants, just for the sake of it. To disrupt the dealers. Sometimes they got lucky and found stuff. Most dealers though, never kept the bulk of the drugs at their homes. They would be stashed up somewhere, or held by a quiet neighbour, paid a small amount of money for the inconvenience. A neighbour who didn't have a drugs habit, or the stash might get smaller. The Police knew this. If you didn't get raided quick time, it normally meant that the Police were investigating you, properly. Targeting you, through surveillance, phone work, undercover officers, grasses and people like me, agents. Or was I kidding myself? Was I just a glorified grass? I shuddered and knew that wasn't the case. I hated grasses.

When the car was completely gone, out of sight, I looked at my target address and felt for my phone in my pocket. Should I call Jackson? No, he would have a fit and tell me to get out.

The security gates were bordered by a brick wall. It must have been about eight feet in height. It was partially covered with some sort of green climbing plant, it looked like Ivy, Ivy that had matured. With no more room to climb it had started to produce side branches that were now at the stage of looking bushy. The wall underneath the Ivy ran a few hundred feet each way and cut back at ninety degree angles, running parallel to the sides of the house. It probably ran all the way around the house.

I stood tall on my toes and ran my fingers lightly along the top of the wall, just where I stood next to the gates and as suspected, felt the jagged edges of broken glass embedded into the top of it. I looked through the gates and could see three cars. Two brand new Mercedes saloons, that looked jet black in the night, were parked neatly next to each other, just outside a double garage that sat on its own to the left side of the house. Another dark car, which looked like an Audi TT sports car, was parked at the bottom of a set of steps that led up to the front door of the house. The house itself was in darkness apart from what looked like a night light on the porch next to the front door. The white UPVC door looked odd and not in keeping with the large old country style house. Neither did the matching UPVC windows.

First job first. I needed to get into the courtyard, so I started to walk around the perimeter wall in the general direction of where the double garage stood on the other side of it. I passed several tall trees, silver birch; none of them were good enough to climb as the branches were too high. The silvery bark with small black notches looked smooth in the strong moonlight. I kept walking, slowly and quietly, until I thought I was at the point where the garage would be on the other side.

I kicked around the earth on the ground, searching for a marker and bent down to pick up a length of broken branch. It was crooked so I was able to hook it on top of the wall. I walked off in the hope of finding something that would help me scale the wall.

About twenty yards from my marker, leaning against some shrubs I found an old green wheelie bin about four feet in height. I dragged it over to the wall and positioned it just under my crooked branch. I then took off my denim jacket and wrapped it around my hand. I reached up with my wrapped hand grabbing the wall. I could barely feel the broken glass through my protection. I managed to heave myself up, eventually planting both feet on the bin. It wobbled on the uneven earth underneath. I looked over the wall searching for motion detection lights. Visibility was quite good courtesy of the moon and dimly lit porch. I couldn't see anything that resembled any such security system, but I wasn't going to take it for granted. I had seen the cameras above the gates at the end of the driveway, so had to presume there was some other form of residential security protection set in place.

I climbed up onto the wall. Both feet balanced on the top, where I sat in a squat position. I looked down. My guess was perfect. I was virtually two feet away from the cement corrugated garage roof. I carefully pulled myself onto the edge of the roof, taking caution not to go too far in. You could never tell how strong this type of roof was from sight only. The cement normally contained a quantity of asbestos which was known to deteriorate over time, causing the roof to become brittle. Once on the roof I carefully walked along the edge until I reached the courtyard, where I gently lowered myself down and put my jacket back on. So far so good.

I crept around, keeping myself low. Around all three cars. The car that stood on its own displayed a private number plate. M0 ALl. The last 'L' had been made in lower case writing and the plate screw above it gave it the appearance of being an i. Clearly the vehicle that belonged to my target.

It was indeed a family household, three cars, one of which contained a toddlers car seat in the back of it. The Mercedes in question told me that there was likely to be at least one young child in the house. Whatever I was going to do would have to wait until he was outside. Never take a fight to a wife or kids.

I sneaked back towards the garage, still keeping myself as low as possible. I looked around the wooden double doors. At closer inspection it was clear that the garage had not been maintained. The thick oak doors showed signs of rot set along the edges. A hook and clasp hung loose between the doors, absent of any padlock. Two bolts were set though, across the top and the middle of the doors. I carefully unbolted them and eased the door ajar. I slipped inside and pressed a button on my phone so it briefly lit up. The garage was cluttered with junk across a solid concrete floor. A wooden counter stretched across the length of the garage also riddled with old tools, bits of wood and large tool bags. The phone light dimmed and I pressed the button again because I had not found what I was looking for.

I slowly walked along the counter with the phone pointed down towards the tools. I eventually came across a pile of old screwdrivers, splayed across the top of what looked like an old canvas tent fly sheet. I picked up a large flat head screwdriver. I sneaked back out and re-bolted the doors.

I headed away from the garage, back towards the main front door keeping alert of any lights that may come on. I was quiet and cool. I pulled my hoodie sleeves from under my jacket, over my hands and pushed the front door handle downwards. It moved, as expected. Surprisingly, despite warnings from the Police, the majority of people never double locked their front doors if they were inside.

I gently leaned against the door with my shoulder and pushed the flat edge of the screwdriver between the plastic door and frame, positioned right next to where the lock should be. I levered the door, maintaining the pressure with my shoulder. Two seconds later, it popped open. Nice and quiet, no noise and no damage. Any small imprint left by the flat edge of the screwdriver, would remain invisible to the naked eye.

I sneaked in. The porch light lit the entrance, just enough for me to see the key hooks on the wall to the right of the front door. I picked out a small bunch, which had four keys on it. Two Yale keys, one Chub key and more importantly an Audi key. It also had a small black fob on it, which I guessed activated the front security gates. I slipped back out of the door and silently headed towards the car. I used the key and not the remote button to unlock the driver's door. I then quickly returned to the house, hung the key up and carefully shut the front door. I remained crouched on the way out and slipped the screwdriver into my inside jacket pocket before carefully opening the car door. No noise.

I pulled at a lever, releasing the driver's seat, so I could climb into the back. An almost impossible task as that model of Audi was not really designed to carry rear seat passengers. I did manage to squeeze in though, and stretched myself across the bucket seats, pulling the door shut and repositioning the driver's seat in front of me.

I figured by now the time must be around five thirty in the morning. Wishful thinking and reasoning had me believe that he would be the first one out of the house to leave for work. At a guess about seven. An hour in this position was going to be uncomfortable, but there was little else I could do. I decided to half shut my eyes. Settle into a half-sleep. Something that I found easy to do. A half-sleep, kept me awake but also relaxed, still alert to any movement. All I had to do now was wait.

Twenty Five

The room was cold, dank and dark. It contained two people. Both currently silent, busy about their own activities. One of them was dressed in all black with a black balaclava over his head. The same balaclava he had previously worn. The other male, was also dressed in all black, with a similar mask over his head, he was stood behind the video camera, connecting electrical leads to various boxes. The same floodlight stood high behind the man to be recorded. It glared back at the video camera at such an angle that it would only slightly affect the recording, a purposeful tactic for further concealment. Creating a more intense dark silhouette of the man in front of it. Bright lights and sharp shadows filled the room.

Soon they were ready and the man spoke directly into the now activated video recorder, held steady by his accomplice.

"There is more terror in a day of life than is at the moment of death. You must now be prepared for an eternity of days of terror. Terror driven into your hearts by my hands. I am like a lone wolf, striking dread and helplessness deep into your lives. I have already taken five infidels, five devil worshippers, five heathens. Five deaths of un-natural cause. Life and death has a price. If I live, then some other must die before his time. Five more untimely deaths. Your weeping has only just started. Walk carefully. Look over your shoulders, wherever you go. Be watchful, but you will not see me. My war has now become my peoples war. My army is growing, day by day. We will pluck you out one by one. Five more will die. All you infidels will cry with fear. All of Islam will rejoice. Fatwa has spoken. Allahu Akbar.

Twenty Six

0600hrs 18th March

The briefing room at Gravesend Police station was crammed. More than it had ever been.

The pristine uniforms, bulled shoes and designer suits, normally saved for best were everywhere. Charlie Jackson felt out of place in his old navy blue t-shirt, jeans and training shoes. He discreetly smelt under his arm pits and secretly wished that he had showered earlier.

The room was largely filled by incompetent buffoons who had obtained high profile ranks in the Constabulary through qualifications, social standing and pronouncing their P's and Q's, as opposed to their skills in policing or criminology. Thankfully there were a small number of individuals present who excelled in the art of crime fighting, Charlie Jackson being one of them.

This meeting was separate from the Cabinet Office Briefing room, the famous COBRA meetings that always took place in response to instances of national crises or threats to national security. It was also separate from the in-house governmental meetings, the ones that always followed major incidents, the secret ones that dealt with issues that could affect potential voters. This was a meeting for the enforcers of the area who had suffered the deaths and was now potentially the target of the new threats, which had gone viral on the internet an hour earlier.

The room buzzed with different conversations between officers who had naturally split themselves up into their own groups of self-importance and cliques. Some discussing the agenda for the meeting, others just spreading gossip, and some talking about anything but work.

The buzz came to a halt, as the door to the briefing room opened again, this time filled with the huge figure of their new Chief Constable. A large man by frame as opposed to over indulgence. Those that were sitting on chairs arose and those that were already standing, stood to attention.

The Chief took his position at the head of the briefing room before he spoke, "Please take a seat gentlemen," he looked around and noticed two female Superintendents and quickly added, "Ahem and ladies."

The seats shuffled and scraped as everyone in the room sat down. A slight murmur of voices sounded around the room, a murmur which soon shut down as the Chief called for the meeting to start.

The meeting lasted three hours, but in all likeliness could have been sewn up in an hour, but for the promotion chasing cretins auditioning their own voices and opinions during this rare opportunity of having the Chief's ears.

The Chief knew this, but let them continue. Sometimes, even idiots came up with bright ideas. He did wonder why there were so many officers in the room, holding such high ranks. How could one area really need three Superintendents and so many Chief Inspectors. What could they all possibly do on a day to day basis. He made up his mind to examine this further, when all this was over, and normality had been restored.

Outside of the auditions, it had been revealed that numerous arrests had been made across the nation of those individuals known to have lost their children to the IS fanatics, those who had managed to sneak their way out of the country to Syria. Search warrants had led to seizures of bomb making equipment, firearms and other terrorist related paraphernalia. What was certain in the wake of the most recent video release was that the one they were after was still out there. Pressure was mounting on all the law enforcement agencies in the country.

Forensic examinations of the dead bodies had not identified for certain what had caused the explosions, but what had been established was that the detonations had occurred in each person's mouth. The public had been warned of buying unknown foods or drink. This on its own had caused some nationwide panic. Identification of exactly what type of sustenance they were looking for had so far proved futile.

Aside of Nicholas Tucker and Paul Baker, who had once been arrested for breaking into a warehouse together, there had been no coherent link found between all the deceased persons, apart from the fact that they all lived in the Borough of Gravesham.

Nationwide the Police services were working extended hours of duty, quelling riots, gang wars and vicious racist attacks, from both white extremist groups and Muslim gangs. All rest days had been cancelled. The United Kingdom was very quickly becoming a nation of unrest and on the verge of civil war.

While the video release gave no indication as to where and when the threats would be carried out, it had to be presumed that the targets would be within the North Kent Policing area. Resources were stretched in an effort to restrain the growing tensions between the Muslims and the rest of the community. So far though Gravesend had been free from riots, although reported assaults were on the increase.

The intelligence unit's Research and Development team were heavily engaged in tracking through crime reports and incidents that could potentially link them to anyone that showed a glimmer of hatred towards the West. Every line of enquiry was being investigated by the team of Detectives set aside for the operation on the top floor at the station. The flow of intelligence however, appeared to be one sided, Police to Secret Services, not the other way round.

Charlie had wanted the Tactical team to execute a search warrant at Vikki Snugs address. The missing girls and the rapes had to be dealt with as a priority, despite everything else that was going on. The request had been turned down by the Area Commander, Chief Superintendent Best, prior to the meeting taking place. Charlie was disgusted by Best's attitude that there were more pressing matters to be dealt with in the wake of the terrorist threats. Far more serious than to, *save a load of junkie kids who were probably earning money as prostitutes anyway.* Charlie was also warned not to make any mention of Operation Alphabet in the presence of the Chief when he arrived.

Outside the briefing room, after the meeting Julie Stokes tugged Charlie to the side.

"Have you had a chance to talk to Eddie yet?" she asked.

"No why is that?"

"Sally Tall called him late last night. Sam Jakobs has got a job with the Yardies as a debt collector."

"He did phone me and tell me he was in with them. So that's how he did it. I didn't get a chance to ask him. Pond had just been discovered dead."

"He's supposed to collect a large debt today. Don't know who from but Sally heard them talking of thousands of pounds," Stokes hushed her voice as a group of officers came out of the briefing room and walked past them.

"OK. That doesn't sound good. See if you can get hold of him and make sure he doesn't do anything stupid." Jackson stopped himself and carried on, "Although, I think you are right about how smart he is. I think he will know his boundaries. Try and get hold of him anyway and let me know what happens. "

"OK boss." Stokes turned around to walk off, but stopped dead in her tracks.

Charlie Jackson followed her gaze. Stood at the end of the corridor at the double wooden doorway was PC Mark Shepherd. He was just stood there, staring right back at her, in his new boy uniform, with his five digit badge. A cocky grin spread across his red spotty face.

"What the fuck are you staring at?" shouted Stokes. Shepherd blew her a kiss, immediately turned away and then calmly walked out through the door. Stokes went to storm after him but was stopped in her tracks by her Sergeant, Charlie Jackson.

"Leave it babe. We'll sort that prick out later."

Stokes was now bright red with anger. She took three deep breaths before speaking, "Yes I will sort that prick out."

Jackson added, "Later."

Twenty Seven

I had shut my eyes for about an hour, crammed in the back
of the Audi. A very light sleep, a half-sleep, being woken
up at every slight sound. The fox that came in, scavenging
around the round metal bin at the end of the garden,
looking for breakfast. The sound of the high top lorry, that
drove speedily for its size, along the narrow country lane
past the house. Now at the sound of the front door to the
house opening, keys jangling in the Asian man's hands.

I watched through the condensation that had spread
across the windows because of my breathing. He looked to
be in his forties. About five feet eight. Ten stone. Athletic
build. Wearing a made to measure designer black suit. His
head was compact and hard with receding short hair. Tight
skin wrapped his bony skull. Keys in one hand and a black

185

leather briefcase in the other. I recognised him. He was the solicitor at the Police station the day I had handed myself in. The one complaining about his clients bail. The day I had met Charlie Jackson and Julie Stokes. The day of the explosion.

He put the briefcase down as he turned to shut the front door. He activated the remote on his keys for the vehicle which bleeped as he did it, locking it. He did it a second time and it bleeped twice as it unlocked. He walked over to the driver's side and threw his briefcase onto the passenger seat before getting in. He shut the door and leant forward to put the key in its ignition. He leant back and my left arm wrapped around his neck. Tight. His beady eyes bulged. I could see the fear set deep in his dark eyes through the interior mirror, a protruding vein pulsed down the side of his temple.

"I'm Sam Jakobs." No sense in hiding who I was, I never did. "I'm not going to hurt you," I growled, "Yet. Unless you do exactly as I say. You got that Mr Ali." I slowly released the pressure around his neck so he could nod.

I carried on, "Open the gates, drive out and turn right."

He did as I instructed. I completely released his neck with my arm and instead I maintained a firm grip on his left shoulder. I pulled the screwdriver out of my jacket and pressed the sharp end to his temple, next to the vein, just to make sure of his compliance. The gates opened and he turned right. I put the screwdriver down next to me, keeping hold of his shoulder.

"What do you want? Please don't hurt me," his voice stammered. Not the type of voice you would want defending you in court I thought.

"You owe my boss money Mr. Ali. He pays me to collect it. He also pays me to hurt people who don't pay. Apparently you have damaged his goods and today is the day you have to pay for it. He says he's thinking of you Mr Ali. You see if it isn't paid today not only do I have to hurt you, but the debt double's each week. Do you understand?"

"Yes, yes I understand. But it was not my fault. She resisted. I was told that she would let me tie her up. She started screaming and I had to stop her screaming. What if someone heard her? It would be bad for your business, no?"

My mind scrambled for a second, like it does when you are drunk, trying to recollect something, but you can't. I focused. This was not drugs. It was clearly something completely different. Something I wanted no part of. Something I definitely did not want to be referred to as my business. I hate drugs, I hate drug dealers, I hate bullies, I hate sex fiends even more. I was right, this was definitely something else.

My hand moved off his shoulder as I saw a clearing to the right, leading to what looked like an abandoned derelict outbuilding and yard.

"Behind the building and park up." I said, my voice deep and carrying genuine menace. My hand now gripping his skinny throat. He drove around, slowly along the building's edge, shaking, hands trembling. He eased the car to a stop behind the dereliction, tight against the wall and parked up. I kept a firm hold of him as we got out, not that he was going to run.

It took me less than five minutes to get a full update from the lawyer, to the effect that he was paying for sex with young girls. Disgusting perverted sex. He had just over two thousand pounds cash on him, in his briefcase, which he handed over to me immediately. I put the money into my top denim jacket pocket. He further pleaded not to be hurt and said that he could get the extra eighteen thousand pounds within an hour. He just needed to go to the bank. That wasn't what I wanted. I now wanted to know where Rebecca Snugs and the other young girls were being kept.

I forced him to drive me to the address, which was still in Gravesend, close to a built up residential area, an area though that I was not familiar with. An old pub, boarded up and closed down. The tattered sign of *The Dog N' Bone,* stretched across the front of the building above the boarded up windows and doors.

The pub sat detached away from the residential houses, some five hundred feet away, next to a large field containing a couple of adult sized football pitches, some five hundred feet in the distance.

I made Ali pull over short of the small car park at the front of the pub. I still did not know what I was going to do with my captive, the perverted law-man, shaking in the driver seat, so I made him cram himself into the boot. I locked the car and walked around to the rear of the pub, questioning my next move. I decided the right thing to do was to call Charlie, which is exactly what I did. Watching the rear door while I waited.

Ali had told me that the rear door boarding had been turned into a door. The board having been replaced by a hinged panel, secured only by a bolt on the inside. The place was always guarded inside. No activity took place in the old bar areas. Everything went on in the spacious residential rooms upstairs.

I could have stabbed Ali with the screwdriver, which was now again in my pocket, straight through his head, as such ending all deviant thoughts elicited from his evil brain. It took all my strength not to.

I retained calmness and sat on a garden wall watching the door. Not covert but not overt. Part of me wanted someone to come outside to confront me. In the meantime, I had to wait for Charlie.

Twenty Eight

Jasper Shepherd logged onto his computer. He was sat in his office on the top floor at City point in Ropemaker Street, London.

The building previously known as Britannic Tower, recently valued in excess of seven hundred million Great British pounds. The head office of Secretus Security International Ltd. The huge skyscraper consisted of thirty five floors. Thirty five floors of shining metal and reflective glass. Secretus Security occupied the most expensive floor in the building. The entire ridiculously priced top floor had been home for Secretus for the past three years.

Jasper's office alone stretched forty feet long. The size of a boardroom. In fact his office was bigger than the adjacent boardroom. His large desk sat in front of the glass front of the building. Looking out into the City. The open window listening to the hum of busy workers striving to make it in this lifetime, the horns of cars

impatiently occupied as always in London, a bustling

clamour that Shepherd enjoyed.

His desk was clean and void of anything apart from his

computer. A sleek thin purpose built device, adapted to

Shepherd's needs. The computer sat comfortably on a glass

topped desk, which had no drawers underneath it. The

whole set up of the room was designed to elaborate it's

expanse of space. Aside of his desk and computer the only

other items of furniture in the vast room were a soft red

leather 'L' shaped couch at the far side of the room. The

couch faced a large flat screen television on the smooth

wall with a waste high sideboard underneath it. The

sideboard shined pure white and housed nothing but an

ornate glass waterfall ornament on it.

He logged into his false e-mail account using his

pseudonym. The one that he always used when carrying out

such activities. The encrypted software programmes on

his hard drive hid his actions, hid them deep within the

lower layers of the dark net.

His message containing the details of the meeting they

had planned for later on that night. He pressed send, the

electronic mail whizzed through its SMTP server, the internet's post office, through its DNS server, the internet's address book, through the MTA server, the postman pushing it through the letterbox, all before the recipients could collect the mail using POP or IMAP. Quicker than a letter. The message delivered simultaneously to thirty three different addresses.

'Meeting 1800hrs 18th March at the Church. Dress code with all appointments'

Shepherd had used his sponsorship of the extreme right wing political groups such as Britain First, UKIP, National Front and other lesser known groups to uncover the most racist individuals of all. People who shared his belief of white supremacy. But also people who were powerful, holding significant positions in the world of politics, globally dominant businessmen or anyone who had something to offer. Something that he might need. People with tribal beliefs that coloured individuals had been placed on Earth by the white God purely to test the supreme beings resilience and strength. That those of dirty skins were no better than scavenging mongrels. He had found people like him, people like his Father and people like his Father's Father.

He then picked up the phone and dialled his brother. The phone rang twice before being answered, *"Jasp, can't talk yet."*

"OK Shrimp, just reminding you. Need those names and addresses tonight."

"Don't call me that Jasp. You know I hate it." The silence on the other side of the phone, from his older brother deafened Mark Shepherd so he carried on, *"OK Jasp, I'll have them for you tonight."*

Jasper Shepherd clicked the phone off. He stretched his arms out and leant back against the leathered upholstery of his desk chair, smiling with satisfaction.

Twenty Nine

The wooden board covering the back door of the 'Dog and Bone' swung open. A man walked out. A white male, thin build, six feet tall wearing glasses. I would put him at about twenty five years of age. He was wearing a long green anorak, similar to the Parkas that the Mods used to wear back in the seventies; he pulled the hood over his head. As he did this he saw me sat on the wall.

No one else came out behind him. He was only about twenty feet away from me, and just stood there for a moment staring at me.

I jumped off the wall and started walking towards him. He looked confused as to what he should do and partially turned to walk off, towards the front of the building.

My footsteps crunched on gravel, not breaking stride, not quickening but also not slowing. The man walked halfway around the side of the building. He then stopped and turned.

"You all right, mate?" he said in a half whisper, "They are open mate, still working," he grinned this time as he spoke.

I was now stood next to him and leaned in close to his ear, "Open for what?"

The man leaned back, partly confused, partly thinking *shit*, "Oh I thought you were here for, erm I'm just joking with you mate. The pubs been closed down for months."

"The girls." I said. My gritted teeth and growl must have made it very clear that I was not there for the same reason as him.

He went to shout out, but was silenced by the left hook I landed firmly on his jaw. Hard enough to shut him up but not hard enough to knock him out, or break his jaw. Yet.

I dragged him away, my hand firmly strapped around his chin, away from where I might be seen by people going to work, out of view of the distant houses and away from the roadside. I pressed him hard, up against the garden boundary wall, my hand now at his throat, making sure the back of his head scraped with force against the concrete. I reminded him of my strength by squeezing his neck again, and threatened to snap it. I knew I didn't have long before Charlie got there.

Thirty seconds was all it took to find out that the upper floor contained six rooms, occupied by six young girls. Sold for sex. At this very moment in time the floor was being looked after by three men, a permanent fixture called H, a giant of a man with a broken arm and wearing an eye patch, who only turned up occasionally and another black man with gold teeth who had a broken nose. The one that paid the girls. My compulsory witness had not seen any guns but he had seen them with baseball bats and hammers. He had also seen a long machete style knife. Five seconds later the 'grassing pervert' had a broken jaw and was lying next to the wall, unconscious.

I headed back to the front of the pub. Back to the Audi and started to contemplate what to do with the lawyer in the boot. How much to tell Charlie. My thoughts were broken by a voice hoarsely calling out my name. That is my other name, Robbie.

I walked towards Charlie Jackson who had brought Julie Stokes with him. She looked unbelievable. She smiled at me and her gorgeousness swelled to the realms of impossibility. We huddled up close, so we could talk quietly.

Julie was the first to speak, "God you both stink. Bath time Charlie," she giggled as she spoke and carried on, "Robbie same goes for you."

"Been a bit busy," both Charlie and I spoke almost in unison which brought a snigger to all present.

I told them most of what I knew. I told them of the debt I had been asked to collect from the Lawyer, Mo Ali. I told them what the debt was for. I told them of the punter that had come out of the building while I was there. I told them what he had told me and what they would find inside. I didn't tell them that the punter was currently laying unconscious with a broken jaw or that I was in possession of Ali's car who had given me two thousand pounds and that he was currently locked in the boot of his Audi TT. I hoped that they would not clock the motor. I did tell them that the main man K, did not appear to be in the building and that if I found out where he was I would let them know. They now had my other phone number, provided to me by K. Charlie told me to delete my last call, the one made to Charlie from the call log, which I proceeded to do in front of him.

"We've got to do this properly Robbie. I know what you want to do, but we have got to do this right. You've got to vanish before we call for back up and go in. You cannot be seen anywhere."

I stood there quiet for a minute. I wanted to go inside with them. Two reasons. One to protect Julie, they had weapons, and secondly, to take revenge on the dirty scum inside. I knew I wasn't getting to do either.

"OK Charlie, Jules. Call your back up now. Don't want another pervert going in there before your back up gets here." I paused then conceded, "By the way there's one of them, the last punter that came out, he's lying sparked out with a broken jaw by that wall."

"And how did he break his jaw?" said Charlie, who surprisingly, didn't actually look angry. In fact he looked quite pleased.

Julie was already on the phone. I just shrugged my shoulders and went to walk off when Charlie called out to me, "Hey, take the lawyer's car back. Don't want no come backs to you," he grinned as he spoke.

I walked over to the Audi. I could hear soft shuffling in the trunk of the car. I got in and started the engine. I waved at the two police officers and slowly moved off.

I drove down towards the Promenade, which took me the best part of five minutes, where I pulled over into a small overload car park, which I knew would be empty at this time of the morning. Again there were no houses that overlooked the car park. An old closed down school building across the road, that looked derelict. Behind the car park, open green fields that led to the river front looked vacant.

I stood on the hard gravel of the car park and opened the boot. Leaning in I dragged the lawyer out, I shook him before letting him go. He stood in front of me, quivering like a broken man.

"What to do with you?" I spoke loudly, both to him and myself.

"Please don't hurt me. I told you, I can get you the money," he grovelled and collapsed down onto his knees, crying.

"You're getting nicked you dirty old man. This is what you are going to do. Take your car, close your business down and when you get arrested admit what you have done. If you don't I will kill you," I grabbed his scruff and lifted him until his face was level to mine, "Look at me you pervert. Look at my eyes and tell me you believe me. ADMIT IT OR I WILL KILL YOU." I dropped him back onto his knees.

"I believe you I believe you," he whimpered and sobbed as he spoke. Urine shooting down his trouser legs, leaving a puddle of yellowish liquid around his knees.

I threw his keys towards the other side of the car park and walked off towards the town.

My mind confused. I had just left a pervert, largely unhurt. How was that possible? I killed people like him. I felt uncomfortable but was certain I had done the right thing. Yet I still felt uncomfortable. I thought as I walked, my walk turned into a jog, I was still thinking, my jog then turned back to a walk when it hit me. I now knew what I had to do.

I headed towards Louise's house, buying an envelope and pen on the way from a garage. I also got myself a cheese roll and a bottle of water. I was hungry. I ate and drank while I counted out one thousand three hundred pounds. I stuck her money into the envelope and wrote out a message for her on the cover. Nothing romantic. Just a message.

Back in the small car park adjacent to the Promenade, Mo Ali sat on his knees. Wet and cold. Wet from the tears streaming down his face and wet from his urine stained trousers. His whole life was about to be thrown into a furnace, burning everything he had worked so hard for into ashes. His brain tried to counteract the negativity and submissiveness breaching every part of his body.

How can this happen to me. I am the man. I have been the man. I am the one who changes people's lives. I am educated. Who is this Sam Jakobs? He is just a gorilla. An ape. Man runs this world, not apes. But this ape has destroyed my world. He cried again. Head in his hands. His brain reacted. *No I won't let him. I have helped so many people in my position. People whose lives were just about to be destroyed. People looking at long stretches. I have given them the stay out of jail cards. Now is the time to help myself. I must think like a barrister. I am the best at that. Sam Fucking Jakobs was just a debt collector. Or was he? He has left without the debt being paid in full. He has taken just two thousand pounds. He has threatened me, told me I will be arrested. An undercover Police Officer? If he is, he is bent. He has taken money, he locked me in the boot. He threatened me. Actions that could warrant the job being thrown out of court. No he is not a Police Officer, then what? A man of principles? A debt collector for a criminal that is suddenly conscience-stricken? No, it is something else.* His brain was now in lawyer mode. *Ah, I have it. Sam Jakobs is a grass. He must be. He is nothing but a filthy grass. I saw him at the Police station. In custody for attempt murder. He had no legal representation and now he is on bail. That is the only possibility.* He smiled at his new found realisation. One that was sure to help. *Now is the time for the people who I have helped to help me. I will show this ape. I will show Sam Jakobs, the grass. He should never have entered my world. I am superior. He is weak.*

He straightened himself, upright, but still on his knees. Thoughts zipping through his mind. *I have done nothing wrong. In my country I would have been paid a dowry to marry young girls. The western world allowed me to pay a dowry for sex. This is not my fault. It is their fault. The western world has taught them this. They consented. They are the ones who allow gay sex, far worse than this, yet it is OK for them. I will be alright. I am too clever and God is on my side. I will be fine. That ape, the grass, Sam Jakobs will not.*

Thirty

Chief Superintendent Best had refused to release *his* Tactical Team; in fact he had refused to release any of *his* other resources for DS Jackson. They were too busy being briefed for the day's anticipated work. The Chief Constable was still at North Kent Police station and Best wanted to impress. He had already prepared his day's briefing for all his subordinates at the station. A briefing that he would deliver in front of the County's head honcho.

The Chief Constable would be ever present at North Kent for the unforeseeable future; for both fundamental and personal reasons. The station was currently under scrutiny from the whole Nation. It was also the principal focus of the National Media, not just newspapers but TV as well. Best was loving it, he had the Chief's ear and if he played his cards right he was certain to get an excellent promotion out of it. *Every cloud has a silver lining.*

Charlie had no option but to call his own team in. Executing search warrants was not the norm for Intelligence Officers, who preferred to keep themselves in the shadows, pulling the strings, but this would have to be an exception. They could not afford to wait.

The Krays, Crayston and Ronnie were sent to get an out of hours search warrant first. Outside the normal Monday to Friday, nine to five opening hours, warrants could only be obtained by way of visiting a Magistrate at home. Each Magistrate with the ability to provide search warrants were listed on a roster within the Research and Development unit.

Today they were lucky. The on-call Magistrate lived in Southfleet. A short drive from Gravesend. It wouldn't take long. Ronnie's first job would be to prepare a written affidavit, outlining the circumstances and known facts justifying the issue of the warrant, he had to do this relying on the small amount of information he had been given by Charlie on the phone. This information would then be laid before the Magistrate after swearing an oath on the bible, a different oath to the one normally taken before giving evidence during a trial.

'I SWEAR BY ALMIGHTY GOD THAT THE
INFORMATION I LAY BEFORE YOU IS TRUE AND
ACCURATE TO THE BEST OF MY KNOWLEDGE
AND BELIEF AND I WILL TRUE ANSWER MAKE
TO ANY QUESTIONS ASKED OF ME.'

After the oath, the laying of the information would take place, Ronnie read his affidavit;

'Information has been received from a tried and tested source,' (CHIS), in this case Robbie Strange, *'to the effect that numerous young girls aged between 12 and 15 are being held against their will at the said address for the purpose of illegal sexual activity. This information has been corroborated by other sources and young girls are known to be missing. Additional information has been received to the effect that the same individuals are also involved in the supply of Class A drugs, namely heroin and crack cocaine. The drugs are stored at the said premises. It is believed that without the warrant, access will be denied and potential evidence disposed of.'*

The Magistrates would then be entitled to ask them questions, but they rarely did at home visits. They would merely just sign the warrant and wish the officers luck. Which was exactly what happened in this case. The retired school teacher had been a Justice of the Peace officer for five years, yet never ceased to be shocked by the depravity of the criminal element who resided within his jurisdiction. *'Teenage girls kidnapped for paedophiles in Gravesend? God forbid what is this world coming to.'* But he had no questions.

Within an hour Charlie had all his team at the scene, by which time the punter with the broken jaw, had been placed in handcuffs and was sat in the back of Charlie's people carrier. By rights, they should have taken him straight to hospital. They chose not to. He deserved some pain, *old school.* Charlie was going to take the rap for the broken jaw. *Resisting arrest.* Stokes didn't argue. Charlie often took the rap for the misdemeanours of his own team. This was the first time he was doing it for someone else. A secret respect was developing for Sam Jakobs. He had been right. He was a good guy and he was proving his worth.

Within another half hour the Yardie monster, H and B were in custody. No fight was offered by any of them. The entry had been both swift, and noisy with strategic commands, "POLICE; GET DOWN NOW; NOBODY MOVE." Swift and noisy installed feelings of panic and fear. Nobody moved, least of all the three Yardies.

All the girls were saved, although saved was not what two of the young thirteen year old girls called it. It was clear that they had wanted to stay there. *"We aren't prisoners,"* *"We're getting paid, so fuck off and leave us alone."*

Girls that were scarcely dressed, in styles way above their years, and their colourful language left little to the imagination.

Rebecca Snugs, one of the girls who didn't want to go home, struggled with Eddie as he tried to lead her out of the building. Despite the black eye and swollen nose she had suffered at the hands of the Lawyer Mo Ali. *'She was being treated like a woman, a grown up, she didn't like the rude things but she had money. Money of her own. Money that Peter Snugs couldn't take from her. She didn't have to watch her Mother sticking that needle in her arm, wondering if she was going to wake up or if she was going to die. It was definitely better than home.'*

"They've been mind fucked," Julie whispered to Charlie, seeing the problems that Eddie was having with her. Moving swiftly to his aid.

Aside of the arrests, the saving of the girls, seizure of twenty two half balls of heroin, weapons and recovery of seven and a half thousand Great British pounds, no paperwork was found, no lists, no evidence of who had frequented the place. The building would have to be forensically examined. A major part of the case would rely on the young girls testimonies, as well as Doctors medical reports. How far they got with the girls would solely depend on bringing them around to understand that they had been used for something that was very wrong. That they were still children and that no money in the world was worth what they had suffered. Plus they had prisoners, prisoners that they would have to get to talk. At the moment, aside of the man with the broken jaw, who was in too much pain to talk, none of them could speak English, apparently.

The main target, who they still only knew as K was nowhere to be seen, which was not a surprise, Jakobs had already warned them that he was not there. Jakobs had also agreed to do his best to find him and DS Jackson trusted that he would.

Charlie Jackson called in the result. He had to warn Custody that he had four prisoners coming in, one of whom may require medical attention, an injury received while resisting arrest. More importantly he had to ensure somebody from the area's Special Investigation Unit was going to be available to deal with the girls. They would need medical treatment, both physical and mental. S.I.U and social services were best equipped to deal with that, his own team were not.

Having heard of the result, Chief Superintendent Best sent out *his* Tactical team to help. Not because he should do, and not because Charlie had requested them, but because the Chief was still at the Police station, and was present when the information had been relayed to him, over the loudspeaker, on his office phone. The Chief was raving about it. This type of result would surely win back some of that lost Public Confidence. They had dismantled a paedophile ring and saved six young girls. He wanted a press release on the incident as soon as possible. He congratulated a gleaming Best on a job expertly dealt with.

Thirty One

1630hrs 18th March

He stood in front of the camera, balaclava donned as before, staring directly at the activated video camera.

"It has begun," he said and signalled to the video man by nodding his head.

The camera rolled down slowly and settled on a figure tied to a chair. The bright orange jumpsuit he was wearing glared in the floodlight, but his features were darkened, not fully lit by the radiating light streaming down from behind him. The man signalled again and the camera zoomed into the captive's face, shadows moved as swiftly as the camera. It settled, highlighting details.

The face was half covered with an untidy straggly beard. Long matted hair fell from the top of his head, partially covering his face. Terror, visibly embossed in his bulging eyes. His left eye, red, caused by a burst blood vessel, subconjunctival haemorrhage, looked worse than it would in normal daylight. His body's blood circulatory tubes were visibly protruding from his naturally thick neck. He strained against the rope wound tightly around his shoulders and chest. The setting could quite easily have been from a fictional film-set, a war movie showing a tortured prisoner, only this was real.

The terrorist spoke, "Tell them your name. Where you are from. What you have done," a long knife glinted in the light as he ran the tip of it down the side of his face. Pressing hard enough to tear the skin, red liquid trickling behind its path.

"I, I, I'm nobody sir. I'm just a homeless bum. Please I haven't hurt you. Please let me go. Plea--" The voice was deep, but quivered, not intentionally.

"Your Name?" shouted the aggressor, stabbing the knife tip deeper into his cheek, now tearing flesh and not just skin.

He screamed and then spoke, "Paul. I'm Paul Gaston. I'm a homeless bum. I've been homeless since I left the army. About eight or nine years ago I became homeless. I'm an alcoholic. I drink. I'm homeless." His head slumped as the knife was pulled out of his cheek, the inch long cut filled with blood.

"Enough. So you was in the army. British army, killing Muslims, killing for power. God has made you homeless because of your crimes," the camera rolled up to the terrorist who continued, "THIS, is how you treat your heroes. This man has fought for your country and you desert him. Leave him on the street to starve like a dog. More proof of what a selfish country you have become." He turned back to Mr. Gaston, "I can see that you must be hungry, dogs are always hungry. We will feed you now before we part company. I will help you eat."

A plate containing a red thick lumpy liquid, with the appearance of some sort of soup, was shoved under his face. The captor took the spoon from the bowl and swirled it around. He then dipped it into the bowl and filled it with the gloop. The terrorist grabbed Gaston by the hair with one hand and forced the spoon into his mouth. Gaston was ordered to eat, his hungry body also ordered him to eat, he took it in his mouth and started chewing, furiously, on a lump of something he did not recognise but hoped it would go some-way to dissolve the hunger pains that gnawed at his stomach, despite his predicament.

Gaston's teeth broke the small capsule inside, he chewed on the lump for seconds, releasing saliva, which added to the reaction inside his mouth, the terrorist, Fatwa, placed a sack over his head. The camera rolled back, focusing on his upper torso.

The explosion was loud. The headless body remained tied to the chair, but now flat on the floor. Blood was splattered all over the camera lens. It zoomed in showing the mangled torso of Paul Gaston, the blood dripping from the screen adding horror. It held the image for seconds, in silence, before it was switched off.

More silence followed, neither living man in the room moving until eventually the one in charge spoke. "Clean it up." The video operator obliged.

A phone rang. It was Fatwa's mobile. He pulled his balaclava up away from his mouth and ear and answered it. A voice that he recognised on the other side of the phone said, "*Sam Jakobs.*" The terrorist left the room listening to the information being provided on his phone.

Thirty Two

1800hrs 18th March

The woods made the evening seem darker than it really was. Branches and leaves sprayed out in all directions, like long arms with hands, trying to catch any light that might break through. Strong winds whistled through the trees, blowing hard enough to give flight to the tree droppings, carrier bags and other scraps dumped by previous visitors, when this forested part of Cobham had been open to public access. The woods stretched some hundred and ninety acres, from the small village on the outskirts of Gravesend to the Medway towns.

Now part of the land had been purchased by the self made, multi millionaire Terry Parke. Twenty Acres of old farm land situated right in the heart of the woodland. He had to pull some strings through his strong Council

216

connections, and rely on his ability to pay healthy back handers. The purchase by Parke was not exactly for himself but made on behalf of his best friend Jasper Shepherd, for his new venture. A venture that was certain to help Parke's own political future.

The Swedish style luxurious cabin had been purpose built by Parke for the very reason it was being used tonight. Cabin perhaps being the wrong word. The size of the building equalled that of a large Church Hall. Inside, the design was very similar to that of a church, or more fittingly Masonic hall. A stage stood at one end of the room and luxury leather padded wooden benches with tall back rests faced the stage. Indeed it was now referred to as 'The Church' by its attendees. The walls were blazoned with large Gold ornaments, Christian crosses, old biblical paintings and randomly placed swastika emblems. Above the stage stood a large Ku Klux Klan flag, with the words, *The blood drop represents the bloodshed by Jesus Christ as a sacrifice for white people*, stretched across it, under the round image, a red circle with a white cross in the middle. A small red tear drop sat in the centre of the cross. The same emblem used by the group since the 1960's.

Outside the cabin about twenty feet from each corner stood four ugly looking thick concrete blocks. Twelve feet square, dull grey in colour. Each block had one heavy duty thick wooden door. Doors that were covered with a large grey metal plate, bare, apart from the mortise style key lock and round rustic door handles. None of the buildings had windows. All of them had a roof terrace, built on a steel roof deck, with a small edging wall around them. The unsightly buildings stood proud, like four watch towers.

Parke had made his fortune through pornography and property development. He had then moved into Politics, starting with the Conservative party. Now he was the new leader of UKIP. His battle to get to the top after his predecessor had proved difficult, not only because of his history in the pornography trade, but because of his extreme right wing and racist views on life, which he never hid, and became apparent while he was a Tory.

Views that he shared with Jasper Shepherd. However the war with ISIS and the influx of refugees had gone someway in resurrecting his career. People were beginning to listen to the truth, his truth. Crime rates had gone up. Refugees were receiving help from the government of a country already in deficit. Help with regards to housing and benefits, while those born and bred in Great Britain were being overlooked. Parke supported Jasper Shepherd and Jasper Shepherd supported him. Tonight however, Parke could not be seen and subsequently held his absence for the upcoming event.

Inside the church Jasper Shepherd stood on the stage. Dressed in a black gown. He looked like a Satanic preacher. The room was packed. There were over a hundred attendees. Thirty three of whom also wore black gowns, identical to Jasper Shepherd's. All thirty three having brought along with them, their appointments, their followers. The room was deadly silent. No murmurs, no conversations. Silence with respect, waiting for Shepherd to speak.

"As I look ahead, I am filled with foreboding. Like the Roman, I seem to see the River Tiber foaming with much blood," Shepherd's words echoed around the room, "April the twentieth, nineteen sixty eight. Enoch Powel was right. He was more than right. In Nineteen seventy seven he made some more prophecies. He warned us. Warned everyone, including the humanitarians among us, the politically correct, those protecting Muslims. A warning not just against the terrorists. Not just the few, who you are led to believe are causing the problems. It was a warning against all Muslims. Because it is all of them who are our problem. They have one goal, one wish. They want to dominate on a worldwide scale. They are moving towards worldwide sovereignty. He warned us of violence. Violence of a catastrophic scale in our own major cities."

The room murmured. Acknowledgements. Agreements.

"He was right. We have suffered soldiers, doctors, journalists, in fact normal people like you and I being killed. Airports, hospitals, buses, nowhere is safe. How many Muslims have you heard come out and condemn those murders. Those that have spoken, just for the sake of publicity have lied. They don't like us. Plain and simple. They don't like our freedom of choice, our British values. I am now going to show you the latest atrocity, the reason for why I have called all of you here tonight. It is time for action if we want to protect what is rightfully ours. Now watch this."

He turned and set the remote control to operate the pre-set video, projecting onto a wide canvas screen behind him. There was silence again as they watched the most recent recording, the one that had gone viral on the internet, a video of an ex-army homeless guy, Paul Gaston being killed. His audience watched in silence.

He switched it off and spoke, "Fucking scum. The man, Paul Gaston fought for our country and was left to rot by our own government. Then this piece of shit Muslim takes him from the street, humiliates him and kills him, for the whole world to see. He say's this will cause fear. I say not. He say's all Muslims will rejoice. I say that they will. In secret. Like they did over nine eleven. Like they did when their scum, their IS, beheaded our people." His voice and demeanour became more animated as he spoke. Like a gospel preacher. Encouraging the hostility to grow within his acolytes. His army who were now waving knives, batons and guns in the air.

He carried on, "Well tonight is our night. Our night for revenge. Our night to strike fear direct into the hearts of these Satanic people. Payback for Paul Gaston and the others. No hold backs. No forgiveness. Just revenge." The room cheered and roared with agreement. "Thirty three locations. All struck tonight. Thirty three mosques all burned down tonight. Thirty three Satanic priests all brought back here tonight. Now is the time for all appointments to join up with your Office for detail. Today is our day."

The assembly roared, a thunderous roar of unity. The thirty three Offices dressed in the black gowns calling in their own appointments so that they could be briefed with regards to their targets. The speed by which this was incredible, un-rehearsed but acted with military precision. Fast, orderly and professional.

Shepherd had selected thirty three of the forty one Mosques in Kent to be attacked in unison. Tonight he was going to cause carnage. He smiled at his brother Mark who had taken a front seat. Not in a gown, but dressed like the other appointments, in casuals.

Mark Shepherd looked in awe at his older brother. He so much wanted to be like him. A leader of men. He also so much wanted to be involved in the attacks tonight. A request that was refused by his Brother, telling him he had more important things to do for the cause. Something that only he could really do.

Thirty Three

0400hrs 19th March

Charlie Jackson groaned and thrashed in his sleep, his thin blanket had been kicked onto the floor. The same nightmare was hounding him. The one that was relentless, the one that never let him go.

He is breathing hard into his son's mouth, resuscitating, pounding on his chest while his son screams, "*Dad, please help me. I don't want to go. I want to be with you. Please save me. You're doing it wrong Dad. Do it properly or I'm going to die.*"

Helpless, he pounds harder, he breathes deeper, but Jackson is still losing his precious baby boy, he is still doing something wrong.

Screaming comes from all around him, from his daughters, who are crying and shrieking together, overriding each other's voices, "*Dad do it properly, don't let Jason die.*"

He presses his mouth hard against his son's, and flinches, because now the skin is cold, death cold, but his son's eyes are open, and Jason speaks, *'It's too late Dad, you did it wrong again, it's too late.'*

Jackson screams, torturous pain racing through his body, drowned with devastation.

He lurched up from his mattress with a start. Sweat and tears streaming down his face, his heart palpitating. He shouted as he always did, "Noooooo! You fucker." The obscenity was aimed at himself.

It took a few seconds for realisation to set in that he was dreaming; the nightmare had been so real, it always was. He knew it was his fault. Why did he have to buy that wretched bike? Why? He knew that he would be tortured for the rest of his life and he would not have it any other way. He deserved to be tortured, he deserved the burning guilt. It was entirely his fault.

Hanging his head in shame, breathless, he became aware of his phone ringing. It hung up before he could reach it.

He pulled it out of his training shoe, which was a few feet from his makeshift bed and looked at it. Six missed calls, all of which were number withheld. It rang again. This time he answered it. He listened to the on call Inspector from CID and said he would be straight in. He would need his team, so he sent a group text out to them all. He wasn't however going to force them in. Those that woke up and read his text would come in. Those that didn't would probably need the sleep after yesterday's long day.

He got up and took a swig of red wine, from the bottle on the floor next to his mattress. His thoughts then turned to his daughters. He hadn't called any of them for three days, despite the missed calls. He had not spoken to any of his Grandchildren. Guilt churned his stomach, feeling like he had a twenty kilo plate sat in the middle of his gut. He drained the remaining wine and made a promise to himself that he would call all three of his girls later on today.

Thirty Four

0450hrs 19th March

As Charlie Jackson pulled up towards the front of the Police station he saw a large crowd outside. Over a hundred gathered together, in some sort of protest, spilling out of the Station's reception, where Baker had blown up, spilling off the pavement outside onto the road. Chanting. He eased off the gas slowly moving around them, turning into the side road giving him access to the car park. A handful of protesters stood there as well, by the blue metal gate. Two uniformed Officers trying to appease them. A young Asian boy, no older than twelve banged on his window shouting, "Save us. Please save us."

Within an hour Charlie had learned that Mosques all over Kent had been attacked simultaneously. Burnt down. Twelve people of Muslim descent had been killed including four Imams. Twenty nine Imams had been kidnapped. No arrests had been made. The attacks had been swift and professional. Their own Mosque in Gravesend, by the Canal Basin had been attacked. The fire was still going strong, being dealt with by fire-fighters at the scene. Two people dead. The Imam kidnapped. Verified by those that had been lucky enough to escape both the fire and vicious attack.

Julie, Eddie and Jazz had managed to read Charlie's text message and were already sitting in the office waiting for him by the time he had left the duty Inspector. Jackson walked in and Julie handed him a mug of coffee, strong, sweet and black.

"Never ending, is it Skip?" she said, in her matter-of-fact tone.

"No it bloody well isn't," Charlie replied, "and before you say anything else, no, I still haven't showered." Charlie was still dressed in the same clothes that he had been wearing the day before, and the day before that, the same ones that he had slept in all night.

"Very quickly, before I brief you. How did CID get on with our Yardies last night?"

Eddie spoke first, "The three Jamaicans wouldn't say anything until we managed to identify them through fingerprints. The two smaller guys are illegal immigrants, still not talking. Apparently they can't speak English. But the other one, the giant, his real name is Lamarr Brown and he is wanted in Spain for drugs, sex trafficking and assault. He has turned out to be the cry baby. He has spilled the beans on K. Real name Kwamie. Surname not known but we will find it. He's wanted with Lamarr. He reckons K will just vanish now unless we get him in time. They both ran from Spain when it came on top for them. They were running heroin, crack cocaine and a brothel for Paedophiles, exactly what they were doing here. Once they've got into the heroin world it's easy according to Brown. Most kids from those families haven't got a life anyway. He said it's easy to turn the kids into prostitutes. They used to pimp women but soon found out that paedos pay the best money. He reckons that K probably won't know we have busted his little operation yet. He's got some big deal going on with his connections in London. He does that on his own, no one else is allowed to be involved, that's why all of this lot were at the brothel. So with a bit of luck he is still at the Snugs address. He's named all the punters that he can remember including that

scumbag lawyer we all knew was bent. Mo Ali, a school
teacher, a traffic warden and an MP. The guy you got with
a broken jaw is a dust man by day and a youth
team football coach on weekends, Alan Price, who by the
way has admitted everything at the hospital. He will be
coming back later today to make it official. He's not
mentioned anything about Jakobs breaking his jaw. He's
shitting himself about going to prison apparently.
Lamarr however did mention Sam Jakobs. He said
that they warned K of hiring him as a debt collector. K
though, reckoned Jakobs was just a bum. Robbing dealers
for money. He reckoned he would do anything for a bit of
cash. Especially with what he was paying him. Lamarr
suspects him to be a grass. Said it's funny how they get
raided so soon after hiring him. Although he did say that
Jakobs would never have been told about the place or
where it was and he's never been there. We really need to
get to the Snugs address early if we want to get K, but with
all this going on, don't know if we are going to be able to
do that?"

Charlie thought for a minute. "Julie. Give Robbie a call.
He might be able to find out if K is still about. Tell him
that is all we want to know. Nothing else. No broken jaws.
Ed, see if you can do the same with Sally Tall."

"Ok Charlie," Julie said holding her nose and breath as she leaned in to him, "Right what the fuck has happened out there?"

Charlie briefed the members of his team, although he had to skip back to the beginning five minutes later when they were joined by Crayston and Ronnie.

Charlie told them to stay put while he found out what was going to be required from them and whether they could get someone out to find K.

Up in the Briefing room it was pandemonium. It was clear that Chief Superintendent Best did not have a clue what to do. His only instruction was to keep the protesters in order outside. CID were currently speaking to the surviving witnesses and he wanted a uniform presence at the fire. Other than that everyone would have to wait for an action plan, which would be provided to the whole County by Force Headquarters. Charlie imagined the same scenario unfolding all over Kent, including Force Headquarters. He felt sorry for the Chief Constable.

Ian Thom tugged at Jackson's sleeve. "No sense in hanging around here Charlie. They will take forever deciding what to do. Go and do what you do best. Speak with CID and see if it's worth any of your team talking to any of the witnesses. Your lot are much better at extracting every drop of info."

Charlie nodded and went to walk away before Thom called him back.

"Hey Charlie, by the way, excellent work yesterday. Best was fucking all over it with the Chief. Taking all the glory."

Charlie Jackson shook his head in disgust, recalling his abruptness and his refusal to help with the job. The man was definitely a prick. He smiled back at Thom and headed back to the office.

Thirty **Five**

0630hrs 19th March

I had left the perverted lawyer in the overflow car park
back at the Promenade. I had then walked to Brandon
Street and posted the money through Louis's door. I
then walked straight back to Nan's house. I needed a bath.
Julie Stokes words had played on me, although it had also
made me laugh. She reminded me a lot of Louise, only a
stronger version. I couldn't imagine Julie Stokes ever
relying on anybody but herself.

I must have been more tired than I thought. I shut my
eyes and slept all through the day and best part of night,
woken up once in-between by Nan just to make sure I
was alright. I was now wide awake, both mentally and
physically, fully refreshed and clean.

Freshly washed clothes thanks to Nan. I sneaked out

early, leaving her another note, promising that I would be back tonight, awake and in my best company keeping frame of mind. First I had something to do. Something that I had to do, to make me feel better, to make things right in my head.

I got a cab to the block of flats called The Hive, a stone throw away from my intended target. I made small talk with the cab driver, lying, talking of being at an all night party and that I was in trouble from the other half when I got in. Talking like I had a normal life. He wished me good luck after I paid him his five pounds sixty pence tariff with an extra forty pence tip. Six pounds.

I didn't stop to think, plan or arm myself. I just went straight for it, pulling my hood over my head. One hundred and forty five seconds later I was at the bottom of the flight of stairs at Wallace Square. Forty seconds later I was at the top, outside Vikki Snugs flat. I was in the mood for it. I braced myself and kicked the door. Hard, straight on the door lock. The plastic frame splintered and the door smashed open.

First door on the left in the corridor, I recalled was the toilet. I knew straight ahead was the kitchen-diner. The corridor shot off to the left. Another door. Bedroom. I walked on, not breaking my stride. As I reached it I heard a male voice murmur an expletive inside. Not Peter Snugs voice. I turned the handle and pushed the door open with force. K was lying on the bed, naked, next to Vikki Snugs, also naked. I kicked the door shut behind me. For a reason. Anyone sneaking up behind me would have to open the door first.

"What the fuck do you think you're doing?" K glared as he spoke. Reaching around, fumbling, his hand moving towards under the bed as he spoke. He pulled out a small black object. He was slow though, disorientated from being woken up to the sound of a door being smashed open, swift and noisy fills them with panic and dread. I kicked hard against his hand. The Glock 17 fell to the floor. The weapon that K had obtained from his London contacts last night, with his new stash of heroin and crack cocaine, just in case he needed it.

He yelped in pain and Vikki Snugs jumped out of bed. "Get him Jakobs. Fucking kill him. That bastard raped me again last night."

"Get dressed and get out of here Vik. I found your girl last night. Phone the Police and find out where she is. You got some mothering to do with her." I heard the noise behind me, and saw the look on Vikki Snugs face, simultaneously warning me of what I was ready for. I spun around, throwing a straight right cross instantly, striking Peter Snugs square on his nose. The Iron bar he was holding clattered to the floor. More noise behind me. I spun back around and drove the heel of my boot down, hard on the back of K's head as he stretched across the floor towards the Glock. His head crunched against the floor, now cut above the eye where my boot had struck him. I picked up the Glock.

Behind me Vikki Snugs proceeded to rain down punches into her partners head, she still hadn't dressed.

"Where's his money Vik?" I said. She shrugged and got up, giving her long term partner one last kick in the head with her bare heel, seemingly oblivious that she was still stood in front of me stark naked.

I picked up a pair of tracksuit bottoms from the floor, which could only have belonged to K. I went through the pockets and pulled out a wad of notes. I handed the money over to her. "This is yours. You never saw me. Don't forget I saved your kid." She grabbed the money nodding.

"What about the prick down there?" she said pointing at Peter Snugs who still wasn't moving.

"Don't worry about him. He wouldn't dare. Not after he sees what I do to this prick. Now get dressed and get out of here."

She quickly picked up a pair of smaller tracksuit bottoms and pulled them over her thin veiny legs. No knickers. A white T-shirt and grey hoodie covered her equally pale, raw-boned, torso. No bra. Finally she slipped on a pair of open toe slippers, then she was gone.

Snugs was still not moving. I knew he was faking. K on the other hand was groaning. I knew he wasn't faking. I gave K a hard kick in the ribs. Winding him and maybe cracking a rib or two.

I turned and dragged Snugs up. By his neck. Squeezing hard. "Two choices fuck head. First one, stay and get what he's getting. I prefer that choice. Scum that protects someone who's just raped his bird and rapes her kid deserves to die. Please stay here. Or second choice, fuck off

out of here. Out of Gravesend forever. Come back and I
WILL KILL YOU. Tell me you understand?" I growled,
mouth within inches of his ear.

"I understand Sam. Please. I'm out of here. You won't
ever see me again. I promise."

I dropped him and he ran. I knew that was it. He was
gone.

I turned back to K and dragged him up. The Glock
pressed hard into his head. "What to do with the fuck
head?" I said aloud.

"You're a dead man," he squealed as my fingers crushed
against his windpipe.

"Don't think so." That was the last thing I said to him as
I dragged him out the door onto the balcony. Thoughts of
the raped kids swirled around in my brain. Kids being
raped! I lifted him up with ease, adrenalized strength, and
threw him over.

I didn't look over the balcony after him. There was no
need to. It was too high to survive. I was too angry to care.
I wiped the gun clean of my prints and put it in K's

tracksuit bottoms. I pulled my hood back up, kept my head down and left. Where to? I hadn't planned. I just needed to walk. One thing I did know though, that feeling of being uncomfortable had completely gone.

Thirty Six

Charlie and his team sat around the office, each busy with their own workload. Charlie started making phone calls to his counterpart Sergeant on CID, Peter Davis. The others sat there typing out witness statements relating to the search warrant that they had executed, and arrests that they had made, and the property that they had seized, and the girls that they had saved yesterday. The room was quiet apart from the sound of the kettle that Charlie had put back on, hissing in the background and fingers typing furiously on keyboards.

"Sarge, can I leave this with you to get someone to drop it off at Force Headquarters?" shouted Jazz, as he threw a packet over in Jackson's direction.

Jackson caught it, putting the phone down having got no reply. It was an evidence bag, "How much?"

"Seven thousand Six hundred quid." came the reply.

"No problem, I'll get one of the civilian drivers to take it," said Charlie, throwing the sealed evidence bag into a cardboard box under his desk. They knew that the Clerks at the Station would not hold it, due to the amount. The money would be subject of an application for a confiscation order, under the Criminal Proceeds Confiscation Act 2002, in the meantime kept in a safe at HQ until it had been dealt with.

The silence was broken by a loud blast. The office shook. "What the hell now?" shouted Charlie as he instantly went for the office door.

Outside a marked Police Skoda, parked closest to the yard metal gates was on fire. Burning ferociously, from what appeared to be some sort of explosion, flames now catching on the nearby bins, billowing smoke rising. Other cars, close to the explosion were also damaged, windows smashed, bodies damaged from flying metal, there was broken glass everywhere.

"Get everyone back," shouted Charlie.

The two Officers who had been at the gate, appeasing the protesters, were on the floor as were a number of civilians. The gate itself, which had been half open, was severely bent.

Charlie and his team went to work. Dragging people away from the fire, ushering others back. They were quickly joined by other officers including Chief Superintendent Best.

"Must be one of them. I want them all arrested. Now!" he bellowed pointing at the protesters.

Chaos erupted all around. Some officers helping those thought injured, others arresting the civilian protesters, who in return were resisting their apprehensions. Questioning the assumptions, assumptions made because of their religion, that they would detonate a bomb in close proximity of themselves. They were protesters, in fear of their own safety. They were not suicide bombers, they were victims. The chaos got worse and fights broke out both inside and outside the sanctuary of Police premises. Back up being requested repeatedly over the radios.

Nobody saw the figure sneak into Charlie Jackson's office, through the door that had been left open. Nobody saw the figure come back out minutes later.

It took at least another two hours before a certain level of calmness had been obtained. Every patrol car that had been out on patrol or busy on calls, had returned to help with the riotous scene. The Police station cells were now full. The overflow of prisoners had been taken to the station basement, awaiting transport to neighbouring stations. The injured had been taken to hospital.

A feeling of dread suddenly filled Charlie Jackson. Things were certainly getting out of hand. They were losing all control of a once relatively peaceful country. A civil war certainly beckoned and he knew things were going to get worse. Much worse. He needed to call his girls.

Thirty Seven

The video was being shown all over the world. The latest in a stream of videos that had taken the world by storm, this one though, was different to the others, this one was from the other side, this one was the one that would most definitely bring the United Kingdom to breakdown.

The new recording was silent. No words, no noise. Twenty eight Imams on their knees, deep in woodland with no landmarks to see. Just trees and earth and a line of the Muslim priests on their knees, heads bowed, hands bound behind their backs.

There was no sound when a hail of bullets flew into their bodies, ripping chunks of flesh, separating muscle from bone, and bone from skeleton, body parts flying through the air. What was left of the bodies collapsing to the floor.

The screen zoomed in around the still, torn, savaged, blood soaked bodies, before it slowly started to fade, darker and darker until it was black. Momentarily black, because then slowly, the focus returned. This time there was no scenery. Just a blank screen, like a computer screen. Letters started to appear across the screen. Letters which finally read, *'FUCK YOU FATWA. THIRTY THREE WILL PROTECT ENGLAND'*.

*

Terry Parke smiled at the end of his press conference. Things were coming together. Fortune favouring the prepared mind. He could turn any disaster into an opportunity. While he had been careful not to condone the terrible retributory actions taken by Thirty Three, he had declared his understanding of what had gone on. The reasons for why such a reaction was inevitable. He had described the current Government as being weak. That they had done everything to encourage such a reaction from the British people. How they had allowed terrorists to slime their way into the Country with their open door policy on refugees and immigration. Putting every British person in danger.

He reminded everyone of Enoch Powell's prophecy that mass migration would lead to mass segregation, and then disastrously to racial and religious division. He reminded everyone of the Muslim riots of Bradford in the year two thousand and one. Of the bus suicide bombing in London in two thousand and five and now of the six murders committed by the Muslim called Fatwa.

He couldn't help himself, he had his beliefs so he went on, and called all Muslims the same. British born or otherwise. He couldn't help but quote, '*Just because you're born in a stable doesn't make you a horse.*' Those British born Muslims were still the ones that wanted Sharia Law imposed here, in Great Britain. No respect for females, anti homosexuality. Even the prisons had been taken over by them. He branded every single Muslim as a hater of the Western world. Haters of Great Britain and everything that stood for Great Britain. He had ended with a warning to all good hard working Christian people that unless they acted now, their Britain, as they knew it, would be gone. Gone for good. It was time to stand up and be counted. Time to end this madness of political correctness. Time to protect what was their birthright. Time to eradicate our enemies. Nothing to do with colour creed race or religion. It was not racist to protect your home from invaders. The Muslims were at war with the world of non Muslims. It was time to act. Time to vote for Terry Parke. Time to vote for UKIP.

Thirty Eight

It felt like I had been walking for hours. Uncertain of exactly how long. My phone rang. The one K had given me. I looked at it. I didn't recognise the number but answered it anyway.

"Robbie it's me Julie. Can you talk?"

I felt confused first, then relief and answered, "How did you get this number? Yes babe I can talk. What's up?"

"You called Charlie off it Dumbo," she laughed. "Just thought that you would like to know that we got the kids. They are safe. We've nicked the three Yardies as well. Just wanted to say thank you. You deserve a good payout for this."

My mind went blank. I had forgotten that I was a paid agent. I had no urge to get paid though. Not for saving a bunch of kids. I didn't say anything.

"Robbie, are you still there?"

"Yes Jules. Sorry. No problem, just make sure you bang them up for a long time."

"Will do Sarge," she joked, "Hey we haven't got K yet, but we have had a three nines call. A report of a black male found dead at the bottom of Wallace Square. We think it's him but will have to wait until he can be identified. Looks like he fell or was pushed off a balcony. Have you heard anything?"

"Not about that but I have spoken to that prick Peter Snugs. He was going to do a runner from Gravesend. He reckons a load of Yardies came down from London. They had a row and a big fight broke out with K, which got really bad. He didn't say anything else. If he's dead though? I don't give a fuck. Someone like him is no loss anyway." I was never going to admit to murder.

"I hear you Sam. We did have information that he was due a large drugs delivery from his London connections today. It must have gone wrong. You sound down mate. Are you sure that you are OK?"

"Yes babe. I'm fine."

"Go and have a drink. It's a job well done. Hopefully we can meet in a couple of days."

"Yeah that would be cool."

The phone clicked off. I thought of tossing it away, but then put it back in my pocket. I felt guilty for lying to Julie but it was a necessity. I fancied a drink but I had a promise to keep. I headed off to Nan's.

Thirty Nine

0830hrs 22nd March

The next two days created unprecedented history. It saw the Special Forces, two thousand army personnel and counter terrorist officers join the Police on patrol on the streets of Britain. France and Germany were also currently in talks with the Prime Minister, in relation to loaning their own police and army staff for assistance. It had come close to a national curfew. Despite pressure from back benchers to do so, the Prime Minister however, right or wrong, remained strong. Not wanting to bow down to the terrorists, from either side.

ISIS had denied any knowledge of the Fatwa attacks but offered their full support to him, hailing him as a hero. At the same time all the extreme right wing groups denied any knowledge of a group called 'Thirty Three' but members were beginning to show signs of allegiance to whoever they were. It had now been three days since any other videos had been offered by either side. The boffins had worked out where the term Thirty Three had come from. In some way it paid homage to the Ku Klux Klan. K being the eleventh letter in the alphabet. Three K's and as such three elevens made thirty three.

The world of Muslims mourned the deaths of the Imams. One still remained missing. Factions of the Community inevitably started to blame the racist Western culture, the Government, and conspiracy theories had started that the 'Thirty Three' murders had actually been committed by the Government, in retaliation to Fatwa.

Reprisal assaults, both ways, were on the increase all over England. It had almost become so that any minor scuffle between different nationalities, were turning into full blown affrays, or even in some cases riots. Justifying the increase in numbers of the personnel that were looking after the streets of England.

Back in Gravesend Charlie had calculated the reward payment owed to Robbie Strange. All informant gratuities were worked out through a nationalised informant payment matrix. The reckoning of the sum of the reward took various factors into account, the gravity of the offence in question i.e. was it a local issue, or a cross border issue or did it have an impact on serious and organised crime. It also took into account the level of work put in by the agent, and the number of arrests, and the level of criminality of those that had been arrested. The total amount could then be increased or decreased by what was called a weighting factor. A decision made by the Controller. The Inspector in charge of the Intelligence Unit. Ian Thom. This would be done by taking into account the entire circumstances of the investigation.

By rights all the factors were on the higher end of the scale. He had helped bust a team of Class A drug suppliers, a child paedophile ring, and saved six young girls who had been kidnapped by coercion, young teenage girls being used for sex, girls that the Yardies had also raped themselves. On top of this the offenders were international criminals, currently wanted in Spain for similar offences. Robbie Strange was due a large payment of ten thousand pounds. A lot of money, but deserved thought Charlie. On the other side of the coin however, ten thousand pounds and Sam Jakobs did not seem to sit right together.

The amount of reward money due, meant a conversation with the head of the Intelligence Department at Force Headquarters, with the Authorising Officer. Charlie placed his request in Ian Thom's tray and went back to his desk. He had given his team a lay in and wasn't expecting them in for work until about mid-day. They were worn out. Early starts and late evenings would always, eventually take their toll. Tired bodies and tired minds meant mistakes. Charlie couldn't afford to have any mistakes. Largely his team had been used to support the Uniform patrols with riot controls and CID with interviews and arrests. In between that, they had also supported the needs of their sources, their agents and their grasses.

The office door burst open and Julie Stokes came barging in. Charlie glimpsed over at the wall clock. It was only a couple of hours into the working morning. She looked furious. Her normally neat and tidy hair was windswept, her t-shirt was half untucked. She did not look her normal perfect self.

"That's it Charlie, I'm going to kill him. He's a wrong one." Her voice quivered as she spoke.

"Calm down Jules. What's up? What's happened?"

Julie Stokes didn't speak straight away. She slumped into her chair and put her head into her hands. Her blonde hair hanging over her fingers that were cradling her head, taking deep breaths in an effort to calm down.

"Julie. What's happened?"

She took another deep breath before speaking. "Charlie, as you know I got home very late last night. I got home and jumped straight in the shower. But I felt strange, it felt like someone else was in the house. I just thought I was tired. I went to put the kettle on and found it was already warm, almost hot, like it had already been switched on. I racked my brain and just thought that I had put it on before I got in the shower, I was tired, I could have forgot. I made a cup of tea and couldn't shake off the feeling that I was not on my own. So much so, that I started to walk around, searching. I started upstairs and my bed was not made up. I always make my bed Charlie. Even then though, I thought maybe I hadn't. I was tired. Then I thought I heard the front door slam and ran downstairs but couldn't see anything. Anyway I went to bed, but had a shit night's sleep. An hour ago I hear whistling. Like a wolf whistle, like in that pub, coming from outside my house. I looked out the window and I saw him. Grinning. The fucker waved at me got in his car and drove off." she broke down crying as she finished.

"Who Julie? Who?" Charlie demanded to know.

Her sobbing slowed down and she looked up, "That fucking sprog, Mark Shepherd."

Forty

Charlie Jackson and Julie Stokes were now in Chief Superintendent Best's Office. Charlie Jackson had felt that there was no alternative but to take it to the head of the area, despite his dislike for the weasel. The room was adequately large. About twelve feet square. A chestnut executive desk occupied one end of the room. The opposite end from the door. A matching chestnut sideboard stood behind the desk, with glass cabinets and drawers. Pictures of the Chief Superintendent shined behind the glass. Shaking hands with the Prime Minister and Chief Constable, another one of him receiving an award of some description. A large fish bowl sat on the cabinet, containing three large orange cold water fish. The desk was reasonably clear, but for family photographs, three children and an attractive wife. It had three chairs around it. One that Best occupied, facing his two officers. They, or Charlie to be more precise, had relayed all of their concerns about Police Constable 'five digit' Mark Shepherd. Everything. The racism and now the goading and stalking of Julie Stokes.

Best sat there listening for the best part of it. Trying to look earnest and interested. Deep down though, he had a dislike of the Intelligence department. He didn't trust them. They were a law to themselves. Did things that he would never condone. They were best friends with criminals as far as he was concerned. They paid the filthiest type of species on this planet. Heroin addicts, thieves, burglars, people who had no loyalty to their own. There actually was *no honour amongst thieves*. Proved by the grasses that they worked with. He did on the other hand have a huge liking for Chief Officers and Ex-Chief Officers.

Charlie finished talking. Stokes had sat there pretty much quiet throughout the meeting. Her head down because she was embarrassed, not wanting to show her red eyes from crying. She was one of the blokes. She didn't want to be seen as the weak, pathetic hormonal female.

Best eventually spoke, "OK Charlie. Thanks for bringing this to my attention. Can I have a private chat with you though?" he indicated with a nod of his head that Stokes was to leave the room.

Charlie looked confused but asked Julie to return to the office. He said, "See if you can get hold of Robbie Strange for me Jules. We need to have a debrief with him. Arrange a meeting."

Best stood up and turned his back to them, he picked up a box of fish flakes and tipped some into the bowl. All three fish darted to the surface, greedily sucking in their food. Best grimaced. He was Chief Superintendent and they were talking code in front of him. He knew that there was no such person called Robbie Strange and that it was a pseudonym. Another secret that he was not trusted with. Who did they think they were? Julie Stokes got up, heaving herself out of her chair and left the room without a word, still with her head pointed down.

Best waited for her to leave before speaking, "Charlie. What do you actually want me to do? We are stretched at the moment as it is. Riots, fires, marches, assaults, protests. Do you want me to go on. Now you want me to suspend the Ex-Assistant Chief Constable's son on the say so of her. Do you know that he's already been put on fast track for promotion? How do you know that they haven't had a thing together? What if it's just a domestic? Sorry Charlie the best I can do is to call him into my office and speak to him. If it is a domestic I will warn him off. I am not suspending or reporting anyone."

"What are you implying? I can tell you Sir, there has been no relationship between Stokes and that creep. I was there when he verbally assaulted those Asians. He is not fit to wear a uniform. I don't care who his old man was." Charlie's voice was raised with malice, which clearly took Best by surprise. He was the Chief Superintendent and nobody spoke to him like that.

"How dare you talk to me like that DS Jackson? Don't you dare forget who you are addressing. You are lucky I don't stick you on. Coming up here, dressed like a tramp. I will be speaking to Inspector Thom about your behaviour. I have told you my decision and that is final. Shut the door behind you." Best's face burnt bright red as he spoke, flushed with blood rushing to the surface of his skin.

"Talk to who you want asshole. Like I give a fuck. Let's see what happens when they find out about your support for racism and your lack of respect for females." Charlie Jackson turned and walked away, ignoring the expletives coming out of the head of the Area's mouth. He stormed out slamming the door as loud and as hard as he could, making Best's Secretary, Ms Beth Roberts jump a little. He gave the shocked secretary an apologetic smile before leaving.

Forty One

I busted through my last set of pull ups at Woodlands
Park. Nine sets in all, using various grips on the outdoor
chinning apparatus before I dropped in a heap onto the
floor. I laid there for a few minutes breathing deep, my
oxygen starved muscles demanding that I breathed faster
and harder.

Eventually I sat up and looked around. The park was
situated just on the outskirts of the town centre. A short
jog from Nan's house. She was currently over the moon
with my frequent appearances. Her love for cooking for
somebody else, especially me had her beaming all day. The
morning was clear and crisp. The green across the park had
been recently mown, and the smell of freshly cut grass
filled the air. The park itself was largely empty, as expected

at this time in the morning, when most children were still at school. There was a young couple sat on a bench, while their daughter went up and down on a slide in the play area, on the other side of the park. Two council workers worked to system, across the green, picking up litter.

I went through my tracksuit pockets looking for both my mobile phones. I still had the phone given to me by K. Julie Stokes had said that they would meet up with me in a couple of days and I was half hoping for a phone call from her. I had no missed calls on either phone.

I stared at the phones contemplating whether I should call her. Just then my own phone rang. The name *Baby girl*, flashed across the screen. Louise. I answered the phone.

"Gorgeous," I said, feeling a pang of guilt for having thoughts of Julie.

"Sam. Are you ok?" she replied.

I could hear concern in her voice. "Yes babe, why?"

"Thanks for that money Sam. It's come in really handy. I haven't spunked it all but I have bought loads of new clothes for Eve. God she needed them. I've also done a massive food shop and I've put the rest in Eve's savings account."

"That's good Princess but that's not why you called me? Is it?"

"No Sam. No it's not. I don't want to ask you where you got the money from or if you are in any trouble because I know you won't tell me. But ...."

"Spit it out babe. What's up?"

"There were four really large Irish blokes knocking on my door asking for you."

"Did they hurt you?" My stomach knotted.

"No Sam. No not at all. In fact they were really polite and well, really polite. They just said they needed to talk to you urgently and left a number. They were nice to me and everything, but they looked nasty. Looked quite evil. I think they were Irish travellers. I told them obviously that I don't see you but sometimes you phone to see how the baby is. They said they wouldn't bother me again. I think they know I will give you the number and that you will call them. Are you in trouble Sam?"

"No babe. Nothing to worry about. It must be about that labouring job that I applied for. I gave your address because they needed an address," I lied, "I'm really sorry. I won't do that again. Honestly it's nothing to worry about. Text me their number and I will call them." Inside I seethed. Who would dare go around my Louise's house? I didn't know any Irish travellers. I always kept away from them.

"OK Sam. I'll text it over to you. Shouldn't really use my address though Sam. I don't want to sound ungrateful. I know you help me loads, but if it gets back to Social they could cut my benefits."

"No worries baby girl. It won't happen again. I'll let this lot know I don't live there." I hung up. A few seconds later my phone beeped and a text message from *Baby girl* came through. The contents of which was just a mobile phone number, and then two xx's.

I pressed the number that she had sent, but hung up straight away. I needed to think first. Where had these guys come from? Who had I fallen out with? I racked my brain. No Irish travellers came to mind. I dialled the number again. It rang. Two rings, then three then four. Voicemail. I never liked leaving messages but on this occasion I had no choice. I didn't want anybody messing with Louise or Eve.

"This is Sam Jakobs. Apparently you need to talk to me. Call me back anytime." I hung up. That's it. They had my number. They would call me back. Just not straight away. They would want me to worry and stew. Worry about not knowing who they were, what they were about and what they wanted. To me though, they had broken that unwritten rule. You never take a fight to a wife with kids on their own doorstep. I would remind them of that when we eventually met.

My phone rang again. The other phone. K's phone. Julie Stokes, I had saved her number. I smiled as I answered it.

"Robbie? Can you talk?" her voice sounded soft and I could picture her gleaming teeth shining through that ravishing smile.

"Yeah. What's up princess?"

"Nothing much handsome. Just catching up, making sure you're alright. Maybe meet up later if you're free?"

"Yeah. That would be great. Just tell me when and where, I've got nothing on."

"Twelve o'clock good for you? We could pick you up at that new Supermarket. The one off Coldharbour Road. In the car park, do you know the one that I mean?"

"Yeah, I know the place."

"We'll be at the far end of the car park. The corner furthest away from the road. Is that OK?"

"That's cool. I know exactly where you mean. Plus it gives me time to have a shower first," I laughed and she giggled as well. I hung up still smiling. All feelings of guilt now gone. This time there had been no talks of cover stories, or ground rules or anything. The meeting had just been arranged.

I set off on a jog, heading back to Nan's. Thoughts of the Irish travellers now gone. I wondered what Julie Stokes would be wearing.

Forty Two

Chief Superintendent Best was still in his office, seething with anger, no not anger but rage. He was red in the face, burnt red, like you get after spending that extra ten minutes on a sun bed. His silver wiry hair no longer in the neat side parting. Clumps of it were now sticking straight up, caused by running his fingers through it, in temper. His heart rate had increased, as had his blood pressure, the heat flush causing him to unclip his neck tie and top shirt button.

How dare he talk to me like that? The Intelligence Unit, as a whole, has no standards. They sit there in the morning meetings like they run the show. Running the show through their seedy underhand dealings with criminals. Criminals who should be locked up, not getting paid for Christ's sake. I've heard those rumours about Charlie Jackson. Yes everyone likes him, or feels sorry for him but that's no excuse. Criminals like him, I wonder why? I've heard of those rumours, of Jackson's drinking habits, an alcoholic, and worse, that he partakes in the consumption of illegal narcotics, drugs, probably brought from his drug dealing informants. Probably also taking back hander's. He was as bent as a nine Bob note. That's it, he won't get away with this. I'll sort him out.

Best picked up the phone and made a call. He dialled an extension number that he knew off by heart. An extension number to an office based at Force Headquarters in Maidstone. An office that he had previously worked in. Professional Standards. The Police-Police. The office that got rid of people like Charlie Fucking Jackson. It only took him a few minutes to persuade Inspector Childs to open a new file on the Detective Sergeant. Charlie Jackson was a name that Childs was all too familiar with. A new file to fit in the ever-growing file that Professional Standards already had on him. Charlie Jackson was bent and they were going to prove it.

Forty Three

1130hrs 22nd March

I had been home, and eaten a huge fry up cooked by Nan, sausages, bacon, eggs, fried bread, mushrooms and beans, all topped up with two cups of Nan's special milky coffee.

I had also suffered a huge lecture of how I should give it another go with Louise. As far as Nan was concerned, the fact that Louise had not moved on with a new boyfriend showed that she was still mine, in heart anyway. Probably waiting for me to grow up. I had tried to explain that we were getting on great as friends, but struggled to talk about any intimate feelings that I had for her. My feelings belonged in one place and one place only, that was my mind.

I didn't say anything about Julie for obvious reasons. That was work, at the moment, or was I kidding myself, I just knew that I had developed feelings for her. Although I was not stupid. I was well aware that fancying someone could give you the same kind of feelings but for very different reasons. I washed up the breakfast stuff and filled her living room fireplace with timber to burn before I left.

I was now almost at the supermarket in Coldharbour Road. The car park was reasonably packed for the time of day. Most of the spaces closer to the store were taken. I looked down and over to the far corner of the car park, where I was to meet Julie and Charlie. Most spaces were vacant in that corner. I couldn't see them. I walked down the roadside flight of steps into the car park. As I reached the bottom I caught the glimpse of a fracas starting up in a parking bay, close to a pedestrian crossing that led to the front electric doors of the store. Three Asian males were stood there arguing with an elderly silver haired man, who in return was doing his own finger pointing and shouting. A crowd was forming, some of whom appeared to be taking sides. I had no choice but to walk in the same direction anyway.

The shouting became clearer as I approached the crowd.

"You're just a bunch of murdering cowards. If you don't like it in my country go home," the silver haired man must have been in his late sixties. It was clear that he had got a little braver with the growing crowd, most of whom were showing their support for him, also aiming abuse towards the Asian men.

"Listen to yourself you fool. We're not even Muslims. We're Sikhs," retaliated the smaller of the three Asians. His voice raised but not shouting. He carried on, but this time his statement directed at the forming crowd. "This fool just barged into our Mum and called her a black bitch and a suicide bomber. It's our Mum. We are British, not terrorists. It makes me sick how quickly you all gang up. It just shows your true colours. What you really are. You're all bloody racist."

"Fucking black bastards," "Fuck off home, you're all the same," "Go on Paki, let's see what you got," shouted back the crowd. It was difficult to see who had shouted what, but it was very quickly turning nasty.

It was clear that the growing hostility in the crowd was not going to do the Asians any favours and the largest of the three, turned around to an older Indian woman who looked to be at least eighty years old, wearing a bright green sequinned Indian dress, "Come on Mum let's go." He took her by the arm and led her into the back of a silver Range Rover. The other two males followed suit, but backing off, keeping an eye on the increasingly growing, confrontational gathering.

I watched the Indians climb into the car and start the engine. They slowly crept forward and were forced to stop when a large ginger haired man stepped in front of them. He looked to be in his late twenties, early thirties, and must have weighed about eighteen stone. Most of the weight being around his waistline and thighs. He slammed his hand down on the bonnet, denting the metal.

"You aren't going anywhere you black fuckers," he shouted, his freckled face colouring, matching his ginger hair.

I would have run the beer-bellied bully over if I was them, but it was clear that they were now pretty frightened in the car. I had to do something myself because it was obvious that nobody else was.

I walked up to Ginger, "Hey. Fuck off out the way. NOW!" My eyes glazed at will, and my psychotic stare drilled into his head. He immediately backed off. I sensed his fear, he was a coward like most bullies. I nodded for the driver to carry on, which he did, thanking me as he went by.

"What's the fucking matter with all of you?" I shouted, staring at the crowd. The group, mostly couples started to melt. People walked away. The old silver haired man didn't budge though. He just stared right back at me.

"Are you mad boy? That lot are here for one purpose only. Destroy us all and take over the world. You'll learn my boy, but maybe by then, it will be too late."

I shook my head and walked away. As I did, I caught Julie Stokes face, stood at the back of the small number of people still remaining. She nodded towards the back where we were due to meet and walked off. I looked at the old man and shook my head again. He returned the gesture and got into his old Estate.

I walked into the store. Eyes had been on me and I didn't want to walk straight over to the unmarked police vehicle. I went to the cigarette kiosk and bought a packet of twenty Benson and Hedges dual cigarettes, the ones that you could click to give it a menthol flavour. I wasn't a

proper smoker any longer. I had given up in the army, but I did smoke, occasionally, and right now I had
that occasional urge to have one. I didn't know why, I just did.

Ten minutes later, having consumed the menthol nicotine-stick I was sat in the front passenger seat of the blue Ford Escort estate with Detective Constable Julie Stokes. The same car she had used when we met in Chatham. There was no Charlie Jackson and she told me that he had been tied up at the Police station.
Incidents exactly like the one we had just witnessed were kicking off all over the area. She said Charlie would join us in an hour, after he had finished his business.

"So what would you have done if the whole crowd turned on you? We wouldn't be sat here now, that's for sure," she said and carried on, "does trouble follow you everywhere you go? because it certainly looks like it does to me."

I couldn't tell if she was angry or not. She was still smiling. I knew Charlie would have been, had he been there. "The whole crowd would never have ganged up on me. Not the whole crowd. I guess you would be on my side," I grinned.

"No seriously Sam. What would you have done?"

"Like I said that would never have happened. Crowds contain too many sheep. Challenge the biggest one, the sheep back off straight away. The big guy was a bully. I could see his eyes melt as soon as I called him. Once he goes the others go. It's just what happens." I replied.

"Or you just keep getting lucky," she argued.

"Yeah, maybe. I'm a real lucky sort of guy. Anyway, where are we going?" I asked, wanting to change the subject, part of me pleased that Julie had turned up on her own, not that I disliked Charlie.

"Fancy a drink Sam? Because I do. I know the perfect place."

She told me of a country pub we were about to visit in Southfleet. She went through the same questions that Charlie had gone through with me for the first meeting. Did I ever drink in the pub? Did I know anyone who lived in the area? She also gave me the cover story that we were

on a date, should we by chance bump into someone that I
knew. A date with a woman that I didn't know was a Police
Officer. A cover story that I liked.

I lost track of where we were. Mostly because of the
company I was keeping. She looked fantastic in her open
neck tight fitting white, almost see through, t-shirt. She
smelt good as well, a clean sharp fragrant filled the car. A
Michael Bolton album played quietly in the background.

We spoke of different things on the journey. Mostly
about my life, Louise, Eve, Nan, my time in the army, my
time in the camper van and about my general lifestyle. She
didn't ask any questions about my family, the druggie
family. She was however, very covert about her own life.
Though I did manage to find out that she was single and
straight. It was no secret that a number of female police
officers were gay, not that I had anything against it. In fact
one of my best friends during my stint in the army was gay,
and tougher than most straight men that I knew. She also
liked Michael Bolton, Elvis Presley and Tom Jones. She
only watched action films and ate anything. That was
about all I could get out of her. She was on the other hand
a great listener and seemingly absorbed all my information
about me.

The Southfleet Farm public house was set in quite a picturesque scene. A pond with ducks swimming in clear water set the scenery across the road and a local Farm shop with huge adjoining barns were situated next door. The public house itself was largely built of timber with large glass windows and did not look out of place in the country setting.

She turned right and pulled her Escort into the car park. That's when things started to go wrong. She saw a man leaning onto a white Lexus RX in the car park. It wasn't parked in a bay, it was just sat in the middle of the car park. He stared right at her, he was grinning, causing her to brake hard. I recognised the face but couldn't put my finger on it. He lifted his phone in our direction and appeared to take a photo.

"Fucker!" Stokes screamed, "Can't stop here Robbie," she added as she almost handbrake turned her car. Her wheels spinning on the gravel. "What the fuck! How did he know?" She was now talking to herself. I could sense anger ebbing out of her every word. Was he an ex boyfriend or something? I thought, but why would I recognise him? I didn't say anything. She span out of the car park and continued driving in the direction we had previously been heading.

"Sorry Sam. Can't go there. How the fuck did he know though?" she said, eyes blazing, with a look of bewilderment across her pretty face.

"I know him Jules. Where from? I definitely -" I broke off as realisation hit me. "He's that copper isn't he? From the Command Inn. The racist!"

"Yes," she replied. "But how does he know where I am? Fucking broke into my house. I know he did."

"What!" I exclaimed, "Turn back Jules. I'll sort him out once and for all."

"No Sam. Can't do that, you know I can't. Let me find somewhere to park. I need to call Charlie."

That was when things got even worse. She turned off into what could have been mistaken for a narrow country lane but in fact was a dead end. A large rusty metal gate blocked our path, which led to nothing but overgrown fields as far as I could see. I heard gravel crunching behind us and the screeching of tyres. I didn't even have time to get my seatbelt off when both our doors were flung open. Balaclava faces at each of the doors. Julie dropped her phone in the footwell midway through its call to her Sergeant.

"Out." The demand came from the man on my side.

I looked at Julie to make sure she was alright. Considering what was happening she was behaving quite calmly. No screams, no fits, just a look of shock. I slowly took my seatbelt off. Turning my head to see how many people we had to deal with. Four hefty looking men. Could the copper have set this up? Was there something between him and Stokes? Then my mind went to the Irish travellers. Had they found me? Was this nothing to do with Stokes? I was grabbed by my left arm, being hauled out. I only offered a little resistance. I wanted to get out.

"In the car," the male holding my arm spoke. Nodding towards the dark blue Range Rover that had skidded to a halt behind us. It wasn't an Irish accent. So probably ruled my theory out, but not for certain.

I looked at the man's other hand. No weapon. I took my chance and smashed him with my right elbow, straight where his nose would have been under the mask. He fell hard. I went to turn but just felt a stunning blow to the back of my head and then the world turned black.

Forty Four

Charlie Jackson tried to call Julie Stokes for the fifth time. He had received a missed call from her, with a long answer phone message. The message was largely inaudible and he couldn't hear any conversation. It went straight to answer phone again. He left another message for her to call him as soon as possible.

He was still in the office, now with the rest of his team. He had not long had a fight with the Chief of Staff with regards to the deployment of his team. Chief of Staff, a group of pencil pushers, was the department who made decisions with regards to the best use of available resources. They had wanted Charlie's team to muck in with the response patrols, answering routine calls. Charlie had won his argument, largely thanks to Ian Thom, who was still holding the rank of Acting Chief Inspector. His team were his to command. At least for the time being.

"I'm getting worried guys, I still can't get hold of her," he said, directing his statement at everyone in the office. He knew that she was going to drive Jakobs to the pub in Southfleet. He had authorised it and was due to meet them there.

"The Southfleet Farm doesn't have much reception skip," said Eddie, trying to offer some reconciliation.

"Yeah I know. But you get reception intermittently and she would have got my message by now." Charlie looked apprehensive.

"Only if her phone hasn't died Charlie," said Jazz, "I know my phones not got much battery life. We have been working such long hours the phones aren't getting enough time to be fully charged."

"Yes maybe," Charlie said. "OK. Everyone get your stuff together. We're all going up there. I just got a bad feeling." Charlie often relied on his gut feelings. When he ignored them things often went wrong. Like when he bought the motorbike for his son.

Charlie had briefed everybody of how upset Stokes had been earlier in the day, because of Shepherd, and of his altercation with Best. All the guys had wanted to go out and find the son of the ex Assistant Chief Constable, to put him in his place. They were a team, a proper team, one that looked out for each other.

About twenty minutes later all three of their cars were parked in the car park at the public house. Crayston and Ronnie searched the parking spaces for her car. The car park was almost full. Jazz raised a picture of Julie on his phone through his Facebook app. Eddie went with him into the pub to check if anybody had seen her, showing her picture to the customers group by group. Charlie just walked around the clientele side of the fairly busy bar, eyes darting from side to side, searching for his friend.

A few minutes later they were outside, with no useful information, despite their endeavours. They circled Charlie Jackson awaiting further instructions. He looked at his phone. He had a reasonable signal and tried calling her again. No reply. He then tried calling Sam Jakobs phones. Both numbers. Both went straight to answer phone.

"Right. Eddie, Jazz. Get searching. Up the country lanes. Take every turning and search up to five miles in each direction. Just in case she's had an accident. Ronnie, Cray, go back to the nick. Call Darenth Valley hospital, same reasons. Then get cell site done on her phone. If you get any shit from anyone, get them to call me. We need to know where she is."

"Where are you going Charlie?" asked Crayston.

"I'm paying a visit to Mark Shepherd. I got his address before I came out. He has got some answering to do."

Charlie got into his car and headed back up the Country Lane towards Istead Rise. Shepherd's address showed that he lived in a flat above the main parade of shops at the top of the Rise in the small country village, about five minutes from where they were.

Six and a half minutes later he was banging on flat number one, which from appearance was the largest flat above the parade of shops. It sat above a large supermarket chain-store. The entry was via a wooden gate with no lock, just a latch, down the side of the shop. A flight of metal stairs had taken him to where he was. Charlie banged on the front door with his fist, ignoring both the doorbell and knocker. The window netting to the right of the door moved and he caught a glimpse of a woman. He held up his Police Warrant card. He heard the sound of a young baby crying through the door. The door clicked open and a young twenty something female with peroxide blonde hair stood on the other side, cradling an infant between her right hip and right arm.

Charlie spoke first, "Hello Miss. I need to speak to Mark Shepherd."

"Oh, that's my landlord. He doesn't live here. We rent the place from him. I would have thought you lot would know that anyway. He works for you. He's a copper as well," she replied.

You lot! Copper! "Oh OK. He's logged this as his home address on the system. Maybe he's moved recently and hasn't updated his personal details yet."

"Can't see that mate. We've rented this place for five years and he didn't join the Old Bill until way after that."

Mate! Old Bill! "That's weird then, why would he do that?" Charlie said, losing a bit of patience with the woman, who clearly had no respect. She had that cocky attitude that he had come across numerous times during his career. She was the type who couldn't wait to take the piss out of the authorities, but was probably quick enough to call when she needed help.

"So do you know where he lives? It's important that we get hold of him," said Charlie firmly.

"No, I've never been to his house. We pay his rent money by direct debit. He comes by sometimes to pick up letters and that sort of stuff. All I know is that he lives with his rich brother somewhere in Meopham."

"What's his brother's name?" asked Charlie.

"Listen mate. You're asking a lot of questions about a bloke who is supposed to be working with you. How do I know you are a Copper? You don't look like one. That ID could be fake couldn't it? No I don't know his brother's name and I am not saying anything else. I got a baby to look after." She shut the door.

There was something amiss about Police Constable 'five digit' Mark Shepherd and Charlie was going to get to the bottom of it. Charlie's phone went off. He answered it without looking. Hoping it was her, Julie.

It was Eddie, "*Sarge, we've found Julie's car. It doesn't look good.*"

Forty Five

Mark Shepherd felt twelve feet tall, completely satisfied. His brother would be proud of him. He had executed the little bomb plan in the police station perfectly. Timed to perfection. It had proved even better, not as planned, the Muslims had got the blame for it. They hadn't foreseen the little protest.

Jasper did not know if he could trust his little brother to do it properly. *'Don't blow yourself up,'* he had said, but he had proved Jasper wrong. He had managed to slip the remote detonating bomb, given to him after the meeting at the Church, under the Police car, right underneath the engine. The one that he had disabled himself, right by the gate. It had taken him seconds to replace the ignition fuse with a dud. No one would be driving off in it. His instructions? *'Don't kill anyone.'* *'Just blow the fucking car up.'*

Mark Shepherd had never killed anyone. He had wanted to be one of the shooters in the firing squad, when the Imams had been killed. His brother would not let him. *'Murder costs your life if you get caught,'* Jasper had said.

He had detonated the bomb perfectly. No one had died. Of course part of him, deep in his brain urged him to do it when someone was close to the car, close enough to die. The urge was strong but his fear of his brother was stronger. He did as he was told.

More than that, with all the commotion out in the yard he had also managed to sneak into the Source Handlers office. Where that stuck up bitch Julie Stokes worked. This time though, for himself, not for Jasper. A quick phone call had identified which one was Stokes mobile phone. It had taken him less than two minutes to download the spy software he had purchased. Software that would remain hidden. Ten seconds to delete his own missed call from it, a quick search of her desk and trays and he was out. He would now receive all of her calls and message data. Even better, he would know exactly where she was through the GPS tracking facility.

Yes, he had certainly had some fun with Stokes in the meantime. Getting into her house. Filtering through her underwear. Stalking her had been both fun and perfect. The bitch had it coming, but Jasper didn't need to know about the spy kit, or his fooling around with her. Deep down he had also wanted to go after Charlie Jackson, but he was a bloke, one that looked like could handle himself. It was better to stick with Julie Stokes.

All Jasper needed to know was that he could be trusted. That he knew exactly what he was doing and that his position in both the company, Secretus, and the upcoming empire, Thirty Three, should be held in high esteem. He deserved a gown and he already had his own appointments lined up.

His call to his brother ended with him being summoned back home before going to the Church. Perfect, he would meet him at the house and push for a position, for a gown. The phone call ended and a glow filled his heart. Jasper was proud of him and no doubt so would their Father be. He imagined his Father, in his Commanding Chief's uniform sat next to their white God, giving him the thumbs up.

Forty Six

1300hrs 22nd March

My head pounded and I could feel damp liquid dripping down my head onto the nape of my neck. That was my first sensation. My eyes were still shut. Then I felt the pain in my shoulders and wrists. My hands were bound together above my head. Clamminess and damp filled the air. I listened as my head rolled slightly, pain shooting from deep behind my eyes, back to the throb in the back of my head. I could hear a soft shuffling noise to my left. My feet were suspended above the floor; I pushed down with my toes which touched what felt like a hard concrete floor. I could feel that I had also been tied around the ankles, tight. I slowly opened my eyes. Blackness. I strained to look all around. A small slit of light about four feet in length ran along the ground to my right. The slit under a doorway. I called out in a whisper, "Jules are you there?"

"Sam, I'm right here. To your left."

"Are you OK babe?"

"Well if being tied to a beam in the pitch black is OK, then I'm hunky dory."

I sensed her attempt at being brave. "Cool. Where are we?"

"No idea mate. Soon as they whacked you, I had a sack put over my head and was bundled in the back of a car. I thought you was dead Sam. That was a massive blow you took on your head. He walloped you with a baseball bat. It smashed in half."

"Baseball bat lost then," I tried to laugh, but groaned at the resurgence of pain pulling at the back of my head. I felt as if I was going to black out again, and wondered if my skull had been fractured.

"How long were we in their car? How long did it take them to drive us here?"

"I'm not sure Sam. I was quite disorientated with the sack over my head. At a guess I would say about twenty minutes."

"OK, so we're still somewhere in or around Gravesend then. Did you see anyone? Have they said anything?" I asked, hoping to make some sense of the predicament we were in.

"No. I didn't see anything until we were hung up here. They took the sack off my head and the door was still open. All I could see was three of them. They had to carry the one you knocked out. They were still wearing balaclavas. We're in a small outbuilding or something. Couldn't see much outside. They didn't say anything. Nothing at all. I even told them I was a cop. They didn't say a word."

I tried to feel the rope or cord that had me tied up around the wrist but numbness had set in my fingers, a tingling sensation filling my fingertips.

"Guess we'll just have to wait and see then. I'm sure they'll be back in a bit."

"That's a great comfort. What's happened to the Superman, I can do anything character? Can't you break out? Turn into the Hulk or something?"

I didn't have time to answer. The door swung open and daylight filled the room. I squinted my eyes blinded by the new found light. Two men wearing balaclavas, carrying a third male struggling and wriggling, trying to kick out against them. Tied feet, lashing out one way then the other. A muffled voice protesting under the sack covering his head.

They had to virtually carry him off the ground, due to his resistance. My eyes were more focused now and I watched them carry the body to the other side of Julie, where they lifted his rope bound hands high over a hook hanging from a metal beam that stretched across the room. He wasn't as tall as me, and his feet dangled in the air, a few inches off the floor. The room itself was bare. Smooth grey concrete walls with no windows. Directly in front of us a large white sheet covered something fairly reasonable in size. I turned back to Julie who was looking directly at me. She looked a lot more shaken and traumatised than how she had sounded in the pitch black. Her eyes almost pleading for help. I could see that the rope was cutting into her wrists.

She had a crate of some sort under her feet. She wasn't as tall as us. I guessed they didn't want her to dislocate her shoulders. Her feet were also bound by rope around the ankles but rested on the crate with more firmness than my toes did on the floor.

"You're a bunch of bitches. Cut me down and we'll have a straightener. All of you verses me." It was all I could think to say. I couldn't bear to see a female in that state. Let alone one I knew, and had feelings for.

One of them turned to look at me. They didn't say anything. He ripped the sack off the man's head and nodded for the others to follow him out. I looked at the new captives face. It was the copper from the Command Inn. The racist one. The one that apparently had broken into Julie's house. His face was red and supported two black eyes and what appeared to be a broken nose. He had now stopped wriggling, and was slumped in defeat. His head turned, he saw Julie and then he looked at me. Hatred in his eyes. He turned away and lowered his head, staring at the floor. His mouth was wrapped over and over with masking tape. Julie had also caught sight of him and turned her face to me, looking dumbfounded, and then back to him. The captors all started walking towards the door but the one in charge of the nodding stopped right in front of me. His punch landed on my cheek, exploding the pain in the back of my head. My head slumped down for a second and I heard them move towards the door.

"You even punch like a bitch," I muttered. They didn't stop, but kept walking. They shut the door behind them leaving us in the pitch black again. The last thing I saw before the blackness was a mist of giddiness, a cloudy white light and then I was out for the count again.

Forty Seven

1525hrs 22nd March

Charlie, Eddie and Jazz stood next to Julie Stokes blue Ford Escort. It had taken them a bit of time to find, as they had initially missed the hidden turn off that Stokes had taken.

The car was just abandoned there with both front doors wide open. Splatters of blood traced across the front passenger window and door frame. The intelligence Unit were the only department on area that did not have trackers set in their cars. A decision that was made to safeguard the risk of being followed and as such endangering the true identities of their Covert Human Intelligence Sources. A decision that would obviously be reviewed in light of what had happened today.

The three of them had no gloves on them so they did not touch her car, worried of disturbing any potential forensics or other evidence it might contain. Charlie had called in the incident to his boss Ian Thom. One of his Detectives had gone missing with an informant. Sam Jakobs would be a suspect that was for sure but Charlie trusted him. Something else had gone on. *Could be something to do with the Yardies,* he thought. After all they had busted a lucrative business. Child sex and Class A drugs supply. Perhaps K had given limited information to the Londoners before they had killed him. He couldn't afford to rely on the only theory that was going through his head.

Perhaps Peter Snugs was involved as well. He had gone missing. He would get Eddie to phone Sally Tall and see if she had heard anything. There were other problems. The informant Sam Jakobs was also missing. With a Police Officer. An informant handler at that. It would not take long for somebody to realise that Sam Jakobs was an informant. A revelation that sometimes warranted a death sentence within the criminal fraternity. Ian Thom agreed with Charlie, that at this stage only those who needed to know, would know who she had allegedly been with.

They waited for their Scenes of crime Officer (SOCO) to turn up. Charlie had sent a uniform patrol to the pub to collate the identifications of all the customers inside, and seize the CCTV footage for the whole day. He also had two marked patrol cars block both ends of the lane, three miles each side of where they were. Blue lights flashing, turning around disgruntled civilians wishing to use the bypass. There were no ANPR (Automatic Number Plate Recognition) cameras along that stretch of road. The last one that Stokes car had driven through was at Springhead roundabout, heading in the general direction of the pub.

Charlie felt helpless. Why had he allowed her to go and meet Jakobs on her own? That would most certainly be questioned, when it all came out. It went against all the best practice protocols. There should always be at least two handlers present when meeting sources, for protection, informants sometimes double crossed their handlers, though not the agent types, just the grasses. Jakobs was an agent. Still, he would most definitely have to answer those questions, and he would, when it came to it. The most important thing at the moment was to find her.

He phoned Cray, who was having problems getting urgent cell site tracking carried out on Julie Stokes phone.

"Cray, any luck yet."

"*Might have Charlie. Got to speak to that liaison officer who has been working upstairs from the Counter Terrorist team. She reckons she could get something sorted within the hour by her lot. Apparently, they have got some top of the range Stingray tracking facility. I'm just waiting upstairs for her to come back now.*"

"That's blinding Cray. Call me as soon as you got some news." Charlie hung up and briefed the two Detectives stood with him, both quiet, both equally as worried as Charlie.

Charlie's phone rang again. Withheld number. He answered it, "Hello, this is DS Jackson," half hoping that it was someone that needed confirmation of what had gone on, to authorise Julie's phone tracking. It wasn't.

"*DS Jackson you have really fucked up this time. I want you in here right---,*" He didn't let Chief Superintendent Best finish and hung up. God that man was a prick.

"You OK Skip?" asked Jazz.

"Will be when we find her Jazz, will be when we find her."

They heard a vehicle and a white SOCO van with its 'Kent Police' and 'Forensic Investigation' markings across the side panels, pulled in behind Stokes vehicle.

Charlie greeted Sharon Gardner, the on-duty SOCO, as she got out. Her face was anxious as she knew the circumstances. Charlie called the boys back to let her get on with her work. He didn't have to tell her to do her best. She was one of the better crime scene officers that they had in the county and was certain to leave no stone unturned.

Forty Eight

1635hrs 22nd March

I came back round, the pain in the back of my head felt worse. Like somebody was boring a diamond drill right through my skull. I found myself in the same pitch blackness as before I had flaked out.

"You still there princess? How long have I been out?"

"Where the fuck do you think I would be Sam?" she replied, "My arms have gone all numb. I can't feel them. My legs ache and I feel like being sick."

"How long have I been out?" I groaned again, agonising pain torturing my head, face, wrists and shoulders. I hurt everywhere.

"Feels like forever. At least the weasel has stopped moaning," she replied, "plus either you still need a bath or he has shit himself."

"I don't need a bath," I laughed, trying to sound brave for her. I knew what she meant about her arms feeling numb. I couldn't feel my fingers, my legs felt heavy and weighed down.

I listened to her shuffling her feet around the wooden crate, trying to bring back some life into them. They wanted us hurt but alive for now. I had read somewhere that hanging in mid-air from the wrists could have the same effects as a crucifixion, it could sometimes lead to suffocation. Something to do with the lungs not being able to function properly. Something that they obviously did not care about with regards to their third prisoner, who was hanging completely suspended. At least I was able to take some weight on the tips of my toes.

I thanked God that they hadn't used the Strappado method. Hands tied behind the back before hanging. Both arms would very quickly be dislocated. An old method of torture used in the medieval days. Thinking about it started to make me conscious of my breathing. I took in a deep breath and wondered if I could lift myself up.

I closed my eyes so I could picture the scene properly from when they last opened the door. I knew the beam stretched across the room. Wall to wall. I knew that we were tied by rope which in turn looped over a large metal hook. I could easily do thirty straight arm pull ups. Surely I could do this. Question was, were my wrists strong enough. They were not designed to hold your bodyweight and they were already cut and sore due to the tightness of the ropes. I pulled hard with the smallest of a push off my toes to help. I slowly moved up, my back arched. I pictured my head coming up almost level to my wrists, which were screaming with pain, so the beam must have been about six inches above my head. I leant my head to the side and pulled harder. The pain was excruciating. The door rattled and I dropped back down opening my eyes. The light shining through the door made me turn away instantly.

Two men walked in. One about my height and stamp. The other considerably shorter. He walked nimbly, light on his feet like an athlete.

"The time has come," he said loudly. Almost as if projecting his voice, like an actor would do on a theatre stage. "Prepare the scene," he said in the same voice to his counterpart. He had an accent which sounded Asian.

The door was still open and my eyes struggled to focus. Trees, bare land and I thought I got the glimpse of a building when the man spoke again.

"Over the next three days you will become Satanic martyrs. You will all die in a different way. With no humility. Lessons will be learned by all infidels."

"Is that so you coward. All big and brave with me tied up like this. Cut me down you son of a bitch and I'll fight you with one hand. Both of you." The threats to kill he had made were not just aimed at me, but also at Julie. I could feel my temper boiling. All of a sudden my eyes were blinded. A flash of light and rays of heat battered my face. My eyes had barely got used to the daylight, I squeezed them tight as the huge halogen floodlight smothered us.

I could hear what sounded like furniture being scraped across the floor. Arms took me from either side and I was lifted of the hook. My arms slumped down. Any thought of a fight was currently impossible. I was swiftly seated on what felt like a hard chair and then felt myself being bound across my waist and arms. Tightly, cutting into my flesh through my hoodie and T-Shirt. My eyes were still forced shut by the heat and light, and I could feel my legs being tied in the same manner, unyielding. I tested the resistance against my chest by trying to lift my feeble arms. Trying was as best as it got. I was well and truly trussed.

I heard more scraping and Julie yelped. "Fucking get off her," I growled.

"OR WHAT?" came the answer.

"I told you, cut me free and I'll show you."

"Sam. Shh. It's OK. Help will be here soon," said Julie.

"Is that so Miss Police Officer and who will be coming here to help you? I do not think so." The antagonist laughed.

"Help will come Mister and when it does you are dead," said Julie.

The man just laughed. A third chair scraped and Shepherd protested through his gag as he was tied and bound in the same manner.

I felt the heat come away from my face as the floodlight was moved. I now watched the assistant move it to a position behind us. The best part of the glare now shining down at the back of Julie's head. She looked awful. Terror etched into every feature of her lovely face.

The assistant moved over to the white sheet in front of us, pulling it back. Underneath was a sturdy wooden table. On the table were a few electrical items. What looked like a video camera, a laptop computer and other stuff that I didn't recognise. Black electrical boxes with various leads running to and from them.

I looked around the room again in the hope of finding something helpful. Despite the light beaming from the floodlight, parts of the room were still pitch black. The room had no lights and no light switch as far as I could see. It must have power though. I tried to trace the leads coming from the floodlight and table top items but lost track as they ran down behind the table. I felt the aggressor, close to my back. Instinct told me he was right behind me. I then caught the glimpse of a large blade flash past my face, down to my throat. Its edge was brought to my skin. I could feel the cold metal press hard against me.

"Will it be you tonight? The big hard fighter. That would be good." He released the pressure on my throat and moved over to Julie. Same move. He pressed it hard into her soft smooth skin just under her chin. Her eyes panicking, her mouth releasing another yelp.

"Fucking told you. Get off her," I snarled, the inside of my stomach churning.

"You are not a hero," he hissed at me, turning his head sharply. I tried looking into his eyes, defiant, not wanting to show any fear or signs of submission.

"He then moved on to Shepherd and re-enacted the same move. Three maybe four seconds. Shepherd's eyes blazing with an expression that showed fear, anger and something else as he tried to turn his head back from the knife. He moved back towards me.

"If I hear one more word from you," he whispered, leaning into my ear, "the girl dies first, after she is raped."

I went to reply but thought better of it.

The man at the table, by the video camera, threw something at him. I didn't get to see what it was. He had clearly caught it behind me as I didn't hear the sound of anything dropping to the floor.

"Precautions," he said. "No hero talk before you die."

I felt my head being grabbed and forced back again. My mouth was gagged. I could hear the tape being wound around and around until it was virtually impossible to breathe through, let alone talk. He moved over to Julie and did the same, wrapping the tape round and round, sealing her mouth. Shepherd was already gagged.

He nodded to his assistant who was now holding the video camera. I saw a red light on the side of it illuminate as he switched it on and the man spoke. He was now stood behind Julie staring directly at the camera. His stance changing. He stood upright, shoulders back, stomach in, like an athlete, and he still had hold of the knife.

"You dare challenge Fatwa," he spoke again in his projected voice, "You dare enter and burn down our places of worship and YOU DARE kill our holy men. I will no longer stand alone in this fight. Because of your actions many soldiers have come, Muslim brothers who have realised the time is right. Brothers, who have been living amongst you, hiding their disgust for your ways. Now ready for the war. The threat you all now face is a thousand fold greater. The tears you will cry, will create rivers of despair. Our threat is very real. I have in front of me, three infidels, three heathens, three of you."

His knife pointed down at us one by one as the video camera followed.

"All three will die. Painful deaths. Deaths that you will grieve. Then there will be more and as my army grows so will my acts of revenge. Death. You will not see me. You will not find me but I will be there. You have on this day declared war on all of my Muslim brothers. A war that you cannot win. We are everywhere. We are unstoppable. HERE!" he shouted, "I have two of your own Police Officers and an alleged Good Samaritan. How is it possible that they can be taken? Police Officers? You will ask. Well I can take who I want, when I want and there is nothing that you, or the Police," he pointed down at his prisoners, "or anyone can do anything about it. Fatwa has spoken." The camera ran along the length of us. It went from Shepherd to Stokes to me and then all the way back again.

Julie was now terrified. I was helpless and Shepherd was struggling harder than before, his chair rocking as he pushed and pulled hard at the ropes. Fatwa moved swiftly, agile, light on his feet, knife held in front of him. I braced myself but he went past me around the front until he was stood alongside Shepherd. Shepherd's eyes opened wide, mixture of bewilderment and fear. He tried to lean back but Fatwa grabbed the back of his head and pulled hard. The knife stabbed deep into Shepherd's right eye. He wriggled and thrashed. Fatwa twisted the knife like a screwdriver. The knife came back out leaving a large hole filled with a mixture of dark, glistening red fluid, bright and dark in the manmade light, blood splurging in all directions. The knife went straight to the other eye and he did exactly the same. Shepherd's chair rocking with his struggles but held firm by the assailant.

The blade came out and sliced smoothly through his throat. Blood spurted in all directions, covering Julie's pale, drained, fear stricken face. Shepherd's body was now still. His head hanging back due to its almost complete severance. Blood continued to gush out of the torn aperture of flesh and veins, as the heart pumped its last few beats. The scene worse than any horror movie. This was real.

Fatwa stood straight and walked over to Stokes. She was now physically shaking, her eyes shut. Screaming into her gag. I strained with all my might against the ropes. I couldn't move.

Fatwa held his knife out and grabbed at Stokes hair. He looked into the camera, "She dies next. Fatwa has spoken." He wiped the bloodied knife against her hair. He signalled and the video camera was switched off.

Even I was stunned at the black-hearted act that I had just seen. Fatwa walked over to the door and called out.

Three men. All wearing the same facial coverings entered as he left. Julie and I were cut free from the chair and hung back up onto the beams. The chairs we had been sat on were moved somewhere behind us. The table was covered by it's sheet. Two of the men lifted the chair with Shepherd's lifeless corpse on it and carried it out. The remaining man flicked the floodlight off and dragged it back into place. He walked out the door and once again we were left alone, gagged and in the pitch black

Forty Nine

1700hrs 22nd March

SOCO had recovered fingerprints and DNA from
Stokes car. Probably belonging to Stokes and Jakobs, but
Sharon Gardener would leave no stone unturned. She had
also taken samples from the blood stains and
collected potential evidential specimens from various
locations in, on and around the car. She had placed
moveable items, a packet of Benson and Hedges cigarettes,
a bottle of half drunk water and an empty CD case in
evidence bags.

The uniformed officers had now collected details of the
forty two customers that had been inside the pub, and each
name was being researched by R & D (Research and
Development team). The CCTV at the public house door
entrance gave no helpful information. No sign of Stokes or

Jakobs. The car park CCTV footage was currently being viewed.

Nobody could get hold of Mark Shepherd, who had taken sick leave on his rostered rest day. All Police rest days had been cancelled throughout the County and Country due to the volatile unrest that was spreading across the nation. Sick leave was the only way to get a day off at the moment, and the small group of habitual sickies were going overboard on it. *Stress* being the common denominator on the prescribed sick notes being produced. Shepherd had not presented such a sick note, but had merely called in his absence with a migraine.

R & D had established that he did indeed have a rich brother. Jasper Shepherd. Owner and Chief Executive Officer of Secretus Security International. One of the largest Security companies in the United Kingdom. Finding a private address for a CEO proved more difficult. He had never been arrested or even ever reported a crime. He didn't register on the electoral roll. Mark Shepherd did, unfortunately at the address in Istead Rise, the one he was renting. They considered calling his office, at Secretus, but didn't have to because they eventually got a break through when an *old school* retired Detective, now a civilian employee, piped up that he had worked in the era of Assistant Chief Constable Shepherd. The original proprietor of Secretus Security International. He had purchased a huge farmhouse in Meopham which in turn had been handed down to his two sons. They would never sell it and in all likelihood that was where they would be living. A quick Google search found the farmhouse in Meopham, appropriately named *Shepherds*.

The Stingray tracking tool had been authorised. It was excellent in locating both Stoke's and Jakobs phones. All three phones were found within close proximity of each other. About thirty yards from Julie Stokes car on the other side of the metal gate that led to the overgrown grass and weeds. The scattered phones had been switched off, which initially caused problems with regards to tracking them down. However SO15 and MI5 now had the same software that NSA and FBI had been using for years. Software that could remotely infect each handset with a *Trojan*, forcing the phones to emit a signal despite being switched off. Unless the batteries had been removed. Which they hadn't. The phones had been switched off and thrown into the overgrown wasteland. They now also sat in evidence bags, waiting for forensic examination.

Charlie was adamant that he be involved in the visit to the suspected home address of Jasper and Mark Shepherd. Chief Superintendent Best had wanted to drag Charlie Jackson's arse into his office, but fortunately had been persuaded otherwise, by the remaining Chief Officers. All that nonsense could be sorted out later.

Charlie got set to go with his team, when his phone rang. He answered it and listened, a few short seconds. He clicked the phone off, white as a sheet. A few seconds later his whole team sat around the television in Inspector Thom's office. Fatwa had broadcast again. They watched in horror as Mark Shepherd was slain. Tears erupted from even the strongest of the men in the office as they listened to the words, "She dies next. Fatwa has spoken." The blood drenched knife that he was holding, being wiped clean on her always pristine hair.

Fifty

The door was shut. It was once again pitch black. He had said we would all die over the next three days. He had said Julie would die next. Meaning, probably tomorrow. Or he could kill her later today. I had to do something now. My arms had regained some strength; having temporarily been taken down from the hanging position; for the sake of the video recording. Blood had been allowed to circulate around my body. I was however aware that my natural strength and energy would have diminished. I hadn't eaten anything since this morning, the breakfast that Nan had cooked for me. Food equals energy. As far as I was aware neither had Julie. What was going through her mind? No doubt she had seen horrific things in her career. Things that would give her some sort of psychological steel, but I would wager nothing compared to what had just taken place.

I needed to do something. My hands and arms were becoming numb, quicker than they did the first time round. I could feel paraesthesia, pins and needles setting in my hands. The rope was still just as tight around my wrists. The rope was threaded through a large hook. The distance from the tip of the hook and the hook's stem was just larger than the width of the rope. I had seen that. The hook was secured to the metal beam above our heads. I shut my eyes to recall the layout. Memory recall is far better with your eyes shut, scientifically proven. The beam was a large beam, about twelve inches wide and probably double that in depth up to the ceiling. The upper edge of the beam ran along the ceiling line.

We had been hung there to drain us of strength. Not fed or provided water to weaken us even more. I could physically feel the strength draining away from me. If I was going to do something I had to do it now. I had to be that Superman that Julie had referred to. I cleared my head. I told myself. I am super strong, I can do anything. I am super fit. I am superman. I repeated those words over again. My boxing coach had called the technique self-talk, don't under estimate the power of the mind. A method used to defeat flight-syndrome, better known as fear. Psychologically making me feel stronger and more

powerful. I could do pull ups with ease. I could do Muscle
Ups with ease. (A mixture of pull ups and dips). I knew
what I had to do, but would probably only have one go at
it; my strength would degenerate if I failed first time. The
word fail started to drain my strength, psychologically. I
repeated the other words, I am super strong, I can do
anything. I am super fit. I am superman, self-talk. Four
times over.

I pulled hard, eyes shut. I was up. I leaned my
head forward and to the side at the point I thought it would
hit the beam taking it just past the beam, my head
now slightly higher than my hands, all in one smooth
movement. My wrists killed me. I continued, one smooth
movement, the jumping chin; lifting my wrists first
backwards, up and then forwards, to clear the hook, fast,
super fast, as if I was jumping onto another beam, like a
gymnast would on the asymmetric bars. One smooth
accelerated motion. I could feel the rope clear the hook.
The rope was tight though and the thrust forward forced
my left thumb against the tip of the hook. I felt it tear. I
didn't care. I landed in a lower squat position, but lost
balance due to my tied ankles and fell forwards. It was a
noisy landing. Not much, but a noise. I laid still for a

second, listening, bated breath. Not knowing if anybody was outside keeping guard. Nothing happened.

I reached towards my ankles, lying on my back, feeling for the rope. It took me a while to free them. The rope had been forcefully knotted. I slowly got to my feet. Until then I had forgotten about the pain in my head. However the roll forward had brought it back to life. It was bad, so bad I had to crouch down again. I breathed deep as the pain slowly ebbed away. I started grappling at the tape wrapped around my mouth and eventually managed to get it off. Next I started to work on the rope around my wrists, using both my teeth and fingers. Eventually I was able to flex my body, I had set myself free.

"Julie?" I whispered. No reply.

I slowly headed back in the direction I had rolled from. Feeling around with my fingers stretched in the air. I found the hook that had held me. I shut my eyes and judged Julie's position. I moved over slowly. As I stepped in her direction my feet kicked the crate under her feet. It felt heavy, as if it was bolted to the floor. It almost made me trip. I managed to settle myself and reached forward. I found her. She started to wriggle, convulsing with panic and terror.

"Julie, Julie it's OK, it's me, it's Sam. Shh. I'm going to get us out of here." I stroked the side of her face as I spoke.

She stopped writhing, but her breathing was fast, through her nose, like a person hyperventilating. I stepped up onto the crate in front of her. My eyes had become accustomed to the dark but it was pitch-black, I could barely see her silhouette. I could smell her though. I could smell her perfume, her hair and also her fear. I put my left arm around her waist and lifted her gently. My right hand up by her wrists. Making sure the rope cleared the hook. I lowered her slowly and gently. Her face brushed against mine as I let her down. Her skin was soft but also wet from sweat, tears and Shepherd's blood.

She was now stood on the crate in front of me. I gently moved my hands up to her face, gave her a stroke on the cheek with one hand, while I looked for the edge of the masking tape around her mouth with the other. I slowly ripped it off. I brushed her lips with my finger, urging her not to make a noise and slowly crouched down, feeling down her legs, until I reached her ankles. I untied her completely. I stood up close to her and then took her small hands. I made her follow me. I felt for the edge of the crate and stepped onto the concrete floor, lifting her off it straight after. I took another two steps back, leading her and then stopped. I freed her from her last piece of incarceration, the rope around her wrists and brushed her hair with my hand, "Jules, princess. I need you to get it together babe if we are going to get out of here, I need you on it. Trust me hun, we are going to get out, but I will need your help."

"Oh Sam, that was awful. He stabbed him in the eyes, he cut his throat, his blood shot all over me and I hated him, Shepherd, and I felt sorry for him, Shepherd, and I thought I was getting the same and....."

She burst into tears burying her head into my chest. I could do nothing but hold her, one hand cradling her head, the other trying to soothe her trembling. We stood like that for what seemed like forever.

Up until then the adrenaline and noradrenaline hormones zipping through my body had upped my pain threshold. However the sudden calm serenity of Julie's head on my shoulder brought my other senses back to life. In particular the agony at the tip of my left thumb. It felt like it had been completely ripped off. I reached around her waist to feel for the damage. I could feel that a chunk of the thumb had been half ripped off, at the end next to my nail. My wrists also burned and felt swollen. Pulling myself up on them had undoubtedly damaged the tendons.

"Princess. We have got to find a way out. They could be back anytime," I eventually said.

"Yes. Sorry Sam. I'm the Police Officer. I should be saying that. Let's do it." Her voice was still shaking but she was bearing up. I didn't know what long term mental damage she would suffer. If we got out.

"OK. Let's do it. I got a good look around when I could. No windows as far as I could see. One door. First thing we need to know is if the door's being guarded. Stand still I'm going to have a listen. Don't move Jules so I know exactly where you are," I said.

I knew the door was on my left now and could see the small slit of light coming from underneath it. I edged over towards it, slowly, as you do in the dark. Hand stretched out in front of me until it felt the cold hard metal covering the door. I edged my hand down towards where the handle should be. I hadn't heard anything indicating the door had been locked when they went out. As far as they were concerned we were racked up in a position of no escape. Bit of luck it wouldn't be locked. I turned the small round bulbous door handle. It turned fully and I slowly pulled at the door. It was locked. I put my ear to the door. I couldn't hear much apart from what sounded like a strong wind. I lowered myself to the floor trying to look through the small gap under the door. Again I couldn't see anything. I pushed myself up and caught my injured thumb on something sharp. I winced in pain holding my breath. I slowly edged my way back towards Julie and found her exactly where I had left her.

"Door's locked babe and I can't tell if anybody is outside."

"What now then?" she whispered.

"Let me think," I said. I wondered if smashing the door open and charging out like Rambo would work. If I was on my own I might have given it a go. But it wasn't just me. I had to think of Julie. I didn't know how many of them were outside or what weapons they had.

Julie broke my school of thought, "Sam, they had a Laptop in here. On a table in front of us."

"Yes I saw it as well," I replied.

"Let's find it," she said and slipped her small soft hand back into mine. This time she led the way, until we came to the table top. I pulled at the covering, slowly, until I had it completely away. I scrunched it up and tossed it towards the back of the table. We both gently groped around the top.

"I think I got it," she said. She opened the computer and blindly started pressing buttons, searching for the power. Eventually the screen lit up. Flashing and whirring into life. It soon settling on a blank pale blue screen with a small rectangular box in the middle asking for a password. "Shit," she said.

"You're a copper, don't you know how to bust passwords or something," I said, "I don't know nothing about computers."

"Well that's two of us then," she said.

The light from the lap top caught the side of Julie Stokes face. Underneath the layers of blood, sweat and tears smeared over her smooth white skin shone a very frightened little girl, trying to be brave for her present company. I wanted to take her in my arms, charge through the door and carry her off to safety.

"Let's use the light from the machine to have a look around," I said.

I unplugged the laptop from its power lead and tried to shine it around the room. The light released from the screen however was poor, so we had to walk around with it. I was looking for anything that I could use as a weapon. I didn't find what I was looking for. I found something better. Fixed to a small alcove in the wall at the back of the prison room stood a metal framed ladder. Similar to a bell tower ladder. About a foot off the rear wall going up in a straight line. I held the laptop above my head facing the ceiling. The light barely reached the top of the ladder but we could see what looked like a hatch door. About three feet square.

I asked Julie to hold the laptop and I climbed up. I reached the hatch and pushed hard. It didn't budge. I felt along its edges in the limited light coming from the laptop. I found a bolt. I pulled it back and pushed up again, it moved, squeaking slightly. I partially opened the door, just enough to look out. It was some sort of flat roof. I carefully and quietly fully pushed it open. Not letting it fall. It was an almost square roof, bordered by a wall. I climbed up and called Julie to follow. She took longer than I did but eventually popped her head out, squinting because of the sunlight. She was still holding the laptop.

"Should have ditched that babe," I said.

"No, we might be able to get some information off it," she replied.

"Ok," I said, half relieved that she was still able to think like a Police Officer. She climbed out and I carefully shut the door. We edged towards the front of the building, crouched down, careful with our steps. I looked over the wall, which was barely four feet high, just peeking my head over. On the other side I could see two men with their backs to us, sat down on a crate similar to the one that had been placed under Julie Stokes feet. Both were dressed in all black combats, both also had balaclavas. I watched as one bent down towards his feet, the back of his top rising, showing his lower back, showing me something else, and just at that moment he stood up. We both ducked and edged away. We backed off to the rear of the building. Over this wall was scant woodland with a number of trails leading to thicker woodland in the distance.

"We've got to go now. Give me your hands and climb down," I spoke while grabbing her hands, they felt good, soft good, skin on skin. She had put the lap top on the edge of the wall. I lowered her, stretching as far as I could and then just dropped her. She landed lightly on her feet but fell backwards slightly into a bush, creating a small rustling noise. She just lay there not moving, holding her breath. I looked about. Thirty seconds and we saw nothing. I signalled for her to come closer and when she was below me I threw the laptop down. She caught it. I then lowered myself down, spinning around so I was facing the wall. At full stretch with just my finger tips clinging onto the edge, holding my injured thumb as far away from the wall as I could. I dropped. Landing square on my feet and bending my legs as I hit the ground, to cushion the drop. We stood still again. My damaged thumb was throbbing, as was my head, so were my wrists, as well as my shoulders.

"Right run," I said and half pushed her along the closest trail. We ran along the trail hugging the cover of random trees and bushes as best as we could. I stayed at the back, constantly turning around to make sure we were not being followed, until finally, we reached the denser part of the woods.

Fifty One

The decision had been made that Charlie Jackson and his team could still pay a visit to Shepherds Farm. Only in a completely different manner, and for different reasons. This would be a death message. So far there had been no confirmation that Mark's brother, Jasper Shepherd, had received the information of his sibling's gruesome ending.

There were still questions that needed answering. Mark Shepherd had been stalking Julie, and now both had been kidnapped by the terrorist Fatwa. Where, when and how was still a mystery. Maybe, just maybe the younger brother had discussed Julie Stokes with his family. Diplomacy was going to be required though. Charlie decided to take Eddie with him. Jazz had offered to go with them but in light of the racial tensions and the fact that Jasper's brother had been killed by a Muslim, Ian Thom had decided that it would be better for Jazz not to attend the scene.

"I'm not a Muslim," the young Punjabi Police Officer had protested, "and even if I were, I'm not a terrorist."

"I know Jazz," Charlie said. "Let's just get this done as quick as possible. Can you check to see if they had any luck with the CCTV in the pub car park instead? Please mate, it might give us another lead."

Eddie drove, in his allocated small grey Vauxhall Astra. Charlie sat shotgun. The journey had largely been silent. It took them about half an hour to find the farmhouse entrance. Only it didn't look like the average Farm.

Huge electronic, gleaming white Security gates guarded entry. The word, *Shepherds*, shaped in raven black wrought iron spanned across the top of them. CCTV cameras were positioned high above the gates on long white metal poles. Matching white railings stretched both ways as far as the eye could see.

Through the railings they could see the ultimate picturesque green lawn. As big as a park. The grass looking more like a plush spongy carpet. The rich greenery was cut in lines, dark green, light green, each band about three yards in width, like the lines found across most Premier league football pitches. Shaped bushes and tall Oak trees dotted the acres of land. The driveway went round in a circle, around the lawn, separated from the grass by a short dark wooden fence. A large house stood at the end of the driveway. It went up three floors, with a large triangular roof, with six dormer windows jutting out from it, equally spaced. White panelled windows of assorted sizes and shapes decorated the visible side of the house. A large glass conservatory was fixed to the far side of the building, hexagonal in shape. Night lights followed the driveway along the fence, switched on, even though night had not yet fallen. About fifty yards to its east facing side stood a large corrugated metal warehouse painted a brilliant white and deep blue. Half and half, the blue band stretching across the lower half of it. Outside the warehouse were two new matching Lexus RX's on personalised number plates.

"They're worth about fifty grand each," said Eddie.

An intercom was positioned to the side of one of the front gates. A white box, with a grilled speaker and two buttons with words above them. Charlie pressed the buzzer with *call*, written above it, and waited. They could hear a monotonous ringing tone. A voice eventually cackled a greeting through the speaker.

"Can I help you?"

"Good evening Sir. My name is Charlie Jackson. I'm a Detective Sergeant at Gravesend Police Station. I wondered if I could take some of Mr Shepherd's time?"

"I'm sorry Sir, but Mr Shepherd is grieving. He is not here and left a message that he will not be taking any calls or messages. I'm sorry but the best I can do is tell him that you called Sergeant Jackson, when I see him next." The voice was replaced by an electronic hum.

Jackson pressed the button, "OK Sir, thank you for your time. Please pass him our condolences," Jackson said, dejected, hoping to have learned more. Jasper Shepherd was aware of the murder. Jackson couldn't even bear to think of what was going through his mind, he must have seen the video. He knew all about grieving and family bereavement.

Jackson and Eddie got back into the Astra, with Eddie in the driver's seat again. He started the engine and his phone rang. Eddie placed it into the hands free loudspeaker, situated in the middle of the consul. It was Jazz. He answered it.

"Ed, it's Jazz. Are you still with Charlie?"

"Yes mate. He can hear you. You're on loudspeaker," replied Eddie.

"Thanks. Charlie, I've checked that CCTV. We got Shepherd turn up in the car park just before two in the afternoon. He drives in, stops his car in the middle of the car park and gets out but just stays there, in the car park, leaning on his car. He doesn't go into the pub. You then get Julie's car just turn up into the car park, it looks like he sees her and aims his phone at her, like he's taking a photo. She turns straight around fast. Wheel spins and everything, she drives straight out. Someone else is in the front passenger seat with her. Probably Jakobs but you can't see clearly. Shepherd leaves a couple of minutes later," Jazz said urgently.

"What car was he driving?" asked Charlie.

"A silver Lexus, index 'Sierra, Hotel, Echo, Papa, Two' SHEP2. Looks brand new."

Charlie looked at Eddie as he hung up. His brain working overtime. *That car, SHEP2, was parked outside the warehouse on the farm. Why was Shepherd waiting at the pub for Julie? How did he even know she was going there? What on earth did it all mean?* He tried to calm down. He needed to make decisions. Shepherd's car had been at the pub and was now on the farm. He could have been kidnapped from inside his house. There could be some clues or evidence to be recovered from inside. The blunt response from the man on the other side of the intercom was an indication of how difficult it was going to be to get inside with consent.

Charlie called Jazz back. "Mate get a search warrant ASAP for Shepherd's address. I don't care what you put on the application, just link it to the kidnapping of two Police Officers. Then get the rest of the team together and meet me up at Shepherd's Farm. Be quick mate."

"Charlie, are you serious, a search warrant? His brother has just been killed mate." Eddie couldn't believe his supervisor's rational.

"We might not have to use it Ed, but we'll have it just in case. My gut is hammering alarm bells, something is wrong. I trust it mate, my gut feeling is never wrong."

Fifty Two

We had been running, walking and then running again for what must have been thirty minutes, but seemed more like thirty hours. The walking was because of me, not Julie. My head was pounding and the thump of each running step was making it worse. I didn't want to pass out again.

We moved as quick as we could, through dense woodland. Both of us had somewhat lost our sense of direction, largely due to the twists and turns in the various makeshift tracks we had followed. As far as we were aware, we could have been running around in circles.

I asked for another walking spell, feeling like I was about to faint, when we came out at another opening. The woods had once again become sparse. I could hear traffic in the distance, so we were not too far from a road. Julie stopped, hands now on her knees and breathing heavy, she placed the laptop on the floor. I had offered to carry it but she knew that I was in a bad way with my head.

"Look, Sam. Over there," she said pointing in the opposite direction from where the traffic noise was coming from. In the distance stood a huge building. It had the appearance of a grand hotel. Twenty or thirty windows stretching across its face. A small narrow country lane leading from it towards us. The road at a parallel must have been about two hundred feet in front of us, just past a steep dip.

"Come on then." I said, taking hold of her hand. I half pulled her along with me, re-energised with the prospect of the imminent safe house.

She was still trying to get her breath back, "I, I think I know where we are Sam. I've been, wait," she paused and took another two deep breaths, "I've been there before. Working. We had to do a protection job there. It's-" another pause and another deep breath, "Some important bloke lives there. We had half the TAC team sat there for a whole weekend because he was under some sort of threat. That was a few years ago. We're somewhere near Cobham."

"That's a house?" I exclaimed, "It looks more like a hotel."

"Whatever it is, they will have a phone," she gasped and we moved on.

The house was further than we thought. It took us a good forty five minutes to get there. Walking, not running. The Sun was setting and it was getting darker.

We reached the front of the mansion. It was even bigger close up than it had appeared from distance. Huge white columns stood tall and proud on each side of the front steps, which were covered by thick, equally white tiles. The steps led to two large white solid oak doors, with frosted glass panels running down each side of them. Two wide-reaching balconies jutted out from the building on the second floor, one at each end of the building. The structure itself, stretched almost a hundred yards long, with two neat rows of windows. Other extension windows jutted out from pitched roof dormers, intermittently, across the main sloped roof. I had only seen houses like this on television before. Drug cartels came to mind.

Julie had scaled the steps and I was a few feet behind her. She rang the door bell. It sent out a chime which we could just about hear from the outside. I stood still, waiting for a butler to answer the door.

The door was opened by a man in a splendid grey suit. A plain white shirt undone at the neck revealed a reddish brown sun-tan. He wore black leather shoes that shined like a mirror. The man had very neat silver hair combed into a perfect side parting. Everything about him was immaculate. Not a butler.

"Can I help you?" he started to say and then stopped. Staring, incredulously at the two of us. Turning his head from Julie to me and then back to Julie again. I could clearly see why Julie would cause such a reaction. She looked a mess and had dried blood stains all over her face, hands and clothes. I didn't know what I looked like but it couldn't have been much better.

"Sir, I'm a Police Officer," Julie said, automatically going for the back pocket of her tight blue jeans, now with dark splatters of dried blood all over the front, which was where she always kept her Police warrant card. But it had been taken with all her possessions when we had been captured. She carried on, "Sir, we need to use your telephone and call the Police station. They will confirm that I am a Police Officer."

"Yes, Yes, Yes of course," he muttered, and stepped back away from the door, his head still darting between the two of us. A look of disbelief all over his face, he carried on, "From the looks of things you could also do with receiving some medical attention. Come in, please come in."

Julie walked in past the man, as did I. We stood inside the hallway, which was more like a room, a huge room, the size of four very large living rooms joined together. The type of hall that could easily accommodate a ballroom dance, it was immensely impressive. Large crystal chandeliers dropped from a high ceiling, set about six feet apart all the way down the length of the hall, which must have been about a hundred feet long and almost as wide. A white *Classic Studio* stand up piano was positioned on one side of the hallway, with gold pedals and gold trims, a length of mirror, with a gold patterned frame ran along the entire wall on the opposite side, broken only by three arched doorways. Extravagant furniture tip toed on the creamy coloured marble floor, with hints of gold emblazoned around the border.

"Please come in." He carried on as he shut the door. "My name is Terry Parke. I'm sure you know that I'm an MP. I run the UK Independent Party. Correct me if I'm wrong but I believe you have been all over the television. Hostages taken by that terrible terrorist."

Julie looked at me, clearly taken aback. She hadn't considered what would be happening in the outside world, in response to their kidnapping. Of course, Fatwa would have broadcast the video recording, of which she was a part of, but for some reason she hadn't given it a thought, that they would be part of the big news. She didn't say anything.

"Please follow me. Forgive me but I have a guest. We've settled in the library. I'm afraid that I have given my staff the day off, but I can help you, with some medical -"

"Thank you sir," interrupted Julie Stokes.

"Please call me Terry."

"OK Terry, but I really need to borrow your phone."

"Yes, yes, yes of course. Please follow me and we can sort everything out." He led the way and we followed. His walk slow, but purposeful. Julie walked close to me, slipping her hand into mine, she gave it a squeeze and then pulled it away again. I could feel the relief inside her. I had seen a phone on a small semi global table by the front door. We were walking in the opposite direction but I didn't say anything. I knew I could do with some medical attention. I feared that my skull had been fractured.

The end of the hall came to a crossroads and we went off to the right. To the left had been a large staircase leading up. Straight ahead were some double doors, but we turned right. At the end of our walkway I could see an open door, we walked on towards it and followed him in.

It was a library. Thirty by thirty, high ceiling. Floor to ceiling book shelves coated two of the walls, all crammed tight with books of different sizes. Thick brown leather furniture accompanied the deep pile cream carpet on the floor. A man sat on an armchair. He looked up as we walked in. Instant look of shock, his mouth gaped wide open. His head turned between us and Parke, several times.

"Parke spoke first, "Uh hum. This is quite remarkable. My friend here is um," Parke seemed at a loss for words.

The man spoke out instead, "My name is Jasper Shepherd. My brother Mark was murdered in your presence today by that black bastard." He offered his hand, which I took. I didn't speak. Neither did Julie.

"How did you escape? Or did he let you out?" said Shepherd. He seemed very calm for a man in bereavement.

"I'm sorry. We can talk in a minute, but I really need to use the phone," snapped Julie.

I noticed Shepherd nod to Parke, who in turn said, "Yes dear. Please follow me."

I went to follow them, but Shepherd put a hand on my arm, "Please tell me about my brother's last moments. How badly was he tortured? Please tell me. I want to know every detail so I can take great pleasure in exacting my revenge."

I wanted to follow Julie and watched Parke lead her out. He shut the door behind him.

I turned around and Shepherd said, "Would you like a drink?" he turned away and reached for a half full decanter which was sat on a small round wooden table, a map of the world etched into the top of it. The table was positioned next to the armchair that he had been sat on. There was something about his voice. He picked up the decanter and walked, nimbly, light on his feet to a drinks cabinet, under a window. There was something about his walk that I recognised.

Through the window I could see an expansive picturesque garden, lit up brilliantly by garden lights. The view, to the rear of the property, went for miles. I watched Shepherd's reflexion in the window.

He pulled out a fresh glass. I had recognised the walk, the mannerism, the voice and I felt giddy.

"Whisky?" he said and just started to pour the liquid into the glass.

"Fatwa." I said, planting my feet, I didn't want to feint, not now.

"What?" he exclaimed, turning his head towards me.

"You're Fatwa," I said. "The people that had us captured were white. I saw that when I escaped. A Swastika tattoo on white skin, on the back of one of your guards. You killed your brother. You tell me how you tortured him. I never forget a voice."

He didn't say anything.

"I never forget a voice. Pretend accent or not. Especially one that belongs to an enemy. You could have been sat in here, in the dark, like in that room. I still would have known. No mistake. It's you.

He didn't say anything. He just stared. Eyes glued on me but expressionless.

"It all makes sense now. You had to drag him in. He was struggling but not with fear. He was angry. Fearful struggles are different to angry ones. I thought that strange right from the start. Not being funny, but I've met your brother. He was a coward. Cowards don't struggle like him. He was being deserted. I saw it in his eyes as well. Just before YOU cut them out. He looked confused and angry, but more-so, he looked betrayed. Yes he looked frightened, but not until the end. Right up to the point he knew what you was about to do. To your own flesh and blood. That's why he was gagged wasn't it? I mean all the others had their heads blown off. No gagging. Not him. In fact I can see it all in your face right now. It was you. You killed your brother."

Shepherd still didn't speak. Not straight away. He just offered me the glass of whisky. I took it from him. Staring into his eyes. Drilling deep into them, my psycho look. This was not a man that was in mourning. This was a man in shock. Shock at seeing us in the library at his friend's house, when we should really be racked up in a concrete cell.

He finally spoke, "Not bad young man. Not bad at all, for a grass." His eyes now turned to steel. Face grimacing and then smiling.

"Call me a grass and I'll kill you." I hated grasses.

"You will not be killing anyone. We have you again. Your friend the Police Officer is well and truly secured by now. Like I said before, you will do as you are told or SHE DIES NEXT."

The voice was exactly the same. Same tone, same accent, same volume, same act. Yes he had us. But not like before. Right now it was one on one. I could take him any-time I wanted. Despite my head. I could take him now, I was confident of that. I chose to wait. I didn't know where the other guy had taken Julie. Also I was curious, I needed to ask him some questions.

"Why?" I asked, "Why all the pretence?"

"You make it sound as if I have done something terrible. The reasons are sound. You must know that. Muslims, fucking Muslims are ruining our country. They started this, from the day they were born. It's them who want to take over the world. It's their way or no way. They are even open about it. Not just the extremists. Speak to any of them. They want the whole world to follow the Quran. Fucking heathens. Filling our schools with their shit, banning Christian plays, Christian values, Christian ways."

"So kill them then," I said. "But you. You've been killing your own. As Fatwa anyway."

"Our own. Yes but I have made martyrs of people who otherwise would have done fucking nothing. People with no lives. People who were robbing their own. People with no morals. Drug dealers, perverts, burglars. People who were as good as leeches to society. No good to anyone whatsoever. Now though, they have done something good. Their deaths are bringing us together. They are bringing us, God's real children together, once and for all. Group Thirty Three is growing. It is almost an army. We have more members now than the entire Police Service in this country. The numbers just keep on growing."

"Your brother, the coward, he got you the details didn't he. A Police Officer with access to records, he gave you the drug dealers, perverts. What about the young girl. What did she ever do?"

"That was an accident. That was meant for her Father. Although it was another fuck up by my brother. I just wanted British scum but he chose the Polish guy. A personal row, then he had to put in a complaint to the Police against my brother, so he just sort of picked himself. He should have gone, not the girl."

"Yes but you killed your brother. Your own fucking brother. What was that about?"

"My brother was a fool. I forgave him the Polish guy but he just didn't get it. Yes he was supposed to get me scum, but I wanted bad guys that would still be English enough to enrage the public. Like the homeless squaddie," Shepherd laughed, "Like you. You're nothing but a low life grass, as bad as a burglar, as bad as a junkie, but nobody knows. He fucked up though. He brought in the pretty Police girl too. He was becoming a danger to us, he had a big mouth, he was a liability. We have too much at stake to afford loose ends and he was a loose end."

"I warned you. Call me a grass one more time and you are as good as dead." I spoke as I went for the door. It was locked. I braced myself to kick it open until I heard that unmistakeable click of a gun.

"You could try and get out. You won't find her. She will be safely locked away in the panic room. Terry had one built after threats to his life. Threats by them fucking left wing idiots, siding up with those dirty black bastards. Our own white people standing up for them. Shocking! Don't you understand? You are going to help Britain to become great again."

He was holding a revolver in his hand. An old one that I didn't recognise. More importantly, it was aimed directly at my chest. He was stood a good seven feet from me. Too far to jump. I slowly moved myself back towards the sofa and stood in front of it. Five feet away but still too far to jump. I took a small swig of the whisky he had poured for me. Adrenaline and Noradrenaline swirling through my system. Thoughts of fainting, or feelings of pain, temporarily gone.

He held the gun steady with one hand and made a call from a mobile with the other, smirking at me while he waited for it to be answered. "Yes, it is me. How have they escaped?" He listened.

"Yes they have escaped you fool. I am holding a gun to the grass right now as we speak." He listened some more.

"I don't want to hear any more excuses. Get yourself over here right now. Four of you." Shepherd clicked off the phone and placed it into his pocket, still smirking.

"OK you got me again. So tell me. How did you do it? The explosions I mean," I had to ask more questions knowing that Shepherd was relishing being back in charge, he could afford to tell me all now, he was showing off. He had the upper hand and could end it for me whenever he wanted. Pretty soon he would have help over anyway.

"Ah, the bombs. Ingenious don't you think. Yes, up until now suicide bombers have hit populated areas. Killed as many as they could. So I had to do something else. A disgruntled Father, losing a traitor son, wanting revenge. Fatwa. A murderer, not a suicide bomber, a murderer of individuals. Like some of the others we have suffered. Soldiers, journalists, people that mattered being beheaded. Big stories. Had everyones heart. I needed to do something similar, but more grotesque, killing normal people. Civilians."

"The bombs?"

"Ah yes the bombs. Ironically that was thanks to an immigrant. A Ukrainian, Vladimir Likhonos, a scientist who had an accident with some chewing gum and a powdered explosive. You see he loved dipping his gum in Citric Acid, but one day he dipped it in the wrong bowl, by compete accident. In an explosive. His own saliva triggered a reaction with the powder. A reaction that blew his own head off. It wasn't hard to replicate, well replicate and improve. When you got money like us, you've got the best science labs. It didn't take long to design our own chewing bomb so to speak. Packets of chewing gum. Ten bits of gum. Nine normal spearmint flavour. One explosive flavour," he laughed. "One lethal combination of chemicals that go BANG. One deadly bit of gum that could be taken anytime. A bit like Russian roulette don't you think?"

He laughed again and continued, "Once gone the rest of the packet would show nothing. Post mortems would show nothing. All traces of our chemicals gone. Ingenious don't you think. Thing is when you target scum like we did, it was easy to give them a pack. That's one good thing about our good old English bums. They will always take anything that is being handed out for free."

"So what now? What you going to do with us?" I said wanting him to carry on talking.

"No change there son. You and the cop will die. You will both be killed by Fatwa. It's a shame about her, but she will have to go as well. It will go all over the news. You will become heroes. Then we will kill some more, really fuel the hate. Once we are ready, that's when the real hero shit will start. Thirty three will come into action. Thirty Three will find Fatwa and kill him." Shepherd became more animated as he spoke, his eyes glazing over.

"You're going to kill yourself?" I questioned, raising my eyebrows.

"Don't be a fool. They will find a terrorist. He will be shot in the head. He will be unmasked and found to be an Imam. The one from Gravesend. The only one that we have kept alive. Thirty Three will be heroes. By then our army will be huge. Civil war against the scum will be in full flow. Terry Parke will become leader of our Country and I will be with him. Like I said Great Britain will be Great Britain again."

"Not when everyone finds out what you have done. You're filth. You aren't British; you're just a mental nutter, who should be in a mental hospital. I hear they got spaces in Stone House. Do yourself a favour and book a room." I needed to agitate him further. He would either just shoot me or make a mistake. I hoped for the latter but I needed to do something soon. I just knew, or hoped deep inside, that he couldn't afford to shoot me in his future Prime Ministers house.

He waved the gun in a circle, "You're very brave son, for the predicament that you --"

My whisky glass struck him hard in the face. Liquid in his eyes and glass smashing on his bony forehead. I swept to my right which was the opposite way from where the gun was now pointing on its circular journey. I smashed a kick into his right elbow. The gun dropped. I destroyed his nose with a left hook, thrusting my hip and shoulder in the same direction. He crashed backwards. I picked up the revolver. Thrust it under his chin, pressing hard. I pulled the trigger and blew the top of his head off.

"I told you I'd kill you."

I checked the revolver. It was full apart from the one bullet that I had just spent. I went to the door. One hard kick on the dead lock was all it took. The frame was solid enough, but it was not designed for the power delivered from the combination of energy and force that my right leg had just produced.

I stopped outside, still, listening. Silence. I strained my ear to no avail. I would have to physically search the house. I stopped to think. Panic Room. Safest and strongest place for a panic room would be a basement. Solid concrete surroundings not afforded by any other floor. I needed to get to the stairs. On recollection they had been opposite the short corridor that had led to the library.

I crept forward, still listening. I reached the stairs. They led up, not down. So I moved around to the other side of them, where I found a door, embedded into the side of the staircase. I pushed down on the gold plated handle. It slid down with smoothness and the door clicked open with an equal silence. Fluorescent lights lit a flight of steps leading down to a room. I listened again. I thought I could now hear a voice. The steps were wood painted white. A matching wooden hand rail sloped down with the stairs. I stepped quietly onto them making sure that my feet were positioned on the outside edges of each step. The outside edges are well supported so should avoid creaking. I could see through the hand rail as I moved down. It was a large room. Used as a wine cellar. Hundreds of bottles of wine sat in racks across the two walls that I could see. I moved further down and could hear the voice a bit clearer.

A male voice, "Now get into that."

I looked around the corner. The lighting was even brighter around the side. Terry Parke was stood next to a large open steel door. A room emitting a very bright light on the other side of it. I could see Julie. She was naked and holding an orange jump suit against her body. Parke was holding a gun in one hand, the laptop in the other. The gun was pointing in her direction.

I was now at the bottom of the stairs and moved quietly towards them. Julie saw me. I nodded for her to move to the left, my left. Parke must have seen something in her eye as she moved over. He managed to half turn before I put a bullet in his head.

Julie Stokes dropped the orange boiler suit she
had held over her breasts. She lunged forward, hysterical.
Wrapping her arms around me. I dropped the gun
and cushioned her head into my shoulder. For the second
time that day Julie was entwined in my arms.

Fifty Three

Charlie Jackson was stood at the front door of the
Shepherds Farmhouse, surrounded by his full team, minus
Julie Stokes. They had been joined at the farm by three full
Tactical teams.

Once Jazz had turned up with the search warrant it had
taken them a good fifteen minutes of conversation with the
man on the other side of the intercom, conversation that
had eventually persuaded him to join them at the front
gates. He turned out to be a resident Security officer. He
had opened the gates fully before Charlie produced the
search warrant. A necessity as the man had made it clear
that nobody would be welcome inside. The man had then
attempted to block their entry to the grounds, and it had
taken Jazz only a matter of seconds to put him on the floor
and detain him for obstruction.

The hard line entry had been decided by Charlie Jackson, questioned by his Inspector, Ian Thom over the phone. Questioned action, in light of the fact they were going into a house where the occupier was in mourning over the death of his brother. A discussion that was only going to go one way. Charlie Jackson had made up his mind and Ian Thom trusted his friend. Charlie went with his gut instinct. He always went with his gut instinct as it had never let him down before. He knew something was amiss. Something was wrong with what had gone on, Mark Shepherd's behaviour, the security guard's behaviour, everything was setting off alarm bells deep in Charlie's intuitive sense, paying no regard to his conscious awareness.

His gut instinct had proved right. They had uncovered Jasper Shepherd's links with Thirty Three. Better than that they had found the missing Imam. Tied up and locked in the corrugated warehouse. Jasper Shepherd himself was missing and nobody was talking. Not the housekeeper, not the chauffeur, not any of the twelve staff members found at the address.

They had details of thirty five members of the group Thirty Three. Thirty five high profile individuals. Millionaires, business men and politicians including the leader of the United Kingdom Independence Party, Terry Parke. Printed documents providing details of thirty three individuals, titled *Offices*, two *Masters*, Jasper Shepherd and Terry Parke. Thirty five members.

They had saved the Imam and uncovered a group of murderers but they still found nothing to identify Fatwa or the whereabouts of Julie Stokes.

"Guys I'm at a loss. I need ideas. I need ideas now," he begged to the remainder of his team. His team sat quiet. All of them at an equal loss. The video they had seen, engrained in their minds.

Chief Officers had now also turned up at the scene, crowing about the result. A large group from the media had assembled at the gates preparing to interview one of the gloating Chiefs. Milling outside like vultures, each wanting their lump of meat, the shot, the headline.

"Let's go," said Charlie, deciding nothing else was to be gained at the farm. Also he was getting sick of the Command team walking around with a swagger, patting each other on the back. Detectives from the Area Major Investigation Team, AMIT, taking over, temporarily.

They all made their way to the gates. Their vehicles were still parked on the other side. The gates were still open but being guarded by uniform officers.

They walked through. The vultures started to shove microphones under Charlie's mouth, questions shouted out at him, "What's happened?" "Can we have a statement?" "Is it true you found the missing Imam?" "How many people have you arrested?"

Charlie turned around and growled, "Fuck off. I've still got an officer missing and we are doing everything we can to find her."

Jazz shoved the microphones out of Charlie's face and Crayston put his arm around his Sergeant, leading him off to the cars. The questions were still being shouted at them but quickly changed direction, back towards the building, away from Charlie and his team, back towards the gates, in the direction of Chief Superintendent Best and his gleaming smile walking towards them.

They climbed into their cars, when Charlie's phone rang. He looked at the number. He didn't recognise it. He answered it, "Hello."

"Charlie. Is that you? Thank god it's you. It's Julie."

Fifty Four

Julie put the phone down. Her Sergeant, Charlie Jackson, fully briefed. She was now dressed in the orange jumpsuit, it was cleaner than her bloodied clothes had been. The last cuddle between us had only lasted seconds. That was all we could afford. I knew that Shepherd had called for assistance. Four men. I had taken her to the phone that I had seen by the front door.

"They're coming straight over. Shouldn't take them long. They're in Meopham at Shepherds house," she spoke with some relief.

"That's great Julie, but we still got some work to do. Shepherds men will be here soon. They've had a head start and aren't as far away."

I led her back down to the panic room and pulled Parke's body out of the way.

"Do me a favour. Lock yourself in here. I don't want to put you in the predicament of watching me do something that I shouldn't be doing." I waved the gun around, hinting at what I meant.

"You are fucking joking Mister Jakobs! You are not locking me in anywhere. We're in this together." She pushed past me back towards the steps.

"OK calm down. Just wait a second. Listen to me. At the moment, all they are doing is coming back to pick up prisoners. Us. They don't know what's happened here. Their guard will be down. It might be all the advantage that we need."

"Let's go then," she said, running back up the steps.

I followed her. My head started thumping again and I almost missed a step. I held onto the banister to steady myself. We went back to the library, where I retrieved Jasper Shepherd's phone. They might try to call him when they arrive, or they would just knock on the door. The phone could come in handy.

"Right, this is a huge house, it's big enough to be a hotel. We need to be upstairs, let's get our heads down. It will take them ages to search the house. By the time they are anywhere near finding us, your back up, Charlie and his team would have turned up. With a bit of luck they'll find Shepherd and Parke and think that we've already escaped. They might just leave straight away."

She acknowledged my statement. It made sense. We went upstairs. We found a bedroom on the top floor, facing the front of the house. I opened a window, just slightly, so I could listen out for when they arrived. I handed her the gun, "We should split up. Two places are harder to find than one. If anyone comes in through that door shoot them." Again she just acknowledged my statement. I could tell that she had never handled a gun before. I touched her face, gently, stroking her cheek, "Jules, just relax babe. We've done the hard bit. The main guys are gone. We're just dealing with their knuckle-heads now. If they come in, aim at the chest and just pull the trigger." The chest was the biggest part of the body, so missing the target might still hit the mark.

I heard a noise outside. The noise of a car. We both looked out. Peeking from behind the ivory coloured jacquard curtains. A Range Rover, with its headlights blazing, was pulling up on the driveway, close to the steps outside. The same Range Rover that had abducted us. The front of the house was well lit, by what looked like mini lamp-posts. Four men got out. All dressed in black combats, but this time with no balaclavas.

"I recognise the blonde haired guy," Julie said. Only one of the four had blonde hair. Like the others, he was about six feet tall, average build and aged in his late thirties.

"It don't matter who he is Jules, they are all the same. Remember they want to kill us. Remember they have already killed. I'm going to shut the door on my way out. Shoot anyone that comes in through that door."

She nodded and asked, "Where are you going?"

"I'll find somewhere to hide. Don't worry. You just do your bit." I left her. Shutting her door fully as I left. The phone in my hand, Shepherd's phone, started ringing, only it wasn't a normal ring tone. A song that I did not recognise, the lyrics of which included the word *nigger*. A name flashed across the screen, *Herman*. I answered it, but didn't speak.

"Jasper, we're outside. Where do you want us?"

I was never one to play hide and seek. I was also never one to run. "Come on in Herman. I'm waiting." My voice was quiet, hoarse but menacing.

"Who's that? Where's Jasper?" I hung up and sped down the stairs. Six flights, three floors. I glanced at the front door. It was shut tight. I ran back into the library, past Jasper Shepherd's empty vessel. I went to the window and pushed it open. I climbed out into the garden and headed towards the front of the building, keeping myself close to the wall, conscious of my shadow in the manmade lights.

The phone rang again. I stopped still and answered it straight away. *"Where the fuck is Jasper? Who is this?"*

"Herman, Herman, Herman. It's all going wrong son. It's time to hit your panic buttons. Police are on their way. Shepherd and Parke are gone, dead and so will you be, unless you vanish now. Or you could always come and get me, which I would prefer. Your choice but don't say that I didn't warn you. I'm in the basement." I hung up and tossed the phone thirty feet behind me, into a brightly coloured flower bed. I walked all the way round.

I got to the front corner of the building. I peeked round. The four men were still there. Deep in conversation, I could sense their panic. The fear of not knowing. I hoped Julie was OK. I stayed where I was. I would wait until they decided what they were going to do. They might just leave.

They didn't, they went to the boot of their car and came back out with weapons. I saw a knife, a crowbar and two baseball bats. No guns. They decided to split up. One walked over to the far side of the building. Two walked towards the front door, including the blonde one that Julie recognised. One walked in my direction, six feet, stocky build, dark hair cut into a Flat Top, despite the receding hairline. He was carrying a baseball bat. I moved back. Just a few feet, into an alcove at the side of the building, where it was dark. I waited and listened, trying to drown out the thumping noise in my head.

I heard him before I could see him. Then I saw his shadow, changing shape, growing larger. He was close and breathing hard. *Shitting himself.* I knew I had to be quick and quiet. Quiet being the most important. He walked past me, just six inches and then must have seen me through the corner of his eyes. He started to swing his bat but it was too late for him. My punch, my favoured left hook, as intended, landed on his throat, with force, enough to cause his larynx to cave in. No noise and right now he couldn't breathe, which meant he couldn't scream. My right cross came over as he stumbled back, catching him hard on the temple, causing his head to snap sideways, his brain hitting the side of his skull. When hit that hard there will always only be one result. Blackout. He collapsed, like his electricity supply had suddenly been switched off. One down three to go. I picked up his bat.

I knew one was walking around the far side of the building. I could go back the way I had come and meet him. That would leave two, who would by then, already be in the house and closer to finding Julie. I opted to go to the front door.

Julie Stokes didn't stay in her room. She now knew Sam Jakobs. He was a hero. He would not be hiding out in a room, hoping not to get caught. He would be out there doing something to stop them getting caught, preventing Julie Stokes from getting caught. He was a million miles away from who she had dated in the past. She had been with the hunks, the gym freaks, the ones who took longer than her to get ready to go out. She had also dated the coppers. The ones that had only gone out with her because she was the new catch at the station. She had stopped dating Police Officers years ago. Sam Jakobs was different from all of them. He didn't care what he looked like, or how he came across. He was who he was, and he was a hero.

'Three things get coppers in trouble. Special property, informants and shagging informants.'

She had gone down the stairs. Into the large hall and through the end arched doorway, closest to the front door, into a room that gave her an excellent view out the front. She had seen the group split up, with weapons. Two walking up to the door. She waited at the archway, hidden from the entrance. A window smashed and she instinctively looked around her cover. She saw a crowbar being pulled out of the smashed window. An arm reached around, through the smashed pane of glass. It reached the handle and fingers fumbled around the lever. Eventually the fingers opened the door. She quickly moved back, wondering how she was going to deal with this, gun held tight in her hand. She wondered where Sam was. She heard the door open. Heard footsteps.

She decided, and stepped out of her cover, "Freeze." She tried to sound authoritative, but her voice stammered. The two men stopped. They turned around to face her. The blonde one, The one that she recognised smiled.

I moved quickly towards the front door. I got there to see it was wide open. A smashed panel next to the door. I heard voices, a male and a female, Julie Stokes. I sneaked through the door. Julie was stood at an archway to my right, pointing the gun I had given her at the two men. The blonde one in return was pointing a gun at her. He must have already been carrying.

"I'm going to count to three and then I am going to shoot you. You can prevent that by putting the gun down and telling me where the grass is." His voice was surprisingly eloquent for a man with a firearm. I looked at Julie, she had her gun held out straight, both hands on the weapon, which was pointed directly at her target, but her hands were shaking.

He started to count, "One, Two...."

I interrupted and shouted, "Three " I threw the baseball bat at them as I spoke, my intervention causing the blonde to turn, with the gun. I heard gunfire. Two shots and felt a searing burn across my right shoulder. I rolled over, hoping to avoid another shot, but also in recoil from the pain.

"Fucking stop right where you are," Julie screamed at the second man. The one that she hadn't shot, the one that was now reaching for the gun that his injured, or dead partner had dropped. He stopped still, but stooped over the gun. He slowly straightened, backing away from the firearm, hands raised in a posture of surrender.

I heard a noise behind me, *shit, there was still one of them outstanding,* I turned, in agony, ready to launch myself at whoever was coming through the door. I jumped, but tried to pull off half way, when I recognised Charlie Jackson storming in, my head exploding with pain.

He caught me in his arms just as I blacked out.

Fifty Five

30th March

A week had passed since Charlie and his team had raced
around to Terry Parke's address to our rescue. My injury
from being shot was just a flesh wound. Luckily the bullet
had just ripped through the outside of my right shoulder.
My head had suffered more serious trauma. Bruised brain,
cerebral contusion, saved by my abnormally thick skull,
but I was still suffering headaches.

They had found the fourth man, hiding in the back
garden. Armed only with a baseball bat. He was easily
apprehended by the Krays.

After the phone calls made by DS Jackson, the search of
the address had been taken over by The Counter Terrorism
Command team, better known as SO15, the team that was

formed by the merging of the Anti-Terrorist Branch
(SO13) and Special Branch (SO12), assisted by MI5. The
local Police having been barred from any involvement,
other than providing witness statements.

The investigation with regards to the men that had been
shot dead by me was now in their hands. There would be
no murder enquiry; after all there had been no murder, self
defence. Julie Stokes involvement had been sworn to
secrecy; mine too, with the threat of a murder enquiry if I
didn't. Which, I had been warned would most definitely
reveal my role as a Police Informant. The word Agent not
being used.

The blonde haired assailant had survived being shot by
DC Stokes. It was no wonder that she had recognised him,
Michael Herman Hart was the current Mayor of the
Borough of Gravesham. She had followed my instructions
and aimed for his chest, but hit him in the leg.

The new investigation team had searched the Church in
Cobham. The scene of Mark Shepherd's murder. The
bodies of the dead Imams together with Mark Shepherd's
had been discovered in a makeshift grave, which in reality

was just a large dug out pit that had then been filled with earth and rocks.

All the computer equipment had been seized and interrogated. A large quantity of the chewing bombs, sealed and wrapped were found in one of the four concrete buildings. Jasper Shepherd had spoken the truth. He had scientists employed, working from Secretus Security's laboratories, building on Vladimir Likhonos's mistake. Each packet of the *Fresh* gum, contained one lethal capsule.

Evidence that two of the three remaining concrete buildings were used as torture chambers had also been secured, details of which were never to be released. Then there was the one that had been used by Fatwa for his videos and murders.

The public had been informed that the group known as Thirty Three, were responsible for all the killings. The Shepherd brothers had been named as the main instigators. For some bizarre reason Terry Parke was not named as an accomplice. He was being blackmailed by the notorious Shepherd brothers, sons of the Ex-Assistant Chief Constable. Perhaps because of his long standing political background with the Tories before he joined UKIP. He certainly didn't look like he was being blackmailed to me.

Jasper Shepherd had ultimately been named as being responsible for several deaths. He had killed as Fatwa and as a member of Thirty Three. All the named members of the group, the *offices*, rich and powerful, were being investigated. Most of whom, somehow were currently out on bail. Denying any knowledge of what Jasper Shepherd was guilty of. Two hundred and thirty four *appointments* had also been arrested. Enquiries still ongoing to identify the others. Most of those arrested, genuinely shocked at the revelation that the British murders had been executed by Jasper Shepherd, that Fatwa was a character of invention.

The people of Great Britain were also shocked. All religious groups, whites, coloureds and Muslims, united again. The Government hailing the efforts of their Police Force and Security Services, working together they had uncovered the racist movement trying to destroy their multi cultural society. *A multi cultural society that would always stand firm, hand in hand, united always, against the evil forces of destruction, such as the group thirty three.*

It had taken Charlie Jackson and the Intelligence Unit's hierarchy as a whole, tremendous efforts to keep the nature of Sam Jakobs true involvement with the Police out of the public domain. A burnt agent is an expensive one with no future use.

Charlie sat in his office, swinging in his chair. He had plans to babysit tonight for his daughters. He hadn't done that for a while.

His phone rang. He answered it. Chief Superintendent Best. He was being summoned to his office.

Fifty Six

I had been paid a considerable amount of money. Rewards for the saving of six young girls, the arrests of drug dealers and paedophiles. Even more money for saving the life of a Police Officer, identifying the murderous group known as Thirty Three, for identifying the terrorist Fatwa as Jasper Shepherd, and for saving a nation from Civil War.

Apparently obscene payments like mine were never made this quick. Nor were they made in one hit. They were normally paid in instalments. Charlie had told me that the powers to be were more frightened of being sued for millions because of the predicament that I had found myself in. I could have blamed Kent Police, sued the Chief Constable. They didn't know me. Deep down I knew I would have done it all for nothing, anyone should. Charlie had said I deserved the money and should take it anyway.

The Police got paid, as did the Government and everybody else that had been involved, so should I. I couldn't be paid cash though. The money had to be transferred into my bank account with a cover story. *Kent Police had made an out of court settlement with me due to an outstanding civil case.* They had made me sign documents that would prevent me from suing them for a larger sum later. I had been told to lay low for a while. At least six months. I guessed that was Charlie's way of telling me that business with me was over. Or more likely he had been told by his bosses that business with Robbie Strange was over.

I had transferred a few thousand pounds to Louise. I did not know what to do with the amount of money that was currently in my control. I'd never had money. I had taken out a hundred quid. That would see me through a couple of weeks. I didn't want for much.

My mind had become a bit of a blur, confusion. I found myself thinking of Julie Stokes. A lot. We had shared a moment together. That night. The twenty second day of March. She had invited me back to hers, after we had both been treated at the hospital. Neither wanting to stay the night as suggested by the Doctor. After we had finished with the investigators. I had stayed the night. We made love several times through the night, in her shower, in her living room, in her kitchen and then in her bed, twice. Both of us high on each other, getting higher with each touch, each kiss, skin on skin with the feeling of being as one.

The next morning though it all went a bit wrong. Both of us were quiet. I felt guilty, almost as if I had been unfaithful to Louise, even though we were not together. Julie was confused as well. She just said that she could get into a lot of trouble. I knew what she meant.

'Three things get coppers in trouble. Special property, informants and shagging informants.'

We had kissed before I said goodbye. I hadn't heard from her since. Now I couldn't get her out of my mind. Charlie had got me a new phone, so that they could maintain periodic contact, to make sure I was alright. I didn't need it but had decided to keep it. Julie might phone. So far she hadn't.

Louise however had called me, grateful for the money that I had given her, but she had some news. She offered to return the money to me if I wanted. She had met a new man. A boyfriend, who she was very fond of. She didn't use the word love, but I knew what she meant, she was in a relationship. A wealthy young man, working in the stock exchange. I could tell in her voice that she was very nervous about telling me, not knowing how I would react. A new man in my daughter's life, in my soul mate's life. I felt sorry for her, for feeling this way. I didn't know what to think. I just told her that I trusted her sense of judgement. If she felt this man was good, who was I to say any different. I wished her luck but felt a heavy emptiness in my gut.

I walked out of Woodlands Park, cutting my workout short. I just didn't feel like it. A tap on my shoulder caused me to stop and turn around.

"Jakobs?" said a tall burly blonde haired Irish man. I looked beyond him. Another three men of similar standing smiled at me like it was a beautiful day.

"Yeah. What's up?" I replied.

"Need you to get in the van with us," he replied.

I remembered the phone call from Louise a couple of weeks ago, and wondered if she had been dating then. 'Four Irish men looking for me.' I looked at the van. It advertised Patios and driveways. Travellers for sure.

"Why would I do that?" I demanded. I tried to give them my glare but I was worn out. I looked at their knuckles. They all looked like fighters. It was a lose-lose situation, although I was sure I could put at least one of them in hospital beforehand. I took a step back with one foot so I was closer to a boxing stance.

"Mate you better do as you're fucking told. We been down your baby's Ma's house. You wouldn't want us goin' back there now would ya?" said the speaker.

I looked in the back of the van. It was almost empty. Two piles of paving slabs sat at the back of the van resting snug against the side panels. I could see a large yellow bucket with dried stains of concrete spilling down its edges.

"OK, I'll get in. In fact I'll fight all of you wherever you want, but only after you tell me what this is about."

They looked at each other and shrugged. The same one spoke, "You busted our brief. You told him to get out of town. He's paying us to do the same to you now. Bust you proper and then make sure you leave town for good. He also told us that you are a grass. We don't like grasses. No one does."

"Call me a grass and I'll kill you."

"Just get in the fucking van."

"Hope he's paid you up front. Because you'll be getting nothing once he goes where he's going."

"Half now and half after."

"Keep the half you got and call it quits. Firstly it will take more than you four to bust me," I growled, feeling my mojo grow inside, remembering the kids and the dirty lawyer, "Secondly, since when did traveller boys protect paedophiles?"

"What do you mean paedophile? Take oath," came the reply.

"I swear the man's been busted for going with young girls. Mo Ali is a dirty pervert. You do this and everyone will know what you boys really are," I growled again. I could feel my shoulder's growing in anticipation.

"First of all, you'll not be tellin' anyone anything about nothing. We will find out ourselves and if he is, we will sort him out. Secondly we're going to bust you anyway, just coz we want to." I saw his haymaker coming a mile off. He had taken too big a swing. I ducked underneath it and rolled to my right, just as he lost his balance from missing me with his clumsy effort. I landed a short straight crisp right cross perfectly on his jaw. He crashed to the floor. I was straight back in my stance as the other three gathered around. I saw a woman behind them, scrambling for her mobile phone. That would mean this had to be quick. *Fights only last seconds.* She was calling the Police, that was for sure.

The three men formed an arc around me, with their friend still lying on the floor. Not unconscious, he was moving. Just dazed. One lunged forward, head first both arms in front of him. Hands open as if he wanted to grab me, probably around the throat judging from their position. I sent out a swift short uppercut, thrusting my hip forward as I had been taught and practised for years. The same way as 'Iron' Mike Tyson threw his uppercuts. It landed straight on his jaw. His legs buckled and I jumped back to avoid being squashed. *Two left* I thought, but then there were three.

The first one was also back on his feet. "You fight good, boy. But not good enough," he said.

They all charged together. I threw a straight left-right, aiming the one-two at those closest to me. My left missed, my right caught the middle man straight in the nose which burst open. The other two were on me though and took one arm each. There charge had pushed me off balance and I smashed into the park boundary railings behind me. They pinned me there, as they coaxed the two on the floor to get up. For the next minute, they took turns in smashing punches into my gut and head. I could feel my right eye closing. The headaches were going to get worse. That was for sure. I was close to passing out and I probably would have but for the Police siren in the background. They stopped punching and let me fall to the floor. Right then I wished that this fight had only lasted seconds.

"Good boy." One of them said.

"You're OK boy, but we will be back if you lied to us. Trust me on my mother's grave. But if you're right he's in trouble," the first speaker said and turned to his boy's, "Come On."

They got in their van and drove off.

The woman who had made the phone call didn't come to my aid, while I lay on the floor coughing and spluttering.

She did talk to the Police Officers though when they showed up a few seconds later.

It took me half an hour to tell the Police that I wanted no further action and no hospital treatment. They pushed for the arrests but eventually conceded that I was not going to change my mind. I wasn't a grass, and that they were wasting their time.

Fifty Seven

1100hrs 30th March

Charlie Jackson rapped on Chief Superintendent Best's office door. He didn't know what it was about, but knew that it was not good.

"Come in," came the response from Best

Charlie walked in. Best was stood to the side of his desk. Hands behind his back, wearing a big fat grin across his smarmy face. Another two men sat at Best's desk, both wearing suits, official, with a number of papers sat in front of one of them. Charlie shut the door behind him.

"DS Jackson. Good morning. I am Detective Inspector Childs and this is Detective Sergeant Warrington. We are from Professional Standards," he put his hand out, offering a handshake.

"I'd prefer not to," said Charlie, leaving the man hanging. "So what's up? What's this about?"

Neither man seemed to be offended by Jackson's response. They were used to it. Officers in general had a hatred for Professional Standards. They got coppers nicked, treated them like criminals, taking their pensions. An understandable distrust for a department that often used underhand methods to get what they wanted. The only department that seemed to treat you as a guilty person right from the onset.

Childs opened up the file in front of him, "A complaint has been made about you DS Jackson. A complaint which has been looked at and has cast huge doubts with regards to your integrity. While I am not in a position to interview you at this stage, I have spoken to Chief Superintendent Best and explained my reservations of you maintaining your role as a supervisor on the Intelligence Unit. For at least while the investigation is ongoing. He has agreed and as such, as of first thing tomorrow you will be asked to work from the Custody area as a Custody Sergeant."

Jackson made no reply. Waiting for either Childs, Warrington or Best to continue.

Childs continued, "I'll be needing your mobile phone DS Jackson as part of my enquiries. It is property of Kent Police and you are obliged to hand it over."

Charlie Jackson took out his phone. He looked around the room. Perfect, he launched the phone into the Chief Superintendent's fish bowl, "There's my phone, now why don't the pair of you clowns just FUCK OFF?" Jackson turned around and walked out. He ignored the orders for him to return from Best, with a smile on his face. "Fuck them," he muttered.

Best's secretary, Beth Roberts smiled at Jackson, "You seem to have a certain effect on him Charlie."

"The man's a prick. Sorry."

"Don't be sorry. I think everyone knows that."

Back in his office he used the landline to call his team in. The Krays were just finishing a meeting with an old snitch from a couple of years ago. The man had just been released from prison for committing a burglary. The meeting wasn't with a view to getting information from him, but instead to warn him off going back on a drug fuelled burglary spree. Eddie and Jazz had met Sally Tall, who was having serious problems with her daughter. Rebecca was now a frequently reported missing person, who had resorted to prostitution for money. Julie Stokes had been to Occupational Health. She had been ordered to have regular counselling after her refusal to take any sick leave after her ordeal.

In the meantime Charlie got a cardboard box from under his desk. It wouldn't take him long to pack. He had no drawers and no locker. His work desk was pretty much like his home life. Messy but ordered.

He had already decided. Custody Sergeant was not for him. He felt tired anyway and needed to sort his life out. He had never taken a day off sick in his career. Even after his compassionate leave, when his son died and then when his wife had killed herself. Now though he would. He would use stress. He would need to do something else that he had never done before. He would need to see a Doctor. He didn't even know who his Doctor was. He would get one of his daughters to sort it out.

He shifted some paperwork out of his in tray and an evidence bag slipped out onto the floor. It was empty. He read the bag's content description. *Seven thousand six hundred Great British Pounds.* It was the money seized from the Dog and Bone. Jazz had counted and sealed it before leaving it with his Sergeant to take to Force Headquarters, where it would be stored pending a confiscation order. Charlie had put it off and then in his usual manner, forgot about it. He remembered putting it under his desk into a box that contained stuff to do later. Now the money was missing, stolen. Professional Standards were going to love this. Worse still, they were going to place his entire team under suspicion of theft. He knew none of them were thieves. He had no doubt about that. He folded the packet and put it into his rear pocket to deal with later.

He had more important stuff to deal with now. He had to tell his team that he was going and there was nothing that he could do about it. He would give them the rest of the day off, in fact better than that, he would take them down the pub instead.

Fifty Eight

18th July

Mo Ali sat in his cell, segregated from the main prisoners on the remand wing at Leeds prison in West Yorkshire, close to two hundred miles from home. Segregated for two reasons. Solicitors who find themselves in prison risk being hurt. Hated by inmates. Almost as much as they hate Police Officers. Secondly, he had been indicted with twenty five counts of sexual offences against minors. Paedophiles are hated everywhere. Reasons why he couldn't be housed at a more local prison. He had dealt with too many of the inmates.

His last attempt at bail, at Southwark Crown Court, was refused by that snotty Judge Hermitage.

A risk of flight due to the expectant lengthy custodial sentence. No address and no ties. A danger to society. Interfere with witnesses.

They had used every excuse to keep him inside until the eventual trial date. He had of course given instructions to his representative. Instructions that had helped so many of his own clients getting bail in the past. Instructions though, that had not worked for him. He had offered to surrender his passport, his sister had agreed to house him and offer a surety. He was of previous good character and that should be taken into consideration. He was prepared to abide by any curfew or signing conditions that the judge saw fit. All of which Judge Hermitage ignored.

His life was ruined. His family gone, divorce papers already filed. Broke, the lovely country house he had worked so hard for now in the hands of his soon to be ex-wife. Never to be allowed to practice law again. He would have to start all over again, and all because of that grassing bastard, Sam Jakobs.

Revenge however, would be his. He in turn would make Sam Jakobs suffer. Suffer like he had never suffered before. First though he would have to wait to be released, and be released he would. He was sure of that.

Kent Police had already given him the way out. Their policy was simple. *We will neither confirm or deny the involvement of an informant.* However cases were dropped, when compromised, to protect the identities of their informants. He knew the informant. Better still, an informant who kidnapped him, locked him in his car boot, stole two thousand pounds, a debt collector for Class A drug suppliers, working for those very people who had provided the girls subject of his indictments.

All of which he would reveal during the *Voir dire,* sometimes referred to as a trial within a trial. A hearing conducted in the absence of the jury, to establish the admissibility of evidence, or the competence of a witness, or the legality of the conduct by the Police, the legality of his arrest. A hearing when he would name the informant, the one that had set him up, threatened him, he would make them squeal. The case would be dropped. That was certain.

Now though he would have to wait, on his own, separated from the uncivilised residents of his current home. He would just have to watch his own back. He didn't trust the guards, they were friends of the Police.

They would love for something to happen to him. They hated him.

Hatred that only fuelled him. He would be released. Then would be the time for revenge. Sam Jakobs time would be up. Not through the gypsies though. Most certainly not the ones that he had already tried, and failed with, and paid for, five thousand pounds not to be hurt. Revenge would be his and his alone.

He rolled off his bunk and pulled out his court papers. He settled back on the bunk, under his covers and read through the charges, slowly. Then through the summary of evidence, slowly, taking in every last word, describing his actions with the young girls, perversely fuelling his masturbation.

*

Peter Snugs held the syringe containing his blood loosely between his fingers and thumb, the tip pressed to his victim's neck. They were stood at a cash dispenser, close to a parade of shops opposite the sea front. The elderly man, who wore a granddad cap that covered his white hair, stood in front of him and entered his pin number. The machine accepted the code and the screen changed; now asking for its next task. Snugs made the old man sit down on the floor, withdrawing the pin from his neck. Sweat dripped down his face, despite the freezing wind blowing in from the sea. His opioid dependence withdrawal-syndrome kicking in. The early symptoms of hot and cold flushes, agitation, anxiety, dehydration, muscle aches and runny nose already in action. Now he could feel his stomach cramping and felt like throwing up.

Snugs had been watching the cash dispenser for almost an hour. Waiting for the right target. Then the old boy, Harold Parsons, turned up on his own. That was when he made his move. He grabbed his victim, Harold Parsons, at the machine. He told him that he had AIDS and threatened to inject him with HIV, unless he did as he was told and didn't create a scene. Of course that was a lie. Snugs did suffer other diseases, such as Hepatitis B, but he didn't suffer AIDS, well as far as he was aware he didn't.

Snugs was now in control of the account, he pressed a button and checked the balance. It took longer, but he needed to know how much he could withdraw. He kept his head down, his jacket hood concealing his identity from the camera that he knew was there. The screen changed and showed him that the account held twelve thousand pounds and so many hundred pounds. His heart fluttered, not believing his luck. He withdrew three hundred pounds, which was the maximum amount the account would let him take from the machine. He put the money and bank card in his pocket and ran, leaving Harold Parsons shivering with fear on the floor. He now had the PIN number and hopefully would get to use it again before it got cancelled.

He ran for five minutes, up narrow side streets, turning lefts and rights, through the seafront town of Ramsgate and then settled in an alleyway. He took the money out. Slipped a twenty pound note back in his pocket and pushed the rest down in his sock. Not wanting to get robbed himself. Twenty pounds would buy him a 0.3 gram wrap of heroin, which at best would only be twenty to twenty five percent pure. The quality of smack was shit here in his new town. One thing about the Yardies, he had left behind in Gravesend, they sold decent gear.

He didn't know what time it was, he just knew that it was late. He hoped not too late for his dealer. He needed his gear now, or he would be *climbing the walls*. This was all that fucking Sam Jakobs fault. The man was a nutter, certainly one to be frightened of. He had ruined everything. That day he had heeded Jakobs advice and left Gravesend straight away, but not before stealing twenty three half balls of heroin from their stash. He had also gone round the street dealers and collected close to eighteen hundred pounds cash. Of course that meant he had to leave. If Jakobs didn't get him the Yardies would. He'd got on a train and went straight to Ramsgate, the famous seaside town in Thanet. He had friends there. Well he thought he did, it's amazing how friends suddenly become associates when you are flat on your arse.

The Yardies heroin and cash didn't last Snugs very long. In fact it only lasted him the best part of a week. He had tried to set himself up dealing, but was robbed himself within days. Now he was left homeless, sharing a squat, shoplifting, burgling and robbing people for money, people like poor Harold Parsons. He had tried to persuade Vikki to come to Ramsgate over the phone, with Rebecca, which would push them up the housing list as a priority. Vikki had told him to fuck off.

He walked towards the public payphone in Queen Street, cursing Sam Jakobs, wishing him dead. He wondered if he could get hold of a gun. Jakobs was a hard man, but a bullet in the head would be harder. He imagined how easy it would be, pulling the trigger, as he dialled his supplier. The phone rang twice before it was answered.

"Yeah?"

"Hi it's Pete. I need a full Rambo."

"Toilet. Ten"

"Thanks. See you in a bit." Snugs headed towards the closed down public toilets, just off the pebble beach, to pick up his heroin, wondering how much a gun would actually cost.

*

Lamarr Brown had settled at Elmley prison with ease. People who looked like him, monstrous, never had problems in prison. The missing eye, only served to add to his frightening appearance. For once though, possibly for the first time in years, Brown was happy, despite his incarceration. He was finally free of Kwamie. Free of the fear of what may happen to his parents back in Jamaica.

Relief from his new found freedom, was partly responsible for him talking to the Police. Providing information about everything that he knew. Details of the other K's in this world, working crack houses, selling sex, guns and slavery. Information that would help them, but would also help him. He had been promised a secret letter from the Intelligence Unit, a letter for the judge. A letter detailing his co-operation, but a letter that would not be read out in open court. The judge would read it in his private quarters. Not even the Investigating Officers would know of its existence. A letter that would include details of arrests made and property seized, as a direct result of his information. It would be a letter requesting a discounted sentence for their informant.

Yes, Sam Jakobs had beaten him, taken his eye and broken his arm, but Brown held no malice towards the man. Sam Jakobs had set him free.

Epilogue

19th July

I had only just started mowing Nan's lawn for her. The grass was now about two feet long. The weather was hot and I was stripped to my waist. I had been training hard, resting right and eating a high protein - low fat diet, I looked good.

I had come to all but moving in with Nan. The thought of staying on my own churned my stomach. The few things I had kept at Tommy's flat were now in my room at the back of Nan's house. Louise had a new bloke and it seemed to be going really well for her. I was happy for her. He was giving her a normal life. Something that I could never give. I had met him, there was unfortunately nothing to dislike. He was friendly, jovial and superb with Eve. He understood that I was her Father and would always be part

400

of her life. He also understood that I was Louise's friend, and would always be part of her life. I understood that he was now Louise's best friend.

Nan hadn't been too well lately and needed frequent lifts to her hospital appointments. I had bought a car. A Kia Sedona, which was quite roomy and comfortable for her. I still had huge amounts of money in my bank that I didn't know what to do with. I had offered Louise a considerable amount but she said she didn't need it. She did understand that I still needed to pay my way for Eve, for my own benefit, but at the moment she didn't want for anything. Neither did Louise.

I hadn't heard from Charlie or Julie for some time. I did however hear from the Police. An Inspector Childs. He'd asked me some awkward questions about Charlie and Julie. I told him to fuck off, I wasn't a grass.

I revved the mower up, when I felt a buzzing in my pocket. I turned it off and pulled out my phone.

Withheld number. I answered it.

'Hello Robbie. It's Charlie. Fancy another job?'

The End

ABOUT THE AUTHOR

Jorge was born in Birmingham, England in October 1962. He has three daughters and eight Grandchildren.

He is an ex-Police Officer having served 27 years in the service. An experienced Detective, who has worked on CID, Prisoner Handling, Drug Squad, Proactive Unit, Test Purchase Operative, Intelligence Unit, Research and Development and Covert Human Intelligence Source Handling Unit. During his time within the Police Force Jorge received numerous awards for Special Operations, Bravery and Professionalism.

Jorge now works for himself as a Private Investigator and Author.

https://sites.google.com/site/jorgegillbooks/

Printed in Great Britain
by Amazon